UNHINGED

NATASHA KNIGHT

Click here to sign up for my newsletter to receive new release news
and updates!

BETRAYED

Betrayed is the Prequel Novella that precedes Unhinged. If you've already read it, the click here to begin Unhinged.

If you haven't read it yet, just turn the page...

1

EVE

Going to the American soldiers for help is my last resort. If my brother finds out what I've done, he'll kill me. But I don't have a choice. It's the only way to save what's left of my family.

I walk into the building where they have their headquarters. It's easier than I expect, actually. All I have to do is tell them my name. Eve El-Amin. The El-Amin family is well known here.

From conversations I've overheard between my brother and his "colleagues," I know there are less than a dozen soldiers here. I've met two now. The guard at the entrance, who was younger than I expected, and another whose title is Commander. I don't remember his name. Now I'm sitting in the interrogation room where I imagine they're watching me from behind the mirror hanging on the wall, like they do on American television shows. And all I can do is try to calm my racing heart.

I glance at the door for the hundredth time. There's a clock above it and every click of the second hand as it moves has me wanting to leap for that door. To run out of here and go back home and forget this.

Only fifteen minutes have passed since the commander left the room, but it feels like fifteen hours. The longer I sit here, the harder it is to stay put. I wonder if they're doing it on purpose, using this tactic to shake me up, make sure I'm telling the truth. I am, but I imagine it's not easy to trust anyone with El-Amin for a last name.

I finish the flimsy plastic cup of water the commander had put in front of me, wipe my sweaty hands on my jeans and begin to rise. This was a bad idea. They're not going to help me. Why would they? My brother is the enemy.

But then I hear it. Talking in the corridor. Two men. Their voices are like thunder—deep and powerful. It's like they were waiting for me to make a move to leave.

As soon as I see that doorknob turn, my stomach churns and I freeze, half up out of my chair. All I can do is watch. My mouth is dry, and my heart is pumping blood so hard through my veins, the sound is deafening. But when the door opens, it's not the commander I see. He's behind the soldier who's wearing fatigues and carrying a thick file. The soldier's eyes zero in on me, take in my awkward position, and when he meets my stare, he does something I don't expect. He smiles.

"Ms. El-Amin," he says, and I know he knows I'm terrified.

He sets his folder down on the table and I straighten, as if I'd merely been standing to greet him. He extends his hand. I look at it, at this enormous outstretched hand, waiting for me to place mine inside it.

"I'm Master Sergeant Zachary Amado," he says while I stand there, stupefied.

I clear my throat and drag my gaze up to his. His eyes are so dark a blue they're like the midnight sky. And there's a kindness inside them. Something that makes me trust him instantly. Makes me like him instantly.

"Eve," I say, my voice sounding almost normal. "I'm just Eve."

He smiles, and his eyes light up. "Well, we're glad you came, just Eve. And you can call me Zach."

I feel my face go red and I lower my gaze. He's still got my hand and he squeezes and when I look up, he gives me a wink.

"Everything will be fine," he says. "You're doing the right thing. We can help you."

I nod, but I'm not really sure why because I'm still not certain this is the right thing at all.

"Sit down," he says, releasing my hand.

I sit. I get the feeling he's used to giving orders and having them followed.

He turns to the commander, the man I met initially. The man who asked me questions for almost an hour. He looks like he's in his fifties and he's not as friendly as Master Sergeant Zachary Amado. Zach. They have a brief exchange but they speak too quietly for me to hear. A moment later, the commander says something to Zach, nods to me, and leaves the room so we're left alone. Zach faces me and gives me that smile again, and I think he's trying to reassure me.

"I know you've already told the commander why you chose to come to us, but would you mind telling me as well? I want to hear the story from you."

"I'm here to save my brother," I say.

"Your brother." He opens the folder before him, shuffles through a few pages before coming to a photo of Armen. He studies it himself for a moment, then looks up at me, and I think he's looking at the similarity in our features. Our eyes, mostly. *Like the sweetest honey*, my mom used to say. The memory reminds me how much I miss her.

I blink twice, hoping to banish the tears I feel gathering.

"This brother, Eve?" he asks, using my name. He's watching me. Has been. I know. I felt his eyes on me from the moment I saw Armen's photograph. He rotates it so it's right side up. "Armen El- Amin?"

I look up to meet Zach's eyes. His search mine and I know he's seen the tears. I nod, too afraid that if I speak, my voice will break.

He shifts his gaze back to the folder, and mine follows. He makes a point of flipping over pages and pages of notes, which I can't read from where I'm sitting. There are a few more photographs in the file. Some of Armen alone. And, more importantly, of Armen with the man he works for. Except that the man's face is hidden behind a scarf. He's always hiding. Always sending others to do his dirty work.

That thought gives me strength. It reminds me why I'm here. Why I have to do this.

Steeling my spine, I sit up straighter. He watches me.

"My family's gone. I've lost my parents and two of my brothers, and Armen has got himself mixed up with a very bad man." I point to the photo. "Malik the Butcher." My voice hardens; I hear it myself. I have so much anger at this man, so much hatred of him. He'll destroy Armen if I don't do this. "I can help you find him. Tell you when they'll meet. If you'll help me save my brother."

2

ZACH

When I walked into the interrogation room, I knew the girl was about to bolt. She was terrified, and still is, but she's not weak. She's here to save her piece of shit brother, but she doesn't know him. She can't. If she did, there's no way she'd be here now because she'd know there's no way in hell we'll "save" him.

Eve El-Amin, baby sister of the El-Amin family. What's left of it, at least. Her father was important politically, and his work aligned with our goals. At least to some extent. But he and his wife were blown up leaving a restaurant some time back. Her other brothers, Rafi and Seth, went missing soon after that. Dead would be my guess. That's when Armen, the eldest brother, went to work for Malik a.k.a. The Butcher.

Beirut isn't a hotbed of activity in the Middle

East. In fact, it's probably one of the safest places in the region. But that doesn't mean men like Malik don't operate here. Don't run operations from the safety of their homes. Thing is, we can't find the bastard. And Eve El-Amin is the best lead we've had in a long time.

"You help us, and we'll be able to help you," I say, not looking at her, rifling through the papers before me even though I've memorized everything in the file. I'm trying to be as honest as possible. I don't want to lie to her, but she has information we need and finding Malik is priority one. It's the reason we're here, like ghosts, a covert battalion of elite soldiers with one mission: capture and kill Malik the Butcher. We don't even want him alive.

When I look up, Eve's big caramel eyes are watching me and I'm momentarily disarmed. She's pretty. I'd established that before she'd even walked into headquarters. We have a file on her too. I won't show her that one, though. And she's innocent. I see it in her eyes, on her face. If I had any doubts before, I know for sure now, seeing her like this. I feel it in my gut.

Although my gut's been wrong before.

I shake away that thought and watch her, wondering if she's aware she's hugging her arms to herself.

She's small, maybe five foot four, and petite. When she shook my hand earlier, hers disappeared inside it. She'd stared up at me then, like she is now, and I know she's searching. She's here to save her brother, but if he got wind of her visit today, he'd be the one she'd need protecting from. I wonder if she realizes that and suddenly, that's all I can think of.

"Does your brother know you're here?"

She shakes her head and reaches out to draw a photograph closer to her. "No."

"But you live in the same house."

"He doesn't know."

"You understand that you can't tell him, right?"

"I know." But the way she says it, she's wavering. Her shoulders slump and she drops her gaze. This is a betrayal of him, her sitting here with me. We're his enemy and she knows it.

I reach over the table and cover her hand with mine. She's startled by the contact, and fuck me, but so am I. We're both looking at it, at my hand on hers, and she's so soft and small and I have to clear my throat to speak.

"Eve, look at me."

She does, and her eyes glisten with tears. She's desperate to save him. She's out of options. That's why she's come to us.

"No matter what happens, you can never tell Armen you've been here." I pause, and I can't drag my eyes from hers. I watch a single tear roll down her cheek. She doesn't wipe it away but I want to, and it takes all I have not to slide my thumb across her face to do just that. "I don't want to see you get hurt, understand?"

She pulls her hand out from under mine. "He wouldn't hurt me. He's my brother."

I watch her, feel a shift in the air as I think about how to handle this. How to make sure she understands that he isn't the man she thinks. That he can and *will* hurt her.

"Tell me what you know about Malik," I say, needing time to study her, learn how she thinks. Figure out what makes her tick.

And, most importantly, remember my team's mission.

3

EVE

It's late when I leave the office. I told Zach all I knew, but I don't have any information on meetings between Armen and Malik. He doesn't usually tell me anything. I only know where he's been when he returns after those days and nights because he's in a mood then. I feel his self-hatred coming off him whenever he comes home, and Zach's words ring in my ears.

"I don't want to see you get hurt."

I don't want to believe it. Or maybe I just don't want to admit he's right. That I don't know how far Armen would go if he found out. I don't know if his loyalty to Malik is stronger than blood.

Zach's easy to talk to. I think he tried hard to make me feel relaxed, but that's an impossibility. I can't relax until I know Armen is safe. He offered to drive me home, but I declined. I like walking in the city and our house is only about a mile outside of it. But I know he's following me. I can feel it, even though when I look over my shoulder, I can't see him in the crowd. I like knowing he's watching. For some reason, I feel safer for it.

I get to the house and notice Armen's car is still gone. That's not unusual so I unlock the door and walk inside. Since mom and dad died, the house feels different, bigger almost. Then when Seth and Rafi disappeared, it got empty. Hollow. Like it too was missing them. Waiting for them to walk in the front door.

I glance at the street once more before I close the door and lock it. Walking through the large living room, I make a point of not looking up at the frescoed ceiling my mom loved so much, and go into the kitchen. I put on the tea kettle and make myself a sandwich. I need to eat something, even though I don't feel like it. I'm still too anxious, worked up over what I did. I've set things into motion now that I can't undo. I've given information to the Americans, and although they may have already had it, I betrayed my brother. My reasons for doing it don't matter. I've gone against my own blood, even though my intention is to preserve what's left of it.

Once the kettle whistles, I make myself a cup of tea and carry it up to my room. It's the first one at the top of the stairs. I don't look at all the other closed doors there. All the rooms that stand empty. I go into my own and push the window open to look up at the darkening sky, drink the first sip of scalding hot tea. The phone in my pocket feels heavy. It's the one Zach gave me. I glance at my closed door once as I sit on the edge of my bed and pull it out. It's old, I can tell, and it's used, but whatever information was in it before has been wiped out because now, there's only one number programmed inside it. His. Just Zach. Not his title, not his last name.

I'm to call him if I feel unsafe at any time. I know he's worried Armen will hurt me if he finds out what I'm doing, but he's wrong. Armen's my brother. He wouldn't hurt me.

Zach asked me about Armen's office. About any paperwork he leaves lying around. He asked me to take photos of whatever I find, even if it doesn't make sense to me.

My stomach feels heavy with the thought of what I'm about to do, but I finish my tea and get to my feet. I take a deep breath and pocket the phone as I head downstairs to Armen's office. The door isn't locked. He trusts me to keep out. It takes me a full minute to come to terms with what I'm about to do. I push the door open and switch on the lamp. He keeps the navy curtains closed here. This room never gets any sunlight or fresh air, and it smells like cigarettes. Like stale smoke.

The first thing I do when I walk around the large desk is dump the ashtray full of butts and ashes in the trashcan. He picked up the habit about four months ago and I can't stand it.

He's taken his laptop with him so I don't have to go through that. He usually takes it and when he doesn't, he hides it. Maybe he's suspected my betrayal all along. Maybe his instincts tell him to keep the computer hidden from me.

I touch the yellow pad of paper with his chicken scratch on it. I'm not sure how they'll make anything out of it, but I snap photos. I flip to the next page and do the same. Once I have all the pages photographed, I open a drawer. It's empty apart from two pens, some sticky notes still wrapped in plastic, and a half-full pack of cigarettes. A lighter is tucked inside.

I open another one. This one contains loose pieces of paper. Some are torn, some have coffee rings on them. I can't tell how old they are or how important. I try the next drawer and find the same thing. He must keep everything and it's all a mess. I close it and open the bottom right one. When I do, I step back, gasping, surprised by what's inside.

A shiny, black revolver.

I know he has one. I've seen it in its holster beneath the jacket he wears thinking he's hiding it from me. The realization that he probably owns more than one strikes me then. He never leaves the house unarmed anymore.

Tentatively, I touch it. It's cool and hard, and for

some reason, I pick it up. Feel its weight. Look at it. And I realize it's not unused and that thought makes me drop it back down like it's a brand. I quickly close the drawer, shove it hard when it gets stuck. I want it out of my sight. I want to be out of this room. I don't want to know what he's done with that gun. Who he's hurt.

I go back up to my room and hide the phone under my pillow before stripping off my clothes and running a hot shower. I feel dirty. I feel...bad. But I haven't felt good in a long time and if doing this will get my brother back safely, then I have to do it. I have to feel bad for a little longer because for some reason, I trust Zach. I know he'll help me.

THE FOLLOWING WEEK, I GO TO THE SAME OFFICE, but this time, I use the door at the back of the building in an alley. The soldier who had stood guard at the other door is at this one today, but he's not alone. There's another one with him and from the first moment, I don't like him. It's the way he looks at me as I pass. The way I feel his eyes on me when the other soldier walks me to the office where I was the first time. Once again I'm seated in that big room with only the table and two chairs. I place the cell phone on the table when the soldier leaves and today, it's only a few minutes before Zach comes in carrying a laptop.

"Right on time," he says with a smile. His eyes slide over the phone before meeting mine. "Let's take a look at what you found."

Zack picks up the phone and quickly scrolls through the photographs. He smiles, nods to me, then opens the laptop and attaches the phone to it with a cable. Several minutes pass before he speaks.

"These are difficult to read, but good," he says.

I know they're not what he's looking for. "I wasn't sure what you'd want. What was important."

He closes the laptop and gives me his full attention. "Anything you find, even if you're not sure how or what it is, could be important. These men use secret codes of communication—"

"These men? My brother isn't—"

"The men your brother is currently working with, well, you said yourself they're...not good."

I just sit there not knowing what to say.

"I'm going to send these to our specialist. He'll look through them carefully and hopefully, there's something useful in them. Now, were you careful?"

"Yes."

"Armen doesn't know you took these?"

"No."

"Good."

He rises to his feet. I do the same, feeling embarrassed. Disappointed. "We'll meet again next week."

He reaches into his pocket, withdraws a folded sheet of paper that he reads over once before handing it to me. "We'll meet at this address. It's a public place. Do you know where it is?"

"Yes." It's a coffee shop on the other side of the city.

"Same day and time."

"Okay." I take a step to the door but he strides over before I reach it. His hand closes around my arm to stop me. The touch is gentle, but deliberate. I look down to where he's holding me and when I look up, his head is bowed and I meet his gaze through his thick lashes.

"You did good, Eve."

I study his eyes, the smile inside them. The reassurance. I know the information is useless, but I find myself smiling.

"I'll get something better next time. I'll look harder."

"Most importantly, be safe."

"I will."

4

ZACH

One week later, I'm waiting at the café. I'm early, but I'm always early. I'm sitting in civilian clothing looking like any other tourist in this busy place. That's why I chose it, the fact that there's a high amount of foot traffic here. We'll go unnoticed. I have a man stationed along the path she'll walk. I want to be sure she's not followed. That Armen doesn't have a tail on her. She's not experienced enough to know herself and I'm not about to let her get caught in his web. Not about to let her get hurt.

The information Eve provided last week wasn't very useful, but it was her first time and it's what I expected. Today, it'll be better. And the time after that, better still. She wants to save her brother. I don't need to give her any more motivation than that.

But she's different than other informants. Maybe because of who she is. Or maybe it's that there's something about her that draws me to her. Something innocent and sweet and vulnerable. It's the reason I'm meeting her today. I should give her more time, this could be a waste of mine. It's what my commander thought. It's not often I'm questioned in regards to my work, but today, he questioned.

She walks in at that moment and my brain switches into protector mode. I watch her from my seat in the corner. She's wearing a short skirt and a T-shirt. Her hair is pulled into a ponytail and if she's got any makeup on, it's minimal.

She doesn't see me right away and I force my gaze from her and look around the room to see if anyone is watching more closely than is normal. She's an attractive girl. She'll draw attention. I know that, but I find I don't like the way gazes linger, the way men sneak sideways glances at her, and I have to remind myself that I'm not here for those men. I'm looking for others. The dangerous kind. The kind with intent to harm. I clear my throat and make a small movement. She sees me and smiles, almost waves, but drops her hand and fixes a serious expression on her face as she makes her way to me.

I wonder if she noticed the soldier who would have followed her. I don't plan on mentioning it but am curious if she will.

"Hi," she says, sliding into the seat across from

me so her back is to the room. Mine is to the wall where I can see everything.

Jared, the soldier who tailed her, walks into the café, newspaper folded under his arm, and orders a coffee. From the corner of my eye, I watch him take a seat at the bar and open the paper. I know he's not reading a word of it though. It's an Arabic language paper. He couldn't if he wanted to, and his mission isn't the news. It's to make sure she's safe.

"You found the café all right?" I ask, raising my hand to get the waitress' attention.

"Yes. I know the city well."

"Good." The waitress arrives. "What would you like?"

"Oh, just a cup of tea please."

I order another coffee and when the waitress walks away, Eve tucks a hand into her bag and withdraws her phone. She sets it on the table and smiles nervously. "There's more this time. I hope it's useful."

Placing my newspaper over top of the phone, I smile. "Were you safe? Does Armen know?"

"You keep asking that. I told you no. And he won't find out."

But Armen's a smart guy. I know she's banking on her innocence to keep her safe while she does what she's doing, but she doesn't know men like Armen El-Amin. He's not the brother she thinks he is.

"Don't take any risks, understand?"

"Yes." The waitress comes with her tea and my coffee. I take the opportunity to drag the newspaper toward me, pocketing the phone and setting the other one I'd brought for her on the table.

"Here you go."

She takes it, glancing around nervously before she slides it into her purse. When she meets my eyes again, there's a long moment of silence. I know it disarms her. I can see it on her face, in the blush that creeps up her slender neck to color her cheeks. She clears her throat a moment later and makes to stand. I don't know why, but I place my hand over hers.

"Sit."

I see her throat work as she swallows. She's nervous. Anxious. Why do I like her like this? I'm abusing my power over her. She's inexperienced. A girl—barely a woman. She's intimidated, but curious. The pulse at her throat is working frantically, giving away her pounding heart, and she licks her lips as she settles back down. She doesn't pull her hand away and her eyes are glued to mine. One corner of my mouth curves upward as I release her and sit back, picking up my small cup of Turkish coffee. I sip the thick black liquid while watching her and maybe it's the fact I haven't been with a woman in a few weeks, but my mind races with images of Eve that would make her face burn crimson.

I clear my throat, but my voice sounds hoarse when I speak.

"Drink your tea, Eve."

She's unsure what to do, what's expected. I wonder if she's ever even been on a date. I doubt she has. But I know she likes this. Likes sitting across from me. Looking at me. Likes me looking at her.

She picks up her tea and sips.

"Good." I'm not looking at her when I say it. Instead, I finish my coffee and reach into my pocket for my wallet, extract some bills and set them on the table. "Stay and finish your drink. Order something to eat if you like. Don't leave until ten minutes have passed. I'll be in touch about our next meeting."

I rise to my feet and make my way out of the cafe, knowing I've confused her, but thing is, I'm confused myself. She's an informant. She's the sister of a wanted man. There's nothing I should be doing apart from gathering information. Keeping her safe is part of my mission, but data gathering is number one. Too much at stake for this to become anything else.

A little over an hour later, Jared walks into my office at headquarters. He's casual about it, barely rapping his knuckles against the door to alert me to his arrival. I've known Jared for four years and although we're not friends, I trust him with my life.

"Was she followed?" I ask when he closes the door and sits down across my desk.

Jared shakes his head. "No. And she did just like you said. Sat there for ten minutes before walking out. Looked a little disappointed you left so quickly. Didn't even finish her tea."

I know from the look on his face that he's digging. I don't give him a verbal response.

"You think she's trustworthy? I mean, she's El-Amin's sister," he says. That's what he was getting at.

I feel my jaw tighten. "Are you questioning my judgement?"

"Of course not."

"Good."

"She's a nice-looking piece though, isn't she? Nice—"

"She's an informant, not a 'piece'. You'll respect her. Am I clear?" My voice is harder than I intend.

One side of Jared's mouth curves upward. I just confirmed what he was thinking.

"Relax. She's a little too clean for my taste."

I don't know if he intended to piss me off, but he just did. I rise to my feet, notice that my hands have fisted. "I asked you a question, soldier."

The chair he was sitting on scrapes the floor as he gets to his feet.

"Yes, sir. Understood."

I slowly sit. He remains standing. I focus my attention on the sheets of paper in front of me, flipping through them. "Is there anything else?"

"Just that her brother's vehicle was parked in the driveway when she arrived."

I glance up. "Did you see him?"

"No."

I hate leaving her in that house with him.

"Any useable intelligence?" Jared asks, changing the subject.

I tap a key on my laptop and the screen comes to life. "Take a look at this."

Jared comes around the corner to look at one of the photos Eve had taken. A picture of a picture. It's the street sign in the corner I'm curious about.

5

ZACH

I'm waiting at a stall near our meeting point. Eve is late, which is unusual. It worries me. She's worried me since day one. The more I get to know her, the more protective I feel of her. The more anxious I am every time she walks into her house while I watch, unobserved. I follow her home after each of our meetings. We've been at this for two months now. I don't like the idea of her walking alone. The moment she enters her house and closes the door, she shuts me out. And I can't stop thinking about what Armen would do if he found out, sister or not.

I check my watch for the hundredth time when I catch a glimpse of her. The moment she turns the corner, I breathe a sigh of relief. I didn't realize how tense I'd grown while waiting. She sees me and gives me a wide smile, and something twists in my gut. That's guilt. That's knowing I'm going to take whatever she's got on her brother and use it to capture both him and Malik. To kill one and put the other away—and that's the best-case scenario.

"Sorry I'm late," she says when she reaches me.

"I was worried." With my hand at her lower back, I guide her between two stalls so we're draped by carpets on one side, and silks on the other. Sunlight is filtered red through the fine cloth and she looks even softer, even prettier for it.

I memorize her eyes, layers of caramel, the shade unusual, entrancing. She's watching me, too, studying me. And my conscience tugs at me. She's not even twenty. Barely a woman if I look at her face, at the trust there. The innocence. I should have sent her away the first day she showed up at headquarters. She's too young, too inexperienced, and we're taking advantage of that. *I'm* taking advantage. And here we are and all I can think about is her face, her eyes, the way they look at me. Her lips. How they would feel against mine. How they would taste.

She blinks, lowering her lashes to the bag she's holding. Fumbling inside it. When she looks up, her face is burning red. It's like she's just read my mind and maybe the thoughts inside hers weren't too far off.

I clear my throat. "What's that?"

She's drawing out an envelope along with the cell phone.

The moment I ask the question, her expression changes. Becomes serious. Almost afraid. "An arms sale happening soon. In two days if I'm reading it right. This is a list of the men who will be there. Malik is on that list."

I take it, open the envelope. Pull out the sheet of paper. It's a list of names and I recognize about half the attendees. I look up at her. "How did you get this?" This is gold.

"It was lying on the floor of Armen's study."

My gaze snaps up to hers. "Lying on the floor? Just like that?"

She nods. "He was in a rush. He must have dropped it."

"And he won't know you took it?"

She studies me. "He told me he'd be gone for four days."

I understand. The sale will take place within those days and she's thinking it'll be done. That this will be over and that it won't matter. Because we'll have killed Malik and freed her brother of him.

"Eve, things can change." I tuck the sheet back into the envelope and hand it to her. "You have to take it back, leave it where you found it. If this sale doesn't happen and he realizes this list is missing, he'll ask questions."

She doesn't take the envelope. She's shaking her head and I see her anxiety. Realize it's been wearing on her all this time. "It can't change. I can't do this much longer," she says, and her eyes are suddenly flooded with tears. "It's too much."

I touch her arms, hold them, and when a tear slides down her face, I draw her to me. It's the first time I've done it. Held her like this. And it feels good. She feels good. Like she belongs right here, in my arms. Her body is trembling as she cries and I know it's stress. How had I not thought about this? How did I not realize how much stress she'd be under doing this on her own? All while living under the same roof as the enemy?

"It's going to be all right, Eve. It *will* be over soon." It's a promise I'm not sure I can keep. "Nothing's going to happen to you. I'm not going to let anyone hurt you."

She melts into me, molding her body to mine. I don't know if she's aware of the tiny movement, but I'm so aware of her, of how she's curled into me. Her breath feels warm against my neck and she feels so small. So vulnerable.

Shouting has me whirl around, and I tuck her behind me as I reach for my weapon. It's hidden beneath my jacket, but my hand easily closes around the pistol, keeping one hand on her as the sound of men running sends women and children screaming as they scramble out of the way. I don't know what the hell is going on, but before I have time to draw my weapon, the sound of bullets flying has me ducking for cover, has me taking Eve with me. I hear her scream and push her to the ground, covering her with my own body as men run past, a dozen of them in fatigues, faces covered.

"Stay down!" I'm about to get up, to chase them, but she's got my arm and makes a strange sound.

I turn to her, my heart struggling to regain its rhythm after that sound.

"Eve!" There's blood. A lot of it.

I drop my weapon and take her arm, touch the source of the bleeding.

"Zach?"

In the background, I realize the sounds of running have receded. The men are gone. I don't know who they were or what they wanted, but one of their bullets grazed Eve's arm and this is too close for my comfort.

I meet her frightened eyes. "It hurts," she says through tears.

Ripping a strip from my shirt, I tie it over the wound and lift her in my arms as I stand. I already hear the sirens of police and ambulances, but I'm spiriting her away from the market, away from the stalls. Away from everything.

I don't stop until we're at headquarters. Until the doctor is cleaning the wound, bandaging it. I just stand there, back against the wall, arms folded over my chest. Eyes locked on her, knowing she got lucky. If I hadn't pushed her to the ground when I did, where would that bullet have struck? How much worse could it have been?

She looks so small sitting there. Small and scared. Even as she's trying to smile I see the effort it's taking her not to cry.

This was wrong. What if her brother's known all along? What if that whole thing had been set up just to do what they did? Scare her? Or maybe worse? How in hell could I let this girl get involved in something so dangerous? Christ, I know better.

"You'll have a scar, but it's a flesh wound. You'll be fine in no time," the doctor says.

I watch Eve slide off the table and stand. I don't miss the wobbling of her knees.

"Thank you," I say. I open the door and wait. Eve is watching me.

She nods, thanks the doctor and walks ahead of me. She stops once we're alone in the hallway.

"Zach? Are you okay?"

I laugh, but it's not a laugh at all. "You just got shot and you're asking me if I'm okay?"

"It's a flesh wound. You heard the doctor. Wrong place, wrong time."

"I put you in the wrong place. I should have protected you better."

She touches my hand and the contact of her

fingers on my flesh sparks a charge of pure electricity. "It was an accident," she says finally.

I drag my eyes from our hands to her face. I shake my head. "You're finished today. No more of this. You need to forget this. It's too dangerous."

"What?"

I take her arm and turn her to walk down the corridor. "You'll stay here until this is over. I don't want you going home until we have your brother and Malik."

"Stay here?"

I nod. "Then we'll get you out of here. Out of Beirut. Somewhere safe."

"I don't want that." She stops, pulls away. "That's not the agreement."

It takes me a moment to swallow back my anger, which is at myself, not her. I don't want to frighten her any more than she already is. "Eve, what happened today, what if it wasn't an accident?"

"What?" She shakes her head. "No. This had nothing to do with me. With Armen."

"Until I'm sure, you're not going back to that house. No way."

"He's not—"

I take her uninjured arm, my grip tighter than it needs to be when I shake her once. "Do you realize what could have happened today? Do you have any idea what would have happened if that bullet had struck a few inches to the left? Do you?"

"Zach—"

I'm so angry with myself, I can't think straight. How was I so stupid? How in hell did I put an innocent in harm's way?

"I care about you, Eve. I don't want to see you get hurt."

I t's the middle of the night when I'm walking home. My arm throbs as the painkillers wear off. I'm still a little shaky from what happened earlier, and I wasn't sure if I'd be walking out of that building today, but Zach and his men are gone. I know it's because of the information I gave them. They're getting ready for the arms sale.

Zach doesn't believe I'm safe. He thinks what happened today had to do with Armen. But he's wrong. There's no way Armen knows what I've been doing. I've been too careful. And even if he did, he wouldn't do something like that to me.

The house is dark. I dig my key out of my purse and let myself in, hearing the echo of my footsteps. I'm alone. Armen isn't here and he won't be for four days. And after that, Malik will either be dead or in the custody of the Americans and Armen will be free.

I walk into the kitchen and turn on the dim light over the stove. I'm starving. After this morning, I'd been too anxious to eat. Taking leftover soup out of the fridge, I pour it into a pot to warm it up and can't help thinking about Zach. About what happened today. When the shots rang out at the market, the first thing he did was push me behind him. He used his body to shield mine. He also told me he cared about me. I'm still trying to wrap my brain around that.

When the soup boils, I sit down to eat, but I only manage a few spoonfulls before anxiety fills my belly, not leaving room for food. What if Zach's right? What if I'm wrong about my own brother? Ever since Zach said it that first day, I've been thinking about it, and gathering that information over the last two months, I've seen things.

I open my purse and take out the envelope. From inside, I unfold the sheet of paper I'd given Zach. The one with all the names. Wanted men, I know. Dangerous men. A shudder runs through me at the few names I recognize. He told me to put it back. That if this sale didn't go through as planned, if Armen realized what I'd done, he'd hurt me. I can't think about that, but I do rise to my feet and make my way to Armen's study. I open the door. It's pitch black inside. I go in—just a few steps, my hand is still on the doorknob—and drop the sheet of paper on the floor where I'd picked it up hours earlier.

And I know in that instant that this is over. That this was the last piece of information I'd give Zach. The realization makes me shudder, the thought that I'll never see him again.

But when I hear the lock on the front door turn, I stop dead in my tracks. My eyes lock on the door handle. I hadn't switched on the lights when I'd come home so the room is lit only by the light from the stove in the kitchen and the full moon shining in through the windows. It's like my feet are glued to the spot when the door opens.

I see Armen right away.

And he sees me.

Me with my hand on the doorknob of his study. Me with one foot inside and one foot outside the office he's forbidden me to enter.

He's casual when he enters the house, like he's not surprised to find me here. Several men follow close behind him. Men I don't recognize. Malik's soldiers, whom he rarely lets into the house.

But seeing them, six of them, file into my parents' home, some with rifles across their shoulders, some with pistols tucked into holsters, my blood chills and I feel the color drain from my face. I meet my brother's gaze and all those men—it could have been two dozen of them—and they wouldn't frighten me as much as the look on Armen's face does. The one that says he's known all along.

They flank Armen and every set of eyes is on me.

The last one closes the door and someone switches on the lights. It's startling, the sudden brightness of the place. It exposes me. Leaves me nowhere to hide.

Armen takes a step toward me. Then another. Then he clucks his tongue and I open mine to speak, but nothing comes. Only a choking sound. I try to clear my throat, but I can't. All I can do is watch him approach, watch the one who follows, and I can't tell who is the meaner of the two. The one I should fear more. The one I should run from.

But I don't run. Where would I go?

"Armen?" I manage somehow when he reaches me.

His eyes, so like my own, study my face, glide down to the bandage at my arm. He dips a finger into his mouth, wetting it, and swipes a smudge of dried blood away. He doesn't look at me when he speaks. Doesn't ask about the bandage. The soldier moves behind me and grips my hair, tugging my head back hard.

"What have you done, little sister?" Armen asks the question as he takes a syringe out of his pocket and uncaps it.

When I open my mouth to scream, the man

who's holding me twists his fingers in my hair and renders me mute with pain.

Armen steps even closer, and I'm trying not to look at the needle in his hand, not to see him depress the plunger to push air out of it before bringing it to my exposed neck, stabbing me with it.

"What have you done?"

UNHINGED

PROLOGUE

ZACH

Finding people who don't want to be found has always been one of my specialties. It's what got me into special ops.

It's also what got me killed.

Well, almost got me killed.

It isn't quite pitch black when I step out of my SUV and onto the street. *Her* street. The full moon shines bright overhead, making the clouds appear silvery, making them cast shadows as they skim past. I don't duck into those shadows, though. I take my time walking to her house. Don't bother hiding. I stroll, in fact—if a guy my size can stroll—right up to 13 Rattlesnake Valley Lane.

Her garden is small, but neat, not a single weed in the lush green grass. The walkway swept clean. Perfect. No cracks in the concrete. It's just like her, actually. Perfect—on the outside. The inside's where the damage is.

It's a warm night, even for Denver, but she has all the windows open. Sheer curtains blow gently, but the breeze is getting stronger. It carries a storm on its heels. An omen.

When I reach her door, I slip my key out of my pocket. I made a copy a few weeks ago. She hasn't noticed I've been coming and going for that long. But she's never been home for my visits. Not yet, at least. Not until tonight.

I turn the doorknob and open the front door. I know the exact point when it will creak, so I make sure I'm in before it does. I don't bother locking it behind me. Locks never keep those they intend to keep out, out. It's naïve to think otherwise.

By now, I've memorized the layout of the small house. It's another of my talents. I see everything, every single detail most people don't even notice. It's what saved my life the night I was meant to die.

The living room is picked up, and utterly impersonal. It's like no one lives here. I wonder if she rented the place furnished because it doesn't look like what I imagine she'd like. This stuff is all too big, too rustic. Too secondhand.

I almost nick my shin in the same spot I have twice before, but move just in time as I make my way toward her bedroom. She sleeps with the door open. I'm guessing it's for ventilation. I wonder why she doesn't run the AC, but maybe it's because of her background, where she's from. She's lived in the desert. Grown up in it. Maybe to her, this is cool.

As I get closer, I can see her soft, feminine shape lying beneath the single white sheet on the bed. She's on her side, face to the window. Long, dark hair is strewn across her pillow. She's got one arm over top of the sheet and I recognize the scar where a bullet skimmed her skin two years ago. She'd been that close to dying. If I hadn't tackled her to the ground when I had, she would have died.

And maybe six others would have lived because of it.

Stop.

I can't go there.

Not now.

Right now, I need answers.

A cloud crosses the moon, casting a shadow over her face as I approach. It's gone as quickly as it came though, and a moment later, I'm looking down at her, at Eve El-Amin. And even though I've been tailing her for weeks, memorizing every detail of her new life, being this close to her, it does something to me. Being near her has always been difficult, dangerous, but this time, it's more than that. Or at least it's different. It stirs up all those old emotions—anger the predominant one—but something else, too. Something dark and twisted inside me.

A thing that wants what it wants.

I close my eyes momentarily, quashing that last part. Shoving it deep down into my gut. It's no use. Not here. Not now. Because too much is at stake to let that side take over.

It's like asking the question of why. It's no use trying to understand why. Did she know that night was a trap? Did she know she was sending us into a massacre? Why would she do that? Why, when every single man who died that night would have laid down his life to protect hers?

I feel my chest tightening, along with my jaw, my fists. Eve mutters something in her sleep. I'm not worried she'll wake. My heart doesn't even skip a beat when she rolls onto her back. That's how far gone I am. That's how little I care if she does open her eyes and sees me standing in her bedroom, looming over her as she sleeps.

And that's what makes me dangerous. Makes this mission—my private vendetta—so fucking fragile.

I need to fucking care.

I need to get my head out of my ass and focus on why I'm here.

If she sees me now, it'll fuck up the grand entrance I have planned. For weeks, I've been going through her house. Drinking her liquor. Eating her food. Leaving empty containers on the kitchen counter. Moving her mail. Little shit that makes her think she's not paying attention or forgetting. Unnerving her. Making her look over her shoulder.

That little shit is changing tomorrow.

Tomorrow, shit gets real.

I look down at her face. She's pretty. Always was. She hasn't changed much in two years, which surprises me. I would have thought sending six men to their deaths would have taken its toll.

But then again, you'd have to have a conscience for that.

Her hair's longer. I bet the thick waves she used to tie in a ponytail reach the middle of her back. Her olive skin is pale for the time of year, still smooth, still perfect, just like her tiny nose, those lush, plump lips. I can see a little glimpse of white teeth behind those lying lips.

I crouch down. I'm so close, I can hear her breathe.

I inhale, taking in her scent, remembering it. Memorizing it. Filing it away as my cock stirs.

"Sleep well tonight, Eve El-Amin," I whisper, and I can't resist touching her, pushing a wisp of soft, jet black hair off her face. "Because come tomorrow, your days are numbered and sleep will become a thing of the past."

Another bad night. Another strange feeling. Almost like I'm being watched. But something's different this time. It's closer. Scarier.

I brew a second cup of coffee and tell myself to shake it off when Miranda, the receptionist, walks into the break room.

"Morning, Eve." She pushes the button on the coffee machine and studies me as black liquid fills her cup. Her head is cocked to the side. "Didn't sleep again, huh?"

I've known Miranda for a little over a year and I'm still not sure I like her. Or trust her. But maybe the latter's my own fault. My own nature. Maybe it's the fact I can't be trusted that I'm unable to trust anyone else.

"It's too hot," I lie.

"Mm-hmm," she says and gives me a wink.

I walk past her and check my watch. "I've got to go. New client Devon wants me to meet."

"I saw him." Miranda waggles her eyebrows. "You always get the hot ones."

I give her a half smile. "You think every man who walks in here is hot."

She turns her attention to her cup of coffee, pouring milk and sugar into it. "True."

I walk to my office, which is beside Devon's. Devon is my boss. He owns Alderson Realty. It's a small, family-run business that goes back almost a hundred years. It was started by his great-great-grandfather, Marty Alderson, and has been passed down through the generations. I've been working here since I got to Denver, which was about six months after arriving in the country. Here, I'm Eve Adams. And to hear me speak, anyone would think I was a native-born American. My looks give away my roots, but apart from one or two questions on background—which I lie about—most people assume I'm second-or third-generation and leave it at that.

My name change, it wasn't my decision. I wanted to keep El-Amin, but couldn't. I needed to become a different person after that night for so many reasons. And I'm trying hard to *be* Eve Adams. But there's that old saying: *wherever you go, there you are.*

And here I am.

No matter how much time goes by, it's like the

past is still right here—my constant companion—
always reminding me.

At my desk, I set my coffee down and take a deep
breath before gathering my folders. The new client
Devon wants me to meet is looking for a large property with lots of acreage. I heard the numbers and if
we can get this job, it'll be a big deal for us. I know
the firm needs the money. Alderson Realty has held
its own for a while, but with increased competition
from larger realtors and the market being what it is,
the future doesn't look very promising.

My cell phone buzzes with a text message. I don't
need to read the display to know Devon's waiting for
me with the client. I'm running late, and he showed
up early. I type a quick reply telling him I'm on my
way, gather the things I need and head to the conference room. Miranda gives me a wink when I pass
her desk and I roll my eyes. Once I get to the conference room door, I double check my appearance in
the full-length mirror on the wall, adjust the skirt of
my suit, then push the door open.

"Ah, there she is," Devon says.

He's facing me, sitting at the head of the table
that seats twelve. He rises and touches the chair to
his right. My usual seat. The client's sitting at the
other end of the table with his back to me, but he's
so close I catch a whiff of his aftershave, which
seems familiar for some strange reason. He doesn't
stand or turn to greet me as I enter.

"Good morning," I start, closing the door. I can only see the back of the client's head. He has short, neatly trimmed dark hair, big, really broad shoulders and thick arms. It's almost as though the chair isn't quite wide enough for his muscular build. "Sorry I'm late," I say, my brain trying to process the memory of the aftershave he's wearing and the odd feeling that accompanies it. I walk around the table, eyes on my folders and the too-full cup of coffee I should have drunk before coming in here.

"No problem," the client says.

I stop. My heart stumbles over a beat as my breath catches in my throat and that feeling of something being wrong, that I'm being watched, suddenly grips me.

"I'm early," he adds.

In my periphery, I see he's rising to his feet and something about that moment—his words, his voice, *him*—and...oh my God.

I remember why the aftershave is familiar.

A brick lands in my belly, and I stumble backward.

"Eve?" It's Devon, he's taken a step toward me.

I clear my throat and feel the blood drain from my face as I look up. I don't look at the client. Not yet. I smile weakly at Devon instead.

"Are you all right? You look flushed."

"I'm fine," I manage, but don't recognize my voice. I hear the old accent creeping back into my words. I turn slowly to face the man now standing beside Devon, watching me intently.

And I feel sick.

He's smiling. I recognize that smile.

It's not the nice one.

His eyes have gone dark, darker than I remember, and I notice scars that weren't there before that night. He looks out of place, too big, too wild, too savage to be wearing a suit that barely contains him. He's huge. Much bigger than before. Is that possible, or is that just my memory playing with me? Guilt fucking with my mind?

Devon comes around the table to take the folders and coffee cup out of my hands.

"You sure you're all right?" he asks with an embarrassed smile.

"I..." I can't take my eyes off him. But it can't be. He's dead. He died two years ago. He died in the explosion along with everyone else.

"Maybe you should open a window," he says to Devon, nonchalantly. "She looks like she needs some air."

"I'm fine." It takes all I have to speak like I've trained myself to. Like an American. My voice trembles, and I lower myself into the chair Devon's pulled out for me. I still can't drag my eyes away from him, though.

"I'll get you some water," Devon says.

"No!" The water station is out in the hallway and I don't want to be alone with him. I can't be.

"All right then. Eve, this is the client I told you about, Michael Beckham. Michael, my top agent, Eve Adams."

Michael Beckham?

No. Not Michael Beckham.

His eyes narrow a little as one corner of his mouth curls upward. I see menace on his face, in his eyes. I see his scrutiny. It's him. I have no doubt. Master Sergeant Zach Amado come back to life.

"Eve, are you sure—" Devon starts.

"I'm fine. Truly." I pick up my coffee cup and bring it to my lips. My hands tremble so much it's a wonder I don't spill the contents onto my lap, but I manage the smallest of sips and it calms me a little. I set the cup down and steel myself. "It's nice to meet you, Mr. Beckham," I hear myself say with a voice that sounds slightly more like that of Eve Adams.

He extends his hand to me. I'd hoped the table between us might save me from having to shake it. I look at it for a moment, then place mine inside his.

"Nice to meet you, Ms. *Adams*, was it?"

He squeezes.

I flinch.

"Eve is fine."

"Eve," he says with a nod, still holding my hand. His eyes are intent on me and I remember how once, one of his men tried to call me *baby* in Arabic and he'd slammed his fist down on the table. He hadn't even needed to reprimand the soldier verbally. I was to be treated respectfully. I was, after all, risking my life helping the American soldiers.

But it turned out I didn't help them at all.

Michael—Master Sergeant Zach Amado— releases my hand.

"Eve pulled some properties for you," Devon starts.

I'm not paying attention to Devon though. I don't know if Zach is either. He won't stop staring at me, and I can't look away. Not until he releases me from his gaze a full minute later. He and Devon begin going over the properties while I open my notebook and pretend to take notes.

I don't understand what's happening. He's supposed to be dead. I don't know how I feel about him not being dead. Good, I think. Relieved? It's one less life on my conscience.

Like that will make any difference.

I sneak a glance. He's facing Devon. God, I remember him so freaking well. Everything about him. Things you never think about, like the cowlick at his hairline. The dimple on his right cheek when he smiles. How thick his dark hair was—is—and how tanned his skin would get in the Mediterranean sun. Darker than the others. But he's half-Italian, half-Portuguese. Born in America and raised in Italy. He has two brothers. That was all I knew about him.

All anyone knew, as far as I could tell. He didn't talk about his family or his past. And for a man in his early twenties, he seemed like he had a lot of past.

"Eve, you won't mind doing that, will you?" Devon asks.

"W-what? Sorry," I shake my head. "I didn't hear you."

"Taking Michael to the first two appointments. There's some personal business at my daughter's school I have to handle," he explains to Michael.

"Oh, me?" I do this all the time. I always take clients to view houses. I love that part of the job most of all, actually.

"Are you sure you're all right?" Devon asks again.

"Uh, I know Miranda—"

The look I get from Devon cuts me off. We both know Miranda.

"If Eve is uncomfortable..." Zach starts.

I wonder if Devon hears the dare in his tone.

"She isn't uncomfortable, are you, Eve?" Devon asks.

"No. Not at all," I reply.

"Good." Devon rises. "That's settled then." Zach stands too, and he towers over Devon. "It's good to meet you, Michael. I have every confidence we'll be able to find you a beautiful new home." They shake hands.

"I have no doubt," Zach says.

They both turn to me and I realize I'm still sitting

down. I nod my head and collect the folders while I rise to my feet. "If you're ready then, um, Michael," I say and the name he's using catches in my throat.

"We'll take my truck," he says.

"But it's—"

He stops me with a look. "We'll take my truck."

"Yes, si—" I catch myself before calling him sir, like I used to.

My faltering makes him smile a little and if Devon notices how weird that was, he doesn't let on. A moment later, Devon is gone and we're alone in the room. Devon's left the door open though. Thank goodness.

I turn my attention to Zach. My throat is as dry as the desert as I look at him, really look at him. He always had tattoos but I see now he has more. Something—a snake, maybe two—winding up along his throat. But that's not what catches my attention. It's the other side of his neck. The scarring there. Burns. From that night.

"Ever feel fire lick your skin, Eve?" he asks.

I realize I've been staring too long. And he's been watching me all that time. I drag my eyes to his. Force myself to look at him.

"Ever smell human flesh burn?" he adds.

I'm sweating, and I feel like I'm going to be sick.

"It's like a fucking barbecue." He laughs, but it's not funny. Not even to him. "Seared hamburger."

What does he know? How much can he know?

He's using an alias, as am I, but mine was given to me by the US government. Mine is stamped inside a passport. He's supposed to be dead. They said he was a casualty of the failed mission.

He sighs deeply. "Let's go."

"It's you, isn't it?" I ask stupidly.

He's already taken a step toward the door, but he stops and turns to me. "In the flesh. Albeit slightly charred flesh. We need to go."

"Where?"

He walks back to the table, then comes around it to stand a foot from me. The only thing between us is the stack of folders I'm holding with a death grip. My heart is racing and I feel a droplet of sweat slide down my temple. His gaze travels over my face, moving down to my exposed neck, pausing at my throat, the pulse there, then drifts to where my breasts heave with every labored breath. He drags his eyes slowly back up to mine, and gives me a smirk. He knows exactly what he's doing to me. How he's making me feel. How nervous I am.

And he likes it.

When his hand moves, I gasp. He freezes for a moment—we both do, then he touches a folder.

What the hell did I expect he'd do?

"To the first house, of course," he says.

"What do you want?"

He leans in close to me. Close enough I can feel his breath on my face. "Careful," he starts in a whisper that sends shivers down my spine. "Your accent's creeping in. You'll give yourself away."

"Oh, good, you're still here." It's Miranda at the door. She stops short when she sees us. Can she feel the tension in the air? This weighted, heavy, almost palpable thing between us? It takes her a moment but she shoots a flirtatious look at Zach, drags it over his thick chest before holding a piece of paper out to me. "Lockbox code for the McKinney property changed. Break-in."

"Oh," I say. But I'm still standing there like an idiot.

"Thank you," Zach says, taking the slip of paper from her.

I look at him, then at her.

"It's no trouble," Miranda starts. "In fact, if you need anything, Mr. Beckham—"

"Michael, please," he says, his tone different.

She smiles like a teenage girl.

"I'm sure Eve here will be happy to help me with anything I may need," Zach says, not missing a beat, his expression still flirtatious though, at least when he's talking to her.

"Oh, yeah, okay." Miranda shrugs. "I'm just right out there, in case." She stands there another minute twirling her hair.

She's so obvious it's embarrassing to watch. And it animates me.

"We should go," I say, wanting to get whatever is

coming over with. I know he's not going to hurt me. If that was his plan, he'd have come to my house. Not here. Not where people would see him.

"Okay then," Miranda says. "Bye." Obviously disappointed, she walks out of the conference room.

He shifts his gaze and our eyes meet.

"It's you, isn't it? Moving things around, in my house."

"You really should get better locks, *habibi*."

Baby. That's the word that had pissed him off when one of his soldiers had used it. It's a term of endearment in Arabic. But he's not using it that way.

No.

He's making sure I know I've lost his protection.

In fact, he's the one I'll need protecting from.

2

ZACH

I have to admit, my entrance was impressive.

I wait for Eve at the conference room door, standing between it and the frame.

"After you," I say, gesturing for her to go ahead. It'll be a tight squeeze for her to pass, but I'm not interested in making it easy. I want her as uncomfortable as I can get her. Today is a big day for Eve El-Amin. It's the day she learns there are consequences to actions. That you can't run away from your past. From what you've done.

She hugs her folders to her chest. She's small, not quite five foot four barefoot. Even with the heels she has on, the top of her head only comes to about the middle of my chest. She takes in the space between the doorframe and me. Glances up at my face. Then tries to squeeze past without touching me. It's kind of funny. I don't let her through, though. Instead, I trap her between the wall and me. All I have to do is touch my chest to hers to do it and when I do, she gasps.

Big, caramel-colored eyes meet mine. I remember those eyes. Like the desert at sunset. I look inside them and remember her from before. Young—not quite twenty back then. Not even college educated, but intelligent. Spoke almost fluent English even then. I knew she'd come to us out of desperation. The El-Amin family was well known in Beirut, especially her oldest brother, Armen. She betrayed him to save him. At least that's what she was thinking. She thought she'd made a deal for her brother. But then he screwed her too. Although I'm still not sure if that was a distraction. If she knew all along what would happen. If I was the fool who fell for the trick, and in my stupidity got six men killed.

I'd underestimated Eve El-Amin, and after that night, I wondered if I had paid more attention to those questions I couldn't quite get answers to, the alarm bells I ignored when it came to her, if my men would be alive today.

Eve's cheeks are flushed pink and I'm pretty sure if I don't give her space, she's going to burst into tears. She's sweating bullets. I can see beads of perspiration along her hairline. I back off, and she passes me.

"I need to get my bag," she says, her voice a squeak.

I nod and wait by the door, but keep an eye on her. The office is small. There's one back exit but there's no reason for her to go that way. Hers is the first office beside the receptionist, and the walls are glass so I know she won't try to make a run for it. It'd be stupid of her to, anyway. She doesn't even know why I'm here. Doesn't know I've got nothing on that night. That it's not official military business that brings me. All I know is that she was the sole survivor of the crew that worked this particular mission, and I was pronounced dead way too fucking fast. No men were sent to look for us. To help. Nothing. I know all this because the doctor who saved my life told me. The army thinks it lost seven elite soldiers that night. Why wasn't there a single attempt at rescue?

Although with all the charred remains in that building, I guess it could have been a mistake. But something told me it wasn't. And I had learned my lesson about ignoring my gut.

When Eve returns with her bag and the folders, I push the glass door open to let her into the parking lot. Heat bombards us as soon as we step outside.

"That one," I say, fishing keys out of my pocket and hitting the button to unlock the doors of the Ford F-150.

She turns to it when she hears the beep and sees the lights blink. She nods but doesn't move.

I take the few steps to the truck and open the passenger side door. "Get in."

She looks inside the truck like the Grim Reaper himself is sitting there and when she turns to me, her eyes are glistening with tears and I see her shoulders shudder. She's white-knuckling the folders.

"I'm not going to hurt you," I say. Not sure if it's the truth or a lie just yet. Maybe I'm sexist, but if she were a man, this reunion would be going very differently. But I don't hit women. Even if they are traitors.

I'm not above using other means to get answers though.

I know she has to force her body along with every halting step, but she gets to the truck. The running board is higher than she's used to, but I don't help her. I watch her instead as she shifts the folders to one hand and hikes her skirt up a little. It's the first glimpse I get of her legs. Pretty. Slender.

I don't hide the fact that I'm looking. In fact, I admire her body openly, slowly sliding my gaze upward, back to her face. I'm pretty sure her eyes can't get any wider.

"In." I grip her elbow to hoist her up.

She sucks in an audible breath at the contact.

A moment later, she's in the truck. I walk over to my side and open the door, slide my jacket off and toss it into the backseat before getting in. She's practically pasted herself to the door to be as far away from me as possible, and her eyes dart from my chest to my arms, taking it all in.

"Seatbelt," I say.

I click mine into place. I know what she's looking at. She can see at least some of the tattoos through the white button-down shirt I'm wearing. They cover the whole of one arm and shoulder, the one without the bumpy, burned skin. I can't wait to see her face when she gets a look at my back though.

She drags her belt across her chest and snaps it into place.

I start the engine and put the truck into drive. The doors automatically lock when I do, and she lets out a startled gasp. It makes me smile as I navigate out of the parking lot. "Standard feature," I say, eyeing traffic to make my way into the stream. I only turn to her once we're on our way. "Don't worry. I didn't have it installed just to kidnap you."

She opens her mouth to speak, and I'm wondering if her nerves will give way to her guilt. If she knew all along what would happen that night. If she agreed to it.

"If I wanted to do that," I continue, "I wouldn't need the locks anyway."

"Do what?" She's visibly confused.

I face her squarely for a moment as we stop at a red light. "Kidnap you."

She swallows a lump in her throat.

"You said you wouldn't hurt me."

I give her a smirk then face forward as the light changes to green. "You're awfully nervous."

"I've just seen a dead man."

"Hmm. What's the address?"

"What?"

"The first house on your list. Pay attention, Eve. You used to be quicker on your feet."

She doesn't have a retort, but opens the first folder and reads off the address. It'll be about forty minutes before we get to the house. I know the area. I even know the house. When I called Devon Alderson, I'd already done my research.

"Out in the middle of nowhere, huh?" I say casually, turning onto the highway. We're only going to be on it for a few minutes though. I plan on taking the long way.

"I thought you were dead," she finally says.

"Surprise."

"I'm glad you're not."

"I doubt that."

No reply, not for a long time.

"What are you doing here, Zach?"

"Zach?" I ask, glancing to her. "Are we old friends?"

Her cheeks flush. I remember how that always happened with her. I'd always assumed it was the heat. "I-I don't know what to call you."

"You almost called me 'sir' earlier," I give her a wink and watch her swallow. "Give me your cell phone."

"What?"

"Cell phone. Give it to me."

"Devon will know if you do anything to me. If I go missing, he'll call the police."

"I'm really good at disappearing, as you should know. Being dead makes it easy."

She rubs her face, then runs her hands into her hair, pulling for a moment. "What do you want?"

I put on my turn signal and navigate to the right to exit the highway. It leads to a barely used service road, and she panics.

"What are you doing?" She's already unbuckling her belt and trying the door. After a few moments of fruitless effort, she turns to me. A tear slips from one eye that she quickly wipes away.

I have to take care not to fall for that. She already fooled me once. Never again.

"I like the scenic route," I say. "You know I've never been much of a people person. Now are you going to hand me your phone, or am I going to have to take it?"

"Why do you want it?" She eyes me warily as she fastens her seatbelt.

"So our time together is uninterrupted. You'll get it back later."

"People know where we're going. You won't get away—"

I give an exaggerated sigh. "Relax, Eve. I just have questions I need you to answer."

"About that night."

"No, about the fucking weather. Yes, about that night."

"How are you alive?"

The right side of my mouth curves upward for a single moment, but it's a hard line when I next speak. "The kindness of a stranger," I say. "After the treachery of a friend."

She has the good grace to bow her head. Reaching down, she picks up her purse from the floor, fishes out her cell phone and holds it out to me. I look down at her hand, palm up, the phone sitting in it. When I take it, my fingers brush hers. She startles at the touch. I switch off her phone and slide it into the glove compartment.

For the rest of the ride, we're both silent. I don't know what she's thinking, but I can feel the anxiety coming off her. If I think back to the few days prior to that last mission, I remember her being off, acting differently. I can't stop berating myself, blaming myself. The signs were there. But I didn't listen, not to them, not to my gut. And it cost six of my men their lives. *She* cost them their lives.

My knuckles turn white on the steering wheel. I need to keep it together. I want her on edge, but she isn't going to be any use to me if she's terrified, and I have questions only she can answer. I'll decide after that what to do with her. What she deserves.

"That's the turnoff," she says, pointing to what looks to be a dirt road but is truly a long driveway.

"I know."

"You do?"

I smile. "I did my homework."

"You planned everything."

I nod and turn onto the drive. It's a mile of dirt leading up to the house, which could use some attention. It's old, huge and very private with several acres of land surrounding it. It's perfect.

"What's going to happen in there?" she asks when I park the car and kill the engine.

"Isn't this your job? Don't you know?"

"You're not here to see this house. We both know that."

I shrug. "Maybe I am." I unbuckle my belt and open my door. "Let's go." After sliding out, I slam it shut. She's still sitting in the truck when I walk around to her side. I'm rolling up my sleeves as I go. I'm guessing since the farmhouse is empty, if it even has AC, it's not running. Before opening her door, I open the back one and take out a black duffel bag. I sling it over one shoulder then open her door. She's eyeing that bag like it's a snake I've just wrapped around my neck.

"Let's go, *habibi*."

That last word makes her flinch.

I reach in and stretch my arm across her body and can't help my grin when she presses her back as far into the seat as possible. Locking eyes with her, I unclick her belt.

"You have a house to show me."

3

EVE

I'm trying really hard not to scream and run, and I can't take my eyes off the black duffel Zach just slung over his shoulder.

When he stands to the side, I slide out, holding onto the door handle to take the giant step to the ground. I reach back in for my purse, but his big hand falls on my shoulder to stop me.

"You won't need that," he says.

I glance at his hand, feel its weight, its power, and it takes me a moment to turn and face him.

"I'll lock the car, and I've got the key code right here. That Miranda's efficient, isn't she?"

I can't speak, but I don't think he's expecting an answer. He slams the door shut, locks it, and heads up to the house. I look at him, at his powerful back, thick, strong legs, and I look around me. We're all alone out here, in the middle of nowhere. Devon may know where I am, but that's not going to do me a whole lot of good. Not if Zach decides to hurt me. Not until after it's too late.

He said he wouldn't hurt me though. I have to believe that. And I was being honest when I said I was glad he was alive. He's here for answers, but what happened that night, it wasn't supposed to go down that way. My own brother betrayed me. Does he know that, though? Or does he think I was part of the conspiracy?

But maybe he's not here for answers at all. Maybe he's here to collect? Because that night, the auction turned into something different than it was meant to be, than I thought it would be. And maybe he's here to collect on what he bought that night.

"Coming?" he asks without looking back.

I follow his path to the front door. The owner of the property died about a year ago and the house has been on the market that long. His kids, all adults now, inherited it, and don't want to lower the price, but they're asking too much considering the location and the condition of the place.

When I climb the porch steps, Zach has already punched in the code to open the lockbox, and he's retrieved the key. He slides it into the lock and a moment later, pushes the door open.

"You really should send a cleaning crew out here," he says as he steps in and holds the door open for me. "It's not going to sell for half the asking price looking like this."

I take a deep breath as I stand on the threshold.

"Eve," he says.

I know once I enter the house, he can do whatever he wants to me.

No. That's not true.

He can easily grab me and drag me in, even if I don't willingly take that step.

"I'm losing patience," he adds when I still don't move.

I take a deep breath and step inside. He closes the door behind me.

He's right. We should send a cleaner to the house.

Turning his back, he walks through the downstairs rooms: large kitchen, living room, a study and a spacious dining room. He chooses the dining room to set down his duffel bag. Most of the furniture has been sold off, but there are a few pieces remaining—an old sideboard and two chairs. He chooses a straight-back wooden chair and sets it in the middle of the room then turns to me.

"Show me around."

"What?"

"The house. Show me the house."

"Is that...I don't understand. That's why you're here?"

"Don't be stupid, Eve."

I don't understand what he wants, but I turn and begin to take him on a tour through the house. This is good, it will give me time to think, and it's familiar. Something I can control. But that control feels like a reprieve. And I know it's temporary.

"The room has been partially renovated, but the original..." I hear myself talking, but I'm on autopilot. All I can feel is him following behind me, too close for comfort. I'm not sure if he's listening to a word I'm saying. All I can think about is him here with me. Us, in this house, alone. He's so close I can feel the heat coming off his body and even as warm as it is in the house, I have goosebumps all along my arms.

As we climb the stairs, when I place one hand on the banister, he does the same, his hand touching mine for a moment before I pull away.

"Am I making you nervous?" he asks from so near, the hairs on the back of my neck stand on end.

"No," I say weakly, but just as I take the next step, the old, rotting wood gives way and I let out a surprised scream, throwing my arms out in front of me to break my fall.

But they never touch down because, like lightning, Zach's arm wraps around my middle and pulls me backward into him. I'm breathing hard, and he's holding me against his chest. His arm is wrapped tightly around me and even after he's steadied me, he doesn't let me go.

I can feel his body behind mine, the muscles of his chest, the power in his big arms. He's warm, his breath tickling my neck, and I remember that last night. Remember the look on his face when Armen, my own brother, did something I still can't believe he did. When he betrayed me. I remember looking over the room crowded with men, dangerous men, most with scarves covering half their faces. Remember the guns slung over their shoulders.

Remember the absolute absence of women.

I don't know how I found Zach among the men. Maybe it was his blue eyes. Maybe it was the difference inside them compared to the lecherous, savage leers of the others. Even with half his face concealed beneath the scarf, I'd found him and locked my eyes on his. It's what had kept me upright.

When my brother started the bidding, the others —all those men—they'd gone insane. Like hungry animals coming upon their first meal.

And I was that meal.

I'd seen the surprise in Zach's eyes at this turn of events. I wonder now if that was the moment he knew something had gone wrong. Wonder if he hadn't been busy trying to save me, if he would have been prepared for what happened next.

"The house is old, Eve. You need to be careful," he says from behind me, interrupting the memory. He hasn't let me go yet though, and I turn my face a little so I can see him from the corner of one eye.

"Thank you," I say.

He releases me and it takes me a minute to compose myself, adjusting my skirt, my hand trembling as I reach out to grip the railing. I'm dripping with sweat now but it's not the heat of the house causing it. It's him.

"There are three bedrooms upstairs," I carry on, telling myself he can't hear how my voice is shaking.

He follows me through each one of the bedrooms as well as the bathroom and when we're done upstairs, I begin to head down, paying extra attention on each step. Some part of me wants him to hold me again, to forgive me. I can't understand why that need is so powerful. But there's another part too, and that part is afraid. Afraid of him. Of what he thinks I've done. What his state of mind is. Why he's here under an alias.

Once we're back in the dining room, he goes to his duffel bag and unzips it. I stand there awkwardly and hug my arms around my middle, glancing once at the front door just a few feet away. He doesn't seem to be worried I'll try to run. I guess he knows he can catch me anyway.

"Have a seat," he says as he turns his back to me. He takes out two thick, worn folders from the duffel.

My legs are leaden as I move toward the chair he set out earlier and obey, sitting down, trying to force myself to look at him.

He faces me, and he must feel my discomfort.

But instead he lets silence hang between us for what seems like an eternity, just standing there, leaning against the sideboard, arms folded across his chest, watching me.

"I didn't do my homework with you," he says, finally. "But even if I had, I don't think I would have heeded the warnings."

"What do you mean?"

"Who you are. What you want. Why you turned on your own brother and became an informant for the US military. Why you then betrayed us."

I shake my head. "I didn't—"

"You didn't what?"

"I didn't betray you. I didn't mean to."

"Tell that to the six men who lost their lives because of you."

"I—"

"I would have believed you were innocent if you'd died that night," he says. "I thought when Armen pulled you up onto that block, when he ripped off your clothes—I thought *he'd* betrayed *you.*"

I feel my face heat at the memory. I'd stood there naked, or nearly so, with more than two dozen men to see me like that. My brother had done that to me. My own brother.

But hadn't I betrayed him too?

And then there was Malik. He'd been playing us all along.

"But when I found out you were alive—alive and well—in the States, living under an alias, a new life? Well, you can imagine I have a hard time believing it wasn't all a setup to get me and my men out of the way."

I have no response for him. How can I make him believe anything I say anyway? He's right, the evidence to the contrary is here, right before his eyes. Me. Eve *Adams*. Alive and well.

He studies me. "Was this your payoff?" he asks, reaching into his back pocket and pulling out a passport. He opens it to the first page. It's mine. "I really didn't realize you wanted to come to the States. You were that good."

"Where did you get that?"

"Your underwear drawer. I like the lace, by the way." He shifts his attention to the passport and begins reading the information there. "El-Amin is better than Adams, though." He glances up at me. "I mean, Adams? Where's the intrigue? And you, Eve, are a woman with intrigue."

"That's mine." I get to my feet, but he ignores me.

"The El-Amin name was well known throughout the Middle East. Here, you're a nobody."

"Give it to me."

"Born in Idaho." He sniggers. "Now that's a stretch."

I lunge at him, wanting to snatch my passport

out of his hands, but he catches me, holding me just out of reach as he continues to read.

"Twenty-two. Your birthday's coming up, if that's the real date?"

"Give me that!"

He shifts his gaze to me and for a moment, I go still. But then he waves the passport up high in the air.

"Are you going to take it from me?" he asks.

I jump to do just that, but he's holding it just out of reach and he's still got one of my arms in his vise-like grip.

"You have no right to it," I say.

"It's not even a good one, really," he says, his attention back on the little blue book.

"What?"

"Is it hard to keep the accent out of your voice? Day in and day out? To pretend you're someone you're not?"

"What about you? *Michael Beckham?*"

He tucks the passport back into his pocket, takes hold of my other arm and draws me to him so my chest is touching his and he's squeezing both arms. His eyes burn into mine and his face is hard again.

He's serious.

Dead serious.

"Six of my men died that night."

My eyes warm with tears.

"Six lives lost. Some with families of their own.

Young kids. One soldier had never even seen his baby girl."

"I didn't mean to..." I start, but trail off, unsure what to say.

"But you did," he finishes my sentence.

"I never intended—"

"It doesn't fucking matter what you intended!"

After his roar, there's a moment of utter stillness. Then the first tear slides down my cheek and all of a sudden, it's like all the anger, the aggression, the noise of the moment before, stops. It's suspended as he watches that single drop progress down my face and disappear. He searches my eyes as if he's trying to find the truth.

"I bought you that night," he says, his voice low, even more dangerous than when he yelled. Suddenly, everything about him is different, like he's someone else. Like something dark just crept into this room and slithered into his body, his head. Something powerful and alive and deadly.

His gaze sweeps down to my breasts. Shame heats my blood and I feel my face burn red, and when he meets my stare again, his eyes are on fire.

Zach doesn't let me go but he watches me closely, and under his scrutiny, I feel like I'll collapse. Like my knees will give out if he lets me go. Slowly, very slowly, I watch him take control again, subdue that savage beast inside him. The wild one. The one I remember glimpsing before.

The one that frightened me.

Excited me.

Made me want.

"When your brother put you on that block, that was the distraction, wasn't it? Did you agree to be stripped naked?"

It takes me a minute. I'm not following him, but then I get it. He thinks I was in on it. That it was my plan.

I shake my head. "No."

"He stood you naked in front of a roomful of men. He offered your body to the highest bidder."

"Stop," I say, feeling my face crumple.

"He was about to sell your virginity."

I just shake my head no.

"Were you willing to go that far?"

"I—"

"Did you know? Was it part of the plan?" He doesn't wait for me to answer. "I fell for it. Hook, line and sinker," he says, sadness seeping into the beautiful blue of his eyes momentarily before accusation sets in, darkening them, stealing their brightness.

I look to my feet, to the dusty old floor we're standing on. I can't look at him. I don't want him to see me like this and I don't want to—no, I can't—take the accusation in his eyes. "It wasn't my plan," I say weakly. "I swear, Zach, I didn't know he'd do that."

It takes me a long time to face him and when I do, I know he doesn't believe me.

"I fell for your innocent act before," he says flatly.

"I swear—"

"Then how the fuck are you alive?"

He gives me a hard shake.

"You're hurting me!"

But he talks over me like he's not listening at all. "How?" he says and his grip tightens. "Tell me how!"

"Please!"

His lips stretch into a narrow line and his throat works to swallow, but he doesn't let up. Instead, he slams my back against the wall and I scream. "Tell me!" It's a roar that demands an answer, one I don't have.

Something happens then. A thought. I know it's not true—I know him—I know he would never do *that*. But it gets the best of me and I think about the auction. About the fact that, like the others, he bid. On me. On my body. My virginity.

"Let me go."

He doesn't.

I struggle against him, but it's useless. He can do whatever he wants to me. Anything at all. I don't stand a chance against him physically.

"Please!" Still, nothing. "Are you here to collect? Is that it?" I ask. My voice is loud, hysterical—or on the edge of hysteria. I can't help it. I'm scared. He's unhinged, he's not the man I remember—the one always in control. Always in charge. Determined.

No, he's still that last one. Determined. Very much so.

It's that determination that scared the hell out of me.

"Is that what you want?" I ask again. "The thing you think you bought?" I have to say the words, but it makes me want to vomit. "My body?"

I don't know if it's spelling it out like that or the tears streaming down my cheeks, but he blinks twice and a moment later, releases me and turns away. He's leaning against the sideboard and I can hear him breathing hard. His heart must be going a hundred miles a minute.

"Six men died because they trusted me." His back is still to me and his voice sounds different, hard still, but blacker. Guilt-ridden.

I don't have anything to say. It's not an apology he wants. It's revenge. But it's not me he should be seeking it from.

He starts to gather up the folders he'd taken out of that duffel bag and puts everything away. I stand there watching him, watching his back as he works. He's in pain, I see it. I feel it. And I want to touch him, lay a hand on his shoulder and tell him it wasn't his fault. That there's only one man to blame, and it's not him. But I can't.

He zips the duffel. "Let's go." Without looking at

me, he slings the bag onto his shoulder and walks toward the front door.

Is that it? He's finished with me? I don't understand, and I'm still standing there when he's opened the front door.

"Eve," he calls.

His deep voice reverberates through me, making me shudder. I shake my head once, confused, but I follow him out of the house. He locks it behind us and this time, he doesn't wait by the passenger side door, but climbs into the driver's seat and he's already started the truck by the time I climb in. He's driving back to the city, but he's not heading to the office.

"Where are we going?" I finally ask.

He doesn't answer right away, in fact, he only answers once he's pulled into the parking lot of a bar that's open before lunchtime. He parks, kills the engine and turns to me. "I need a drink," he says.

He pulls the keys out of the ignition, opens the door and gets out. He's messed up, I can see it. He's not the man who sat so confidently in the conference room this morning. Maybe he didn't expect what happened today to go down like it did. Maybe he just expected to ask his questions, demand answers, maybe punish me for my role.

"Zach?" I say when he turns away. It's like he's forgotten I'm still sitting there.

He faces me, but he's a thousand miles away.

"Are you...okay?"

He snorts at that, pausing for a second, and he almost replies, but decides not to. Instead he walks away, closing the driver's side door, leaving me alone in his truck. I watch him disappear into the rundown bar and I sit there for a minute, confused, then open the glove compartment and take out my phone. I'm about twenty minutes from the office. I arrange for a ride with Uber, not sure if he's going to come out and drag me into the bar or what. But nothing happens as I gather my things and climb out, and when the Uber driver gets there, I get into his car. Zach doesn't reappear, and I'm soon back at the office.

I make an excuse to Devon that Michael didn't feel well and have to catch myself when I almost call him Zach and not Michael. Devon's disappointed and I'm not sure why I lied to protect Zach, but I did. I spend the rest of the day in a daze trying to figure out what the hell happened. He still has my passport, but I have a feeling today won't be the last time I'll see him.

I HAVE A DINNER MEETING THAT NIGHT AND AM anxious throughout. Seeing Zach Amado alive, the way I did, the way he came back, is messing with me. He's unpredictable and I don't know what to expect, what he'll do. But I'm also curious about him and as much as I know the best—safest—thing for me to do would be to see him gone, I don't want him to go. I want to talk to him. I want to explain. I don't want him to hate me, but I know that's selfish. I didn't know what would happen that night. It wasn't my intention for his men to get hurt. To die.

That doesn't mean anything, and you know it.

I do. Because they did die.

I thought they'd capture Malik. I thought I could free my brother.

"Eve?"

I blink. It's Devon.

"I'm sorry, I guess I'm not quite myself today."

"I can wrap up here, why don't you go home and get some rest?" he says, excusing me from the dinner meeting.

"If you don't mind, I would appreciate that."

"Go. Check in with me tomorrow."

"Thanks, Devon."

I'm anxious when I arrive home, but don't see the truck anywhere on my street. I'm not sure if it's disappointment or relief I feel. It's dark as I walk up the drive and get inside. I'm not sure what I'm expecting, honestly, but the house is empty. He isn't here. Did I think he would be? Did I want him to be?

It's hot inside, the windows have been closed up all day, but I don't like running the AC—it's too dry as it is here—so I open the windows instead. Denver cools down in the evenings anyway, but this summer has been weird. Global warming, I guess.

The house is small, just a single bedroom, a reasonably-sized living room and a kitchen with a breakfast nook. I like it though. I like small and cozy, and the backyard is great. Completely private. I rent the place from Devon, actually. It's how I met him and eventually got the job at the office.

In the bedroom, I strip off my suit and hang it up, then make my way into the bathroom for a cool shower. My hair is so thick, I have to wash it at night for it to be dry by morning. I'm not about to blowdry it in this heat and don't like spending time on styling it anyway.

Once I'm done, I switch off the water and push the curtain aside to grab a towel off the rack. I squeeze the moisture from my hair, wrap the towel around my body and step into the hallway.

A gasp catches in my throat when I do, and I stop dead in my tracks. He's here. He's sitting in the middle of my couch, legs spread wide, one arm resting over the back of the sofa, the other holding a beer. I hadn't switched on any lamps, so I only see him from the light of the bathroom and I can't quite make out his eyes.

"How did you get in here?"

He reaches out to switch on a lamp. It's dim though, and casts an eerie glow on his face. He only answers me after taking a long drag of beer. "Front door."

"I locked it." I know it's stupid as I say it. He's been inside before. He's been coming and going for I don't know how long. He took my passport. He's been through my things.

"I already told you that you need better locks." He drains his beer and sets the empty bottle down on the coffee table before standing.

I swallow as he rises to his full height, everything looking almost comically miniature around him. He's too big for this house and when he moves around the coffee table, I think he's going to stub his shin, but he sidesteps it. He moves quietly, stealthily. It's the military training he's had. He was taught to move like a ghost. His eyes are set on me as he makes his way down the hallway. I clutch the towel tight to my chest and take a step backward, but my back hits the wall. He only stops when he's a few inches from me.

"Have you been drinking all day?" I ask, craning my neck to look up at him. He's a foot taller than me and I'm not wearing shoes, so I feel even smaller. More vulnerable.

He searches my face, then his eyes drop to my chest, moving up to my mouth before returning to meet my stare.

"You look good. The same."

He's drunk. He has to be. "What are you doing here?"

He looks me over again, and he's too close. But when I try to scoot away, he puts one hand on the wall beside my head so I can't.

"We have unfinished business," he says. He doesn't slur his words. He's so big that maybe he just doesn't get drunk no matter how much he drinks. His eyes have a look inside them that unnerves me. That makes my belly feel funny. Makes me very aware the only thing between us is the towel I'm holding. All it would take would be one tug from him, and...

"Zach?" I say, before I go down that road.

"Eve," he replies, his voice a deep contrast to mine.

We stay like that a little longer, neither of us saying another word. He leans in closer, too close, our faces almost touching.

"You better go put some clothes on," he says in a low rumble, but makes no move to release me from the cage he's made with his body. I just stare up at him, my heart pounding so hard, I can hear the blood and adrenaline pumping through me.

Then, as quietly as he'd crowded me, he steps back. I exhale the breath I've been holding, and I notice he's not wearing the dress shirt he had on earlier. He's wearing a black T-shirt which he's pulling over his head. I stand there watching, my mouth dry. He doesn't make a move to shield himself from me. My gaze travels over his torso, thick and muscular, one half of him tattooed, the other...

Oh my God, the other half.

His skin, it's badly damaged. Monstrous, almost. Burned flesh healed into bumpy, hideous scar tissue.

I remember what he asked me earlier today. If I knew what it felt like to have fire lick your skin. If I had ever smelled human flesh burn. How much pain had he been in? How had he survived at all?

As if he's given me all he's willing to share, he walks into the bathroom.

And...I gasp in shock at what I see there. My stomach turns. My hand moves to cover my mouth.

I didn't think anything could be worse than what I saw on the front of his body, but what's on his back makes the front pale in comparison. Partially burned flesh gives way to tattoos. More of them. Words this time. Words inked in a neat script.

Names.

Names I know.

He switches on the shower and when he turns to face me, he looks stone-cold sober.

"You going to join me?" he asks in that rumble of his, reaching to unbutton his pants.

My eyes drop to his hand as he unzips and I quickly shake myself out of it. Force my gaze back up to his.

He gives me a grin. No, it's more of a smirk. Then

he raises his eyebrows as if still waiting for an answer. I quickly turn away and practically run to my bedroom, hearing his laughter behind me before I slam the bedroom door shut and stand with my forehead leaning against it, trying to catch my breath.

His back. What I saw there, it's a graveyard. The names of his men, those who died that night. Six rows of ink immortalizing his friends.

All those names.

All those lives.

My heart is racing and I think I'm going to be sick, but I force myself to take deep breaths in. Tell myself to calm down. I knew the past would catch up with me, didn't I? All along, didn't I know it? Here it is. In my house. Having a shower.

Hurrying, I put on my pajamas—a pair of shorts and a tank top which seem entirely inappropriate now that he's here. But before I can think, I hear the shower switch off.

There's no lock on my bedroom door, but even if there were, he'd probably have the key. I consider calling the police. Calling Devon. But my cell phone is in the living room and besides, how would I explain this?

"Knock-knock," Zach says just before opening the bedroom door.

I stare at him like a deer in headlights, frozen to

the spot, not sure what to say, to do. Not sure about anything at all.

His hair is wet and all he's wearing is a towel slung low on his hips. He's dripping water on the hardwood floors, but I know he doesn't care.

He looks me over, but his expression doesn't change and I can't tell what he's thinking.

"What do you want with me?" I ask stupidly.

He walks into the room and I instinctively back up when he approaches me. One side of his mouth curves upward and when he stops, he's so close that water drips off his hair and onto my shoulder. What I see in his eyes makes my mouth go dry.

Desire. Want. Need. Lust. All those things are there, and some part of me shares those things. Those feelings.

Only there's one difference.

In his eyes, fear is absent. And I do feel afraid. This man whom I once trusted with my life scares the crap out of me right now.

"I bought you," he whispers.

I can't breathe. I can't think. And the sound of blood pumping through my veins, pulsing inside my ears, is almost louder than his words.

"To save you from all those men."

I don't know if I'm disappointed by that.

"I wanted to kill him when he stripped you," he continues.

I'm breathing again, short and choppy. His chest

touches mine with every inhale he takes, and I can smell alcohol on his breath.

"If he hadn't pulled you up on that stage, everything would have been different. We would have attacked."

I know that. I know.

"But he did, and I failed to give the signal. And then there was the explosion and I thought you died anyway."

"Zach—" I reach out a hand and touch his face, but he gives a shake of his head. My hand drops when he steps back and when he looks at me again, his eyes have gone hard.

"Get on the bed, Eve."

I shrink backward, not sure I've heard correctly.

"Don't stand there like you don't hear me. Get on the goddamned bed."

I'm trembling as I slide along the wall and to the bed. My hand shakes when I reach out to find the headboard. My belly heaves like I'm on a roller coaster. Never taking my eyes off him, I sit, hearing the familiar creak of the old box spring.

"Lie down." He's watching me, but he hasn't moved any closer.

"Why?" I ask and my voice breaks. Every hair on my body is standing on end.

"Because I'm fucking drunk and I need to get some sleep."

I wait.

He understands my hesitation, what I'm thinking.

"Don't worry, I'm not going to collect on that night," he says.

I exhale.

"Not now," he adds.

I swallow, unable to speak. He's staying here. With me. In my bed. It goes without saying. I draw back the blankets and lie down, my eyes never leaving his.

"I know you sleep on the other side, Eve."

God. He's been here when I was sleeping?

I scoot to my side and he nods, then takes a step toward the bed, sits, lies down. His weight has me rolling toward him—the mattress is old and I never bought a new one. He stretches out and turns to me before I have a chance to pull away so we're lying on our sides, eye to eye for the first time. Neither of us speaks. I look at his face. Rugged, good-looking. Rough. Like he's been through hell and back. And I guess he has.

"How did you survive?" I ask in a quiet voice.

"Local doctor found me. Carried me to his home. Took care of me. Hid me."

For the first time, I reach out a hand and touch the scar on his face, the one that splits his eyebrow in half, then put my hand on his shoulder, on the bumpy skin. He tenses, but a moment later relaxes, and he doesn't even blink. He lets me feel it, lets me run my fingertips over scar tissue, but when I reach his hand, he abruptly catches my wrist.

I gasp and we lie there for a minute, my heart racing, his eyes dark and intense. He then rolls me over so my back is to him and draws me into his chest. He's still got my wrist and he keeps hold of it, his arm heavy across my middle. I feel him at my back then—feel his hardness—and I realize he's naked. He'd only had on a towel and it must have fallen away because now he's naked behind me. His thick cock is pressing against my ass, my lower back.

"Don't worry," he whispers huskily, his voice hoarse. "I told you I won't collect. Not tonight."

4

ZACH

I don't know what the hell I'm doing.

She's asleep, but barely. Her sweet ass is glued to me, and the only thing keeping my rock-hard dick from sliding into her pussy is a flimsy pair of shorts she calls pajamas. And all I can do is lie here and hold her, and with every fucking inhale, I smell her, her hair, her skin, the heat coming off her.

The acrid scent of fear is gone. It dissipated when she finally fell asleep. I like knowing I scare her though. It's fucked up, I know, but some twisted part of me likes having that power over her. Years ago, it hadn't been fear she felt around me. She got anxious. Nervous. Like a girl with a crush. Now, things are different between us.

At the house today, I'd meant to interrogate her.

To sit her down and get the answers I needed. But those questions, they got confused, everything got muddled. What happened that night two years ago was cut and dry. We'd been betrayed. She'd been a traitor. She'd set us up to save her brother. I believed that for the last year and a half when I'd learned she'd survived. Hell, I'd fucking mourned her death, only to find out she was living in the US. It didn't fit. She'd cut some kind of deal, but with whom?

We'd been watching Armen El-Amin for years. He came into the picture after their parents died several years earlier. Shot down coming out of a restaurant. After that, their two other brothers, Rafi and Seth, disappeared. Fucking vanished into thin air. Eve was the only girl in the family, and the youngest sibling. When she'd come to us, she hadn't been quite twenty. She'd been scared as hell. Fucking trembling. But she'd been desperate to save her brother Armen—the only family she had left.

I still remember the first day, seeing her sitting in that stark office after being questioned, waiting while we figured out if what she was telling us was true. To have El-Amin's sister turn up and give us information just seemed too unbelievable. Too good to be true.

I watched from behind a one-way mirror. She'd sat there picking at her fingernails, and looking so fucking pretty. Innocent. Like she needed protecting.

And she would once her brother found out what she'd done.

I was assigned to work with her. Well, I volunteered. It was foolish, I know, but I had to. I still remember how some of my soldiers would look at her. I had words with a few of them. She never knew it.

She came to trust me—at least I thought so— fairly quickly. That should have been a red flag right there. The intelligence she gave us was good though, and that's why, the final night, the night we were supposed to take Armen down, I didn't take enough care with things. I should have asked more questions.

The reason she came to us at all was to save Armen. She foolishly believed he *could* be saved, but her brother was a piece of shit. An assassin, essentially. But he wasn't the big fish. We wanted the man he worked for. Malik, or as the locals called him, the Butcher.

A flash of memory from that night brings up the image I can't seem to forget. A face. Eyes. Eyes I know, but can't place.

I truly did believe she was part of the setup. Part of me still does, maybe. But seeing her today, seeing how she reacted to my questions, I'm not sure. No, I'm confused as fuck. Could it be that she wasn't involved? That her brother had set her up? Or that he'd found out what she'd done and was willing to punish her the way he did? Stripping her naked in front of all those men. Selling her.

Thing is though, it doesn't matter.

The names inked on my skin burn as I turn over to stare at the ceiling, as if calling me traitor for forgetting them.

Again.

It doesn't matter because they died. And the reason they died is because I got distracted. I put the mission second. Second to her.

I failed them.

But that night, I couldn't let what was happening to her go down. And I couldn't open fire when she was in the room either, up on that fucking block, an easy target.

I turn back over to touch the small scar on her upper arm. I'd saved her from a bullet once. If I'd done my job that last night, given the order, she would have died. But my failure to do so killed six men loyal to me.

Fuck.

I wish I could sleep. Have some relief from the guilt, the regret. I haven't slept a full night through in years. And now, it's because I'm doubting.

Again.

Was I wrong to come after her?

Is she innocent?

Will she be able to lead me to the true villains?

Suddenly irritated, I toss the sheet back and get out of the bed. I won't be getting any sleep tonight. I grab a pair of sweats, a T-shirt, and running shoes out of my bag and go into the living room to get dressed. It's almost dawn and I need to sweat. Run, and for one hour, empty my mind.

I go over that night again and again, and I need a fucking break.

WHEN I GET BACK TO THE HOUSE, THE SUN IS breaking through the few clouds in the sky, coloring them a deep orange. The neighborhood is still quiet but when I open the front door, I smell coffee.

Eve turns to face me. She's sitting at the kitchen table with a steaming mug in her hands. She isn't wearing any makeup, her hair is in a ponytail and she's still wearing that little pajama set. I'm not sure she realizes how much of her it leaves exposed, but I decide not to mention it. I'll enjoy the view instead.

"Morning," I say as I close the door behind me and walk into the kitchen.

"How long are you going to be here?"

I give her a lopsided grin and help myself to a cup of coffee, opening the fridge as I sip and taking out the bacon and eggs.

"Help yourself," she says.

"I will. Have been." I get a frying pan and set it on

a burner. I know where everything is, and I wonder if she realizes how many times I've been in here the last few weeks. I slide six strips of bacon into the pan and crack four eggs before turning to her.

She shrinks back a little when I do.

"I have to go to work," she says, but she hasn't made a move to rise.

"Tell your boss you're taking me to see the other houses on your list and that I'm picking you up at home."

"I don't want to lie to him."

"Fine, then tell him I slept over."

She looks scandalized. "I can't do that."

I shrug. "That's really not my problem." I drain the coffee from my cup before pouring a second one, and flipping the bacon over. Her chair scrapes across the floor as she rises. I don't bother turning around.

"Sit down."

"I told you I have to go to work."

I glance over my shoulder. "And I told you to sit."

She hesitates but reads the warning in my eyes, and sits.

"Good girl."

"I'm not a dog."

Ignoring her, I get two dishes out of the cabinet and divide the eggs and bacon. Finding forks, I set the plates on the table and take the only other seat opposite her.

She looks at the food like it's poison.

I pick up my fork and start eating.

"Breakfast, Eve. Eat."

"I'm not hungry." She pushes the plate away.

"You know better than to waste food. Now eat."

She picks up her fork and pushes the eggs around. "How long are you staying?"

"As long as it takes."

"Takes for what?"

"For me to get what I need."

"What do you need?"

"Answers."

She lowers her gaze back to her plate.

"Eat, Eve." My food's already gone.

She takes the smallest bite of eggs possible. I watch her as she chews and I know she has to force herself to swallow.

"That's not so hard, is it?"

Her purse is on the coffee table. I get up and instead of bringing it over, I look through it to find her cell phone, and take it to the kitchen.

"Call your boss."

"No."

"Fine." I know her password so I punch it in, then scroll through her contacts and put the phone on speaker as it starts to ring.

"What the hell?" She's up trying to grab it out of my hands, but I grip hold of one of her wrists.

A groggy voice comes on the line a moment later, and her eyes go wide.

"Hello?"

She stares up at me and I smile, gesturing to ask who's doing the talking.

"Um...Devon," she starts.

Good girl, I mouth with a grin I know looks evil.

She tries to take the phone but I hold onto it, and to her.

"I'm sorry to call so early, but I wanted to let you know I'm on my way to pick up Mr. Beckham and I'll take him out to see those other properties this morning."

"Oh, okay, that sounds fine. I'm glad you're feeling better." He sounds half asleep.

"Thanks. Um, go back to sleep, Devon. Sorry again for calling so early. I didn't realize the time." She gives me a glare at the last part.

I smile wide.

"Bye," she says.

I hit end, release her, then switch her phone off and set it on the kitchen table.

"Again, not so hard, is it?"

"You can't just do that! This is my job we're talking about."

I'm walking away though, into the bedroom. I need something from my bag and she's not going to like it. When I return, she's already switched her phone back on.

"I'll take that."

"No," she turns her back, her thumbs working frantically, but I reach over her and close one big hand over both of hers.

"I said I'll take it." I look at the screen. She's in the middle of changing her password. I just shake my head, and this time, slip the battery out and tuck it into my pocket. "Now sit."

She's furious but when she sees what I've got in my hand, she backs away.

"What are you doing?"

"I need a shower and I don't trust you'll be here when I get out, so I'm making sure you will be." I hold up the handcuffs.

"No! No way!"

"I have a gag too," I offer as her voice rises.

She's confused for a second, and it makes me laugh. "Sit your ass down. You'll finish breakfast while I have a shower. Then we can get down to business."

"I said no!"

She sidesteps and makes a run for it, but I catch her easily, and instead of sitting her at the kitchen table, march her into the bedroom. She's struggling and making too much noise for my liking, so I pull her back into my chest and lift her off her feet. One of my hands is covering her mouth, pressing the back of her head into me, the other is wrapped around her middle.

"What are you going to tell your neighbors if anyone gets curious about the noise coming from the house?" I ask, unfazed, easily moving her along. She won't want anyone involved. It'd cost her too much. I know it, and I know she does too. Still, I like the feel of her body against mine, and her struggles, well, they only make my dick hard.

I know the instant she feels it because she stills.

Setting her down so she's standing, I keep one hand over her mouth and rifle through my bag to get the ball gag out. When I see how wide her eyes go, I smile.

Without speaking, I toss her onto the bed. She's on her belly, but before she can flip herself over and get up, I've straddled her and reach around to put the ball of the gag into her mouth. "Open up, *habibi*."

She's sealed her lips and is frantically turning her head from side to side. At least until I pinch her nose shut.

"Open the fuck up."

The instant she does to take a breath, the gag's in place and I secure it behind her head.

"Now, this could have gone differently," I say, sliding her toward the headboard so she's sitting up. "You could be eating a nice, quiet breakfast." I cuff one of her wrists then slide the cuffs through the bars of the headboard and secure the other. "But you chose to do it the hard way."

I get up off the bed and look down at her. She's

struggling against the cuffs and is saying something, but it's all muffled sound. I smile wide.

"Try to relax," I say. I turn my back and walk into the bathroom, whistling a tune, enjoying this, enjoying myself more than I have in a long time.

5

EVE

I can't believe this. I'm bound and gagged and freaking drooling all over myself while Zach's in the shower, singing! It's been twenty minutes. I'm going to kill him when he unties me. I'm going to strangle him!

It's useless trying to get free. My wrists hurt, and this gag is humiliating and uncomfortable as hell. I try to wipe at the drool that's dripping down onto my chest but only manage to make a bigger mess.

Ten minutes later, the shower switches off. I don't know if I'm relieved though because for all the whistling and singing, I know he's serious about getting answers. I don't know what he'll do when he realizes I don't have what he's looking for. What he thinks I did, if he knew why, he'd understand. But he has to know I was betrayed too. I didn't intend for what happened to him or his men to happen. I didn't know what Armen would do. I was tricked. Set up and used by my own brother.

My back is straight and I'm glaring into the hallway when Zach walks out of the bathroom. He's drying his hair with one towel and he's got another one wrapped low around his hips. Like last night, I can't stop looking at him.

He tosses the towel he was using on his hair aside so it's all standing up around his face. He cocks his head to the side and looks at me like he's sorry for me, and walks toward me.

"You've got a little drool..." he trails off as he wipes some of it away, but he's only smearing it across my cheek.

I twist my face away, embarrassed when I should be angry.

"You know what though?" he asks, sitting down so I have to scooch my legs over so his aren't touching mine. He pets the back of my head then uses my ponytail to make me look at him. He leans in close, runs the scruff of his jaw across my temple, then moves his mouth to my ear. His breath is hot and he's tickling the ridge of my ear with the stubble on his chin. "I like it wet," he whispers.

I go rigid as he lingers there, warm and close. Too close.

When he finally releases me, my chest is tight and I have to force my lungs to take in air. He rises to his feet and I can see the outline of his cock. He stands there, watches me looking. Lets me. His eyes are hard when I turn mine up to his and for a moment, my head races to the conclusion that he's here to take what he thinks is owed him. What he thinks he bought that night.

No. He won't do that. He won't take if I don't give. I know him, and he's not a monster.

He turns away and fishes out a pair of boxer briefs and jeans to get dressed. When he drops the towel, I force myself to look away. I won't be caught watching. It's what he wants, I'm sure.

When he turns back to me, I face him. He's got his jeans on and has to adjust his cock to get them zipped. He pulls a black T-shirt over his head. It strains to contain him.

"Ready for me to take it out?" he asks.

For a minute, I'm not sure what he's talking about. But then he gets that cocky grin on his face and points to the gag.

"The gag, *habibi*. What did you think I meant?"

I mutter a curse.

"What's that?"

I repeat it.

"It's really hard to understand you with that thing in your mouth. You want it out?"

I nod once, angry.

"Are you going to scream?"

I narrow my eyes, glaring at him.

He sits down on the bed again, head to the side,

studying me. "I'll ask you again. Are you going to scream?"

I shake my head once, but I'm still glaring.

He smiles wide. "Good girl." He reaches back and I think he's going to take it off, but then he pulls away and I know he's playing with me. "Do you know what will happen if you do scream?"

I make a noise. It's me telling him to go fuck himself, but I can't actually form the words.

"What's that?"

I say it again.

"I'll tell you what. You scream, and I'll gag you until lunch and we'll try it again then. Understood?"

My shoulders slump, and I nod. If there's one thing I trust, it's that he means what he's saying.

He reaches behind me and a moment later, slides the ball out of my mouth.

"Fuck," I say, closing and opening my mouth, the muscles of my jaw sore. I try again to wipe the drool off on my shoulder, but he takes the towel he just discarded and wipes my face with it. I realize it's the one that was just wrapped around his dick, and feel my face heat up.

"What is that, your little bag of kinky sex toys?" I ask, gesturing to the duffel.

"You like kinky sex toys?" he counters.

"Uncuff me."

"I don't think so. I like you like this."

"My arms are sore and my wrists hurt."

"Then you'll know for next time not to struggle."

"I hate you."

He shrugs and goes into the bathroom. I hear water running and I assume he's washing the gag because when he returns, it's dry and he sets it on the nightstand.

"In case we need it again."

I have no doubt he'll use it again the moment it suits him.

He stands and moves around the room to close the windows. He then takes the single chair from the corner, brings it closer to the bed and sits down on it. Any joking or laughter is gone from his face when he folds his arms across his chest and studies me.

"Why did you decide to turn informant on your own brother, Eve?"

I'm surprised by his question. It's not the directness of it. It's just I guess I'm not expecting that one. Because why would he care?

"My parents were dead. My two other brothers had disappeared. Armen was all I had left, and I knew what he was doing was going to get him into trouble. Or worse."

He doesn't speak, just sits there as if waiting for more. I know he's versed in interrogation techniques, and for a moment, my mind wanders to other methods. Darker ones. I think he knows what I'm thinking, and there was a time when I would have said no, Zach Amado would never use those tactics. But now, after yesterday, seeing his reactions, seeing how unhinged he's become, knowing what he's been through in the last two years, I'm not so sure anymore.

"I-I wanted to save him. It was my deal. The man I dealt with before you, he promised—"

"He lied."

I just watch him. I guess I knew that was a possibility back then. And it doesn't matter anymore anyway. Armen's dead.

"You were naïve."

I shake my head. "No, not naïve. I was out of options. And besides, I trusted *you*." I feel my eyes fill with tears.

This time, it looks like he's the one surprised by what I just said. It takes him a moment to continue with his impromptu interrogation. "Save your tears, Eve. They won't sway me. What you said—you trusting me—it means nothing. It doesn't matter anymore."

But I know it means something. And it does matter.

"You were willing to give up your brother, knowing he'd be taken into custody? Jailed? Or worse?"

"The worst happened. He's dead."

"Is he?"

That stops me. "Y...yes. No one could have survived that night."

"You did. I did."

My eyebrows knit together. "But—"

"Did you see him go down? Did you see his body?"

I shake my head. "I didn't see anything. Something hit me on the head. I thought it was a bullet, that I was dead, but I was just knocked out. I saw pictures of the place later. Saw the bodies. My brother was blown to bits."

He shakes his head, watching me, unblinking. "Are you certain it was him? Did you see *his* body?" he repeats slowly.

"Is he alive?" Something like hope—a thing I've not allowed myself to have for too long—begins to bloom within me.

"I didn't say that," he says, unfolding his arms and putting one bare foot on the chair, resting an arm on his knee. And just like that, with those few words, he quashes that hope of only moments ago.

"You like messing with me? Like having me tied up and hanging hope out there only to obliterate it seconds later? Does it make you feel good?"

"No, Eve, it doesn't. Not much makes me feel good anymore."

"You're hateful."

"Who saved your life that night?"

"I don't know."

"What do you mean, you don't know?"

"I told you, I was knocked out. When I woke, I

didn't know where I was. I dealt with one man. I didn't know him. I'd never seen him before. He told me passage for me to travel to the US had been arranged. Said it was the safest thing. Said it was my payment for having helped you. 'Helped the American effort' were his exact words." I've never forgotten them, or the way he said it. How he answered my questions about survivors. I've never forgotten how terrible I felt that day.

Zach's face hardens and he's sitting up again, forehead creased. "What nationality was this man?"

"He sounded American. Looked...I don't know, American."

"Looked American how?"

"I don't know, Zach! Blond hair, blue eyes. I can't remember. I didn't care—"

"If you're lying to me, I swear—"

"I'm not. Why would I?" I pause, but he doesn't reply. "I never wanted to come here. I never wanted this life. I just wanted my brother back and I wanted us to be free."

"What happened that day? Before the night? Your hands were tied when Armen hauled you onto the auction block. It was after the arms sales. When business was done."

I feel the tears coming now. "He found out what I'd done, but what he did, I think he was made to do it. The man he worked for—"

"Malik."

"Malik the Butcher. I never met him, never even saw him. He only came to the house a handful of times, and he always stayed in his car. Armen went to him when they would meet. The man never even got out of his car when he did come, and the windows were tinted almost black. I couldn't even see shadows, outlines of people inside."

"Tell me what happened when your brother found out you'd snitched on him."

"He was furious. He said I was going to get him killed. Get myself killed. That you were all liars. Murderers. He said I needed to tell him what I'd told you. I wouldn't, not at first, but then he told me why he was working for that man. He said Malik could find Seth and Rafi. That he was working on saving them. He said he could get them back that night if I told him what you knew. And Armen also said Malik would have our brothers both killed if he failed." I drop my head, tears warm in my eyes. "That's why I told him."

Zach is staring at me, but I can't read what's in his eyes. He must hate me.

"I chose my family over you, and I can't apologize for that."

He keeps on studying me, not saying a word, but I mean it. If that was my choice again, I'd choose the same way again.

I continue, it's all I can do. "He told me later that I'd be punished. That Malik required it, but that he'd negotiated my life would be spared. I didn't know what he meant. Didn't know he'd..." *Sell me to be raped*.

I can't say that part out loud. My own brother, a man who should have protected me, put me on that auction block, stripped me naked...

I'm not looking at him when I hear him rise. A moment later, he's wiping my face, my eyes and nose.

"Thank you," I say before I catch myself.

He grunts, then sits back down and he's studying me again.

"Your other brothers, Rafi and Seth, did you ever see them?"

I shake my head.

"What happened to them?"

"I don't know. I would guess your military knows more about them than I would."

"It's not *my* military." There's venom in his words. Betrayal in his tone.

I realize something then. "Do they think you're dead? Is that why the alias?"

He takes a long time to answer, and when he does, it's a slow nod.

Now it's me who has questions. So many questions. He was betrayed that night, and it wasn't just me who did the betraying. But does he think it's his own people? And what does he want now?

I shake my head at myself. I can't be stupid. I

know what he wants. I saw his naked back. Saw the graveyard there. He's here for vengeance. And I have the feeling he's willing to do anything to get it. Even die. He's unhinged, unpredictable. Desperate. And I know if I want to survive, I can't be anywhere near him when the bomb ticking inside him goes off. Especially now.

His questions about Armen though—if I saw his body—they make me think. I saw photos of the scene. The man who gave me my passport showed me. I just assumed...

But maybe, just maybe, he is still alive. I assumed Seth and Rafi had been killed after that night, too. But maybe I was wrong. Maybe that's why I'm here, because why else? Who else would bother saving my life? I'm not worth anything to any of them. Why save me when everything would be a hell of a lot easier if I'd just died that night?

"My wrists really hurt, Zach."

He gets up and fishes a key out of that bag. He moves beside me, and I lean forward as he uncuffs my wrists. He leaves the cuffs attached to the headboard and I swing my legs off the bed, rubbing my sore wrists. I'm not sure what I'm supposed to do but when he walks out of the bedroom and into the kitchen, I follow and sit across from him. I pick up my fork and eat the now-cold breakfast he made me while he watches. He's right. I don't waste food. I've known hunger.

HE DOESN'T TALK TO ME MOST OF THE DAY. HE SPENDS it on his laptop instead, and I find myself tiptoeing around my own house. I can't stop thinking about what he said. That maybe Armen isn't dead. Maybe Seth and Rafi are alive, too.

I don't have the privacy I need to search through his things and get my passport. He doesn't trust me enough to leave me alone just yet, and I can't try to leave without it. Once I have it, I'll disappear. If there's any chance my brothers are alive, I have to go back. I'm not of any value to him anyway. I don't know anything. Even if I did, I'm not sure I'd give him the information because he's on a suicide mission, even if he doesn't know it himself. And for some reason, I want to save him from that.

"Where do you live?" I ask that evening.

He's still absorbed in whatever he's doing on his computer and it takes him a moment to reply. "Here, for now."

"When did you get into the States?"

"A few weeks ago."

"How did you get the passport? Michael Beckham's, I mean?"

He shrugs. "I know some people. Maybe the same ones who made yours, Eve *Adams*."

"What happened that night? After the explosion?" I ask.

We'd been in Beirut. It's where I was born. In comparison to other Middle Eastern countries, Beirut was safe. But still, we had our own militant groups and the man Armen was working for was involved in arms sales to other groups. Terrorist groups.

Zach is studying me over the top of his laptop. After a long time, he draws in a deep breath, closes the lid and sits back to watch me. "A local doctor saved my life. I was badly burned and I'd been shot. All I remember was the pain. He and his son somehow dragged me from the rubble of the place and had the foresight to hide me."

"You're lucky."

"I guess I am in comparison to the others."

"Does it still hurt? The burns?"

He shakes his head. "Some numbness, but like you said, I was lucky."

"I'm sorry."

"For what?"

"For what happened to you."

He only studies me, and it's unnerving. Like he wants to crawl inside my brain. Learn everything.

"Can I see?" I ask, the words slipping out before I can think. My heart picks up its pace at the thought of it, of seeing him bared, his scars, his regret.

I can't make out what the emotion in his eyes is. He's so very schooled in hiding what he's thinking.

"What do you have to drink?" he asks.

I guess that's a no. I get up and open a cabinet and realize this could be my opportunity. "Only a little bit of wine." I hold out the nearly empty bottle.

"No whiskey?"

I shake my head. "There's a liquor store two blocks away. I can run out—"

"I bet you can run." He stands. "Get dressed. We'll go together."

I fold my arms across my chest. I'm not as afraid of him right now. I know he won't hurt me. "What do you plan to do with me, exactly? I told you what I know. And I don't think I filled in any of the blanks. You can't stay here forever. You can't just walk into my life and—"

"Get fucking dressed or I'll gag you and bind you to the bed while I go on my own. You have two minutes."

I glare, but he taps his watch so I turn and walk down the hall and into my bedroom.

"Door stays open," he says, just as I'm getting ready to close it.

Fine. I know I'll have one chance to do this. If he catches me looking through that bag for my passport, he will cuff me to the bed, I have no doubt. So I get to my closet to choose clothes, which is when I notice the two suits hanging there. His. When the hell did he do that? I touch them, then lean in and smell them. Smell him on them. Abruptly I pull away, annoyed with myself.

Leaning my head out, I make sure he's busy in the living room and kneel on the floor to push two stacked shoeboxes out of the way. I open a third one and lift the tissue paper out to find the small pistol I bought when I got here still tucked neatly inside. I've never had to use it. I'm not even sure why I bought it, or if I *can* use it.

I take it out of the box and feel the weight of it in the palm of my hand.

"Time's a tickin', Eve," he calls out from the other room.

I quickly take it over to the bed and slip it between the mattress and box spring on my side, then put on a summer dress and return to the living room.

He's waiting for me by the front door. My heart is racing and I'm sweating. If he notices how anxious I suddenly am, he doesn't let on.

"Do I need to tell you how to behave?"

"No, I got it."

"Good."

Even though the liquor store is within walking distance, we take his truck, and he's holding my hand tight the whole time we're inside, like he's warning me. Afterward, we drive through a fast food place to pick up dinner.

"Sorry it isn't more fancy," he says in a tone that tells me he's not sorry at all. "What would you like?"

"I don't care."

He orders two meals, and we drive home. There, he sets the food on the coffee table and gets two glasses. He pours me a drink and sets it beside his.

"Come here, Eve."

"What's going to happen tomorrow?"

"We'll see tomorrow. Sit down."

I do. He hands me my drink and I accept it, take a sip after he touches his glass to mine and drains his. Maybe he'll get so drunk I can walk out of here, but I doubt that. He's eating his burger when I hear a buzz and he reaches into his pocket to take out his phone. I can't read the text message from where I am, but whatever it says has him sitting upright. He types something back before pocketing the phone and glancing at me.

"You'd better eat while it's warm. It's barely palatable when it cools."

I unwrap my burger and take a few bites, then abandon it to pick at the fries. He pours me another drink and I can feel his eyes on me.

"So what do you do besides work?" he asks.

I glance at him. "We're making small talk?"

"I guess we are."

"My life isn't all that interesting."

"Boyfriend?" he asks, and from the look on his face, I know he's messing with me.

"No. No juicy stories for you to get off on. Sorry."

"That why you wanted me to take my shirt off earlier?"

I see laughter in his eyes. "I'm going to bed," I say, standing.

He catches my wrist. "It's early."

"I'm tired."

The way he's looking at me is unnerving.

"You can sleep out here," I tell him.

It's like he's trying to read me. I wonder if he can see right through me. But a moment later, he lets go of my wrist.

"Door stays open." He picks up his laptop and pours himself more of the whiskey. It's his third glass.

I nod, and walk back toward the bedroom. It'll be tricky to do what I want with the door open, but I'm hoping he'll be distracted and that the whiskey will relax him. At least a little. Enough for me to get my passport. I won't try to escape tonight, but I need to be ready to go tomorrow.

I don't trust her. Not for a second. But I'll give her the opportunity to try something. That way I can show her what I mean when I tell her she'd better do as she's told. Actions speak louder than words.

My phone buzzes again, and I take it out of my pocket. I still have a contact in Beirut, a man who can get me answers. That doctor who saved my life? He came looking for me that night. Came looking to clean up after Malik was finished with his work.

I know the man Eve's brother worked for. Malik the Butcher. No one's ever seen his face. He has contact with very few, and those few usually turn up dead within a few months. Armen El-Amin was an exception to that.

The US military has been gathering intelligence on Malik for years, but they could never get close enough. I know he was there that last night. I felt it in my gut. I know he likes to watch the destruction as it happens. Likes to see the blood drain from a body, likes to watch the life seeping out of it. He's a sick bastard.

But the piece about her other brothers, about Armen working for Malik in exchange for Malik's help to find and free them, is that true? It sheds a new light on Armen. Still, he fucked me and my men that last night. He needs to pay for that. Eve's betrayal, if she truly did it for her brothers, I'd understand, but I'm not sure. My gut says she's innocent. Although when it comes to her, my gut's fucked up.

I read the text message from my contact: *Paper isn't a match. Different maker.*

Crap. I was hoping this would be easy, but nothing ever is. I was hoping the jerk who made my passport—Michael Beckham's passport, I mean—had made Eve's, because it's a fake. And that's another thing right there. Who the hell saved her life? And why pose as an American agent? Assuming he was posing.

Back to the drawing board.

I reply with my thanks and ask about news on Malik. Thing is, there hasn't been anything in two years. Not since that night. But I can't believe he died in that room. I've learned not to believe anything unless I see it with my own two eyes.

A creak from the darkened bedroom gets my attention. I know what she's up to. She has to know I expect her to search for her passport. She won't find it, but I'll have some fun.

I give her a few minutes and even get up and go into the kitchen, turn on the water in the sink to make some sound. The hallway lights are out and I walk quietly toward the bedroom. I'm not really trying to be sneaky, but I know how to be invisible. And she's not a trained soldier.

When I get to the bedroom door, I see the shadow of her hunched over my duffel. She can't see much, it's pretty dark in there, but she's feeling around.

"Looking for something?"

She gasps, and jumps back.

I flip the light switch and she lunges toward the bed, reaching her hand between the mattress and the box spring and fuck if I'm not surprised to see her straighten with a gun in her hands. A gun aimed at me.

My training kicks in, years of it, and given her inexperience, it takes me all of two seconds to cover her hands with my own, and draw her into my chest as I maneuver the hand holding the gun downward. I don't want that thing going off by accident, and I'm not sure if she's even loaded it or has the safety on. I'm not taking any chances though.

"That was stupid, Eve."

But she's not done yet because she uses the fact I'm holding her close to ram her knee up into my balls. I'm not ready for that and with a groan, I drop us both down on the bed. I still have both her wrists and I don't let go as I crush her beneath my weight.

"You want to fight dirty?" I ask through clenched teeth when the worst wave of nausea passes. I'm squeezing her wrist until she releases the gun and I hear it clatter to the hardwood floor.

"I can't—"

She can't breathe, is what she's trying to say.

I lift myself a little, but it's not to help her out with breathing, it's to haul her higher on the bed. I drag her arms over her head and the whole time she's fighting me with all she's got. I'm keeping my thighs glued shut this time. The cuffs I'd used earlier are still at the top of the bed, and I when I release one wrist to bind the other, she's clawing at my face, my shoulder, my arm, anything she can get at.

"Let go of me!"

"I can fight dirty too, Eve," I say, binding her other arm so they're both over her head. When that's done, I get up on my elbows, but keep my face close to hers. "In fact, I like fighting dirty."

I draw back and look down at her. She's still wearing that summer dress she had on earlier. That's a mistake because it's ridden up to her belly during our struggle and I can see black silk panties beneath.

She begins her struggle anew when my eyes

linger too long, this time twisting and turning and trying to kick her legs this way and that. She's still yelling for me to let her go.

"You want the gag?"

I pick it up to show her and she zips her lips the instant I do, shaking her head.

"You sure?" I ask.

She opens her mouth to say something, and I make like I'm about to shove that ball in there so she shuts it again.

I put it down and lean over the edge of the bed to pick up the pistol. It's smaller than anything I've used before, but it's loaded and just as deadly. I empty it of bullets and set it on the nightstand before turning my attention back to her.

"What, were you going to shoot me?"

"I just want my passport back."

"So you'd shoot me over a fake passport?"

Her forehead creases, and her big caramel eyes study me. I search her face, I can feel her heart beating against my chest. Watch the little pulse work on her neck. I'm hard again. It's been a long time since I've had a woman, and Eve lying beneath me, half exposed, all warm, soft skin, her chest rising and falling as she labors to breathe, well, yeah, my dick's hard. And this time, I want to play.

Her mouth is open and I can feel her breath on my face. I don't remember the last time I kissed a woman. Even when I fuck, I don't kiss them. I never want to. Her though, I don't know what the fuck it is with her, but she makes me want to.

She makes me want. Period.

And I decide to take, just this one little thing.

I close my mouth over hers. Our eyes are open and I kiss her, just her lips at first, soft and slow. I swallow her gasp of surprise and take it deeper, touch my tongue to hers. I'm testing, seeing if she's going to let me or if she'll bite. I hope for her sake she won't, and she doesn't. She's lying still beneath me, her struggles having ceased, and staring at me with those eyes like the fucking desert, vast, and golden and forever.

I moan, tasting her mouth. My hands find hers, close over them, and I think I'm going to disappear in this kiss.

I draw back and look down at her. Her lips are swollen and she's breathing hard.

The night of the auction—I *bought* her. I still catch myself trying to figure out what I was thinking. What I thought would happen. I knew the instant I called out the number, the one that had everyone stop and turn, I knew I'd fucked up. That I'd fucked it up for my men. I remember knowing in that instant it was a trap. That I'd been played. That was when the first explosion had blown out the wall behind me.

"Zach?"

I shake my head, open my eyes. I guess I'd closed

them. I know it's PTSD. I don't have the nightmares anymore, but that's only because I don't sleep. Instead, I have these moments, these flashes of memory flooding back, and every time, I relive that night. The whole of that night, or as much as I can remember. And every time I get a little piece back when I do. Like suffering through it again and again is the price I have to pay to get new bits of memory back. Like my brain doesn't think I can handle it all at once. And maybe I can't.

Or maybe I'm a coward because part of me doesn't want to remember.

"Zach?" she repeats my name.

I blink. She sees what just happened, but she doesn't know what it is. She can't. I look her over, slide my hands back down over her arms as I sit up, straddling her. I can't stop looking at her, at her eyes, her mouth, all that skin. Soft and pretty and mine.

Mine for now, at least.

My gaze slides to the flesh of her belly.

She squirms, but she isn't going anywhere.

I touch her softly with the back of one hand and make her gasp as I draw my knuckles over the point of her pelvic bone and down the hollow of her stomach. Her panties are soft, dark silk and I swallow as I draw them down.

She makes a sound, but I don't look at her face. I can't drag my eyes from her belly. From the skin I'm exposing. It's lighter here, there's a slight tan line. I see a corner of neatly trimmed dark hair and my chest tightens. Her panties are caught beneath her hips and I have to tug once to get them off.

She's breathing hard now, and she's got her legs sealed tight.

I meet her stare for one instant, then, like a fucking magnet, return it to her pussy. I get up off the bed and slide the panties down her legs and off her feet, tuck them into my pocket before sitting down again.

"Please. You said you wouldn't hurt me," she manages in a small, trembling voice.

But I need to see. I just need to see.

She lets out a small scream when I touch the hair between her legs, splay my fingers through the mound.

I look up at her. "I won't hurt you," I say.

Her gaze is moving from my eyes to my hand, then my cock and back, and I know she doesn't believe me.

"I won't hurt you," I repeat.

When my fingers slide over the seam of her sex, her breath catches. I want to open her, look at her. I already smell her and she's aroused. I feel it too as my fingers dip between her thighs and touch the moisture there. I drag them up to her swollen clit and trace a small circle, closing my eyes for a moment, imagining it's my tongue on her, tasting her, circling that hard little nub.

"Please don't," she whimpers.

I open my eyes.

"Please."

But her pupils are dilated, and she's licking her lips.

My fingers still, but I don't pull them away.

"I bought you that night," I say without looking at her. "Bought this. Everything happened because of this."

"Zach?"

It's like I'm back there again and she's on that makeshift stage and I've just called out a bid that doubles the highest one made. And I know I've fucked up, but right that second, some sick part of me has come alive with the knowledge of what I've just done. What I've just bought.

"It's mine," I say again, rubbing her clit, shifting my eyes to hers.

"Please don't."

I'm watching her. She's crying, but she's not struggling. She knows it's useless.

"I wanted you that night. I wanted this." My touch turns into a pinch and she gasps. "My men died because I wanted this."

She shakes her head no. "It wasn't your fault."

"Then whose fault was it?"

"This isn't you, Zach. You can't do this."

"I can."

"You won't."

Our eyes lock, and I don't know what I'm doing. What the hell I'm thinking. I just know what I said, that I can do this. It's more true than I want to admit and I can't let that be.

I pull my hand away and stand.

"You don't know me, Eve. You don't know what I've become."

I turn and, without looking back, I leave her bedroom and get out of the house and I walk. I walk for what feels like hours, and all I can think about is her. Her that night. Her now. Her almost naked.

Her brother stripped her then, I did it now. I can still feel how she felt. Fuck, I can still smell her. I can almost taste her. If I put my fingers in my mouth, I will.

I fist handfuls of my hair and tug. Who the fuck am I? What kind of monster have I become? How far would I have gone tonight?

I'm standing outside her house again. It's quiet. I want her. Fuck, I want her. I want to be inside her. It's like that's become the only thing now. I should stop drinking. Should get what I need from her and move the fuck on fast because all of this—her—being this close to her...it's muddling things. It's confusing what was once clear. I have a mission. I have to remember that mission. Get the truth, find out who fucked us, and kill them. What happens after that doesn't fucking matter because I know this is big. And I know I won't cheat death twice. Someone wanted me dead that night. Wanted to wipe out my team. This is a suicide mission, and I have to finish it.

My back burns. It's like every name traced onto it is reminding me of my mission. Reminding me of that life. Of what I owe each of those men.

I won't survive this. I know it. Always have known it. It's just this is the first time I'm admitting it.

Something nags at me. It's been bothering me since she told me her contact after that night was an American. Why the fuck did she survive that night? Who wanted to keep her alive? And why?

I take a deep breath in and make my way back up to her front door. I walk inside. She's lying on her side and watches me closely. She doesn't look surprised or even frightened right now, and I guess I'm relieved for the latter.

Her shoulders must be killing her. She doesn't speak when I enter the bedroom and uncuff her. She just lies there, eyes on me, as she rubs her wrists.

I strip down to my boxer briefs. She's watching me, and I'm watching her. I don't know what she expects, but I'm not a rapist. I'm just fucking tired. I lie down on the bed, my back to her.

"I'm fucked up, Eve."

It's quiet for a long time. She doesn't move. Doesn't pull away. She's so close. I can feel the heat of her body, and the memory of how her pussy felt haunts me. I'm staring at the wall, the window. I'm almost startled when I feel the tips of her fingers at my back. It's when she starts tracing the names that I squeeze my eyes shut. I wonder if I could cry if it would be better. Easier. I can't though. There's no room for tears. All I have is rage. And it makes my vision go black.

"I knew them all," she says, her voice so low it's almost a whisper.

"I know."

I'm holding my breath. I think she might be too. When she's traced every name, she touches the bumpy skin on the other half of my back. Then she does something that genuinely startles me. She kisses it, that scarred, hideous flesh. I suck in an audible, broken breath. Her lips are so soft. So damn soft.

I turn to face her and something in my eyes must frighten her because hers go wide, and it takes her a minute to settle down.

"I recognized you that night. When the bidding began," she says.

All the men covered their faces so only our eyes peeked out from beneath the scarves wrapped around our heads.

"It was your eyes. The horror inside them."

I remember. And—my God—what I'd give to forget the look inside hers.

"Armen used me to find you in that crowd."

She's started crying and sits up. I follow, studying

her so closely, but she won't look at me. Not right now. She's focused on her hands, nervous, just like she was the first time I saw her in that interrogation room.

It takes her a long time to speak, and her voice sounds strange when she does.

"The day of the arms sale—the auction—Armen was different. He was stressed. Anxious. That afternoon, he came with others. He called me a whore." Her voice breaks. "He said I was the Americans' whore. And it was time for my punishment. He knocked me out with some sort of drug, and when I woke up, I was at the auction." She doesn't look at me when she says it, and I feel that rage building inside me. That's good though. That's what I need. Anger. Fury. I need the strength to obliterate my enemies.

"Look at me."

She shakes her head.

I touch her chin, lift her face to mine. She's struggling to keep from sobbing, I can see it.

"See, you're right about something," she says, tears sliding down her cheeks and falling on my arm. "It was my fault. If it weren't for me, they'd all be alive."

I want to tell her she's wrong. That it's not her fault but mine, but I have to remember she could be lying to save her neck. Trying to make me believe she's sorry. Make me trust her so she can slip away.

At that thought, I slide my hand down her chin and close it around her throat. Her eyes go wide when I push her backward against the headboard. Her neck is at a strange angle and I know it hurts her, but I get up on my knees and straddle her.

I have to remember why I'm here.

She's a weakness. I have to keep a tight leash on the chaos she wreaks inside my head. And the way to do that is to see her, all of her. Not just what I want to be true.

"Were you part of the setup?"

I realize her hands are clawing at my forearm. Her nails have broken my skin, but I don't feel it. It's my damaged arm. I loosen my grip a little.

"Did you know all along?" I ask and my voice is so low, so deep, she shudders with the question.

She shakes her head. Or tries to.

"Because you know what I can't wrap my brain around, Eve?"

She's still trying to drag my arm away. Her face is red, her eyes redder. I'm squeezing too hard.

"How the hell did you survive that night?"

I know the answer the instant I ask the question: *because she's a trap.* She'll be my downfall. Not once, but twice.

I stare at her, almost not seeing her as this realization dawns on me. I draw my hands away, releasing her before getting off the bed and grabbing my jeans. I need to get out of here, out of this room. I can't be this close to her. Not right now.

At the bedroom door, I turn to find her kneeling in the middle of the bed rubbing her neck, watching me. When I speak, my voice is level and I sound much calmer than I feel.

"I can't figure out what your role is. I don't know if you're lying or if you're a pawn in this too. All I know is you're alive, and everyone else is dead. You don't get a free pass like that, not from people like Malik the Butcher. Not from covert US military operations. And until I figure it out, you're mine. You will do as I say, and if, when all is said and done, I believe you're innocent, you'll be free to go."

I take a step toward her and she plasters herself against the back of the bed.

"But if I find out you're a fucking liar, I'll kill you. I'll fucking kill you."

I notice the pistol and ammunition from earlier. I gather it all up along with my duffel bag, and walk out. I don't have to warn her not to try anything stupid. She will, at some point. And I'll stop her. And if I need to, I'll punish her.

7

EVE

I wake to sunlight pouring in from the bedroom window. I'm sweating and I want to say it's because the windows were closed all night long, but I know that's not it. I'm amazed I got any sleep at all after what happened, and even after all of that, all my mind goes back to is him cuffing me to the bed. Him on top of me. Kissing me. Touching me.

I squeeze my eyes shut because I know what I should feel is hate. Anger. Fear at his final words. But all I can do is remember his touch. How gentle he'd been, at least at first. Before his memories took hold of him. Made him remember why he was here.

But it's the part before that moment my mind keeps going to.

The bedroom door is open. He didn't sleep in the

bed with me. I don't know what he did after he walked out of here. All I know is his behavior only confirms one thing: he's on a suicide mission. And this thing—his need for vengeance—it owns him.

I get out of the bed. My dress falls to my knees, reminding me I'm naked underneath. Reminding me he took my panties.

Barefoot, I silently creep down the hallway, but he's not here. Not in the living room, kitchen or bathroom. I peek out the windows and don't see his truck, but I'm not sure that means anything. My cell phone rings and I realize he left it on the kitchen table. I run to pick it up. It's Devon.

"Hi Devon," I say. I haven't checked in with him since yesterday.

"Eve, good morning. I'm glad I caught you. I tried calling last night. Left several messages."

"I'm sorry, I..." I run a hand through my hair. "Just had a long day with Michael."

"A productive day, it sounds like. He's meeting you at noon to see the McKinney house again?"

What?

"Think he'll make an offer today?" Devon asks before I can get my thoughts straight.

"Oh, I don't know about that." Zach's been in touch with Devon? "I'll let you know as soon as I do, though."

"Well listen, it's a shorter drive from your place

so I figure you'll head straight there rather than coming into the office first."

"Devon, when did you talk to him?"

"Michael?"

"Yes."

"This morning. He got here a few minutes after I did. Seems excited about the property and was very positive about you."

I'm confused, not sure what to make of this.

"Anyhow, I'll let you go. Just wanted to tell you good job and if you need anything, I'm here."

"Thanks. I'll see you this afternoon, I guess."

"Oh, you had a couriered package arrive by the way. I signed for it. Remind me to give it to you when you get here."

"Couriered?"

"It's on my desk, but you know how my memory is."

"I'll remind you."

"Good luck today."

"Thanks, Devon."

We hang up and I sink down into one of the kitchen chairs. I'm not sure what the hell is going on. Zach wants me back at the McKinney property? Why? He can come and go as he pleases here, that's clear. So why have me meet him out there?

My phone buzzes with a text message. I look down at it. It's from a number I don't recognize. I swipe and enter my code to read it.

Don't keep me waiting and don't do anything stupid.

It's him.

He's set this up for me to meet him at that house. Is it because it's so remote he wants to meet there? What does he plan to do to me?

I get up and walk back into my bedroom. He won't hurt me. Not yet. If that was what he wanted, he would have done it last night. He wouldn't have told Devon he'd be with me today if he had any intention of hurting me. He wants to make sure I come.

Choosing a suit, I quickly get dressed, pull my hair into a messy bun at the back of my head, dab on mascara and lip gloss, and head out of the house. I'm not going to run. I can't. He still has my passport. And besides, I won't run. I'm as involved as he is in this, whether I like it or not. Something is going on, it's almost like someone expected him to be alive. Knew it. Because hadn't I asked the same question he did last night?

Why had I survived that massacre when no one else had?

Why was I alive?

I drive the thirty minutes to the McKinney property and park behind his truck on the driveway. He knows the lockbox code so he's already in the house. My heart is racing as I walk up the porch steps, and I don't bother to knock. Instead, I walk inside.

As I pass the kitchen, I see two empty beer

bottles and a bag of takeout food, and realize this is where he'd come after he left my house.

"Zach?"

He doesn't answer. I walk into the dining room and come to a stop. All I can do is look at all the walls, the photos he's posted along them. He has one of two men, well, of their backs, and he's drawn a red question mark over top one of the men. Next to it are several shots of my brother, Armen. I walk toward them and goosebumps cover my flesh as sadness fills me up. There are photos of him before he began to work with Malik, but only a few of those, and then there are the ones after. I'm shocked to see the differences in his appearance. Had I seen it back then too? Or maybe it never registered since living together in our family home, we saw each other almost daily.

My other brothers are here too. These look almost like mugshots. I reach out and touch those, Rafi and Seth. Younger than Armen, but older than me. I don't have any photos of them. It's been years since I've seen them, and I miss them so much. If I knew what happened to them, even if that meant finding out they were dead, would it make it easier?

"Closure doesn't help."

I jump and spin around to find Zach watching me. It's like he read my mind.

He's wearing dress pants and a button-down shirt with the sleeves rolled up. I look at his hands and remember them touching me. Remember them wrapping around my throat and strangling me.

I shake off those thoughts. "You can't just stay here," I say, forcing myself to meet his eyes. "It's not a hotel."

He shrugs. He eyes me once before he walks into the dining room. "You'd rather I stay with you?"

"That's not what I meant."

He goes directly to the six images along the back wall. I watch him stop before each one. I wonder what I'd see if I could see his face right now.

"You also can't call Devon and give him the impression you're buying this place just to get me up here."

He turns to face me. "You think I need to do that to get you here?"

My heart is thundering against my chest but I refuse to show fear.

He steps toward me, and it takes all I have not to take two steps back. But when he reaches out to touch me, I flinch. One side of his mouth rises as he tucks a strand of hair behind my ear.

"If I want you somewhere, you'll be there."

His voice is so deep, so low, it sends chills through me. His gaze wanders to my mouth and I catch myself licking my lips. My body is betraying me. It thinks it wants him. Wants to be close to him.

Dropping my head, I take that step back.

"What is this?" I ask, stepping toward the back wall. "Another graveyard?"

The instant the words are out of my mouth, I regret them. Zach corners me against the wall, trapping me with his body to my front and his hands pressed to the wall at either side of my head.

"I'm sorry," I say quickly. "I didn't—"

A moment hangs between us and I'm not sure what he's going to do, how he'll react, but when he smashes his mouth against mine, all I can think about is him, his hardness, the contrast between it and the softness of his lips, even as he takes the kiss without my permission. My hands are pressing up against his chest but I'm not sure if I'm pushing against him, even as my brain screams for me to. For me to get the hell away from him.

When he breaks the kiss, he takes my jaw in one hand and turns my face away, just a little. His forehead is against the wall and he's breathing hard against my ear.

"I don't understand why every fucking time I see you, every time I'm close to you, all I can think about is this."

When he releases me, I remain as I am. He's rubbing the scruff of his jaw against my cheek. I don't move. I stand utterly, completely still, my heart racing, every breath drawing him in. And I don't know what I should do, what I'm supposed to do, what I want.

I can run. Right now, I can run. Slip under his arm. I don't think he'll stop me. But I don't want to.

He moves a little so we're facing each other. His head is bent low and our foreheads are almost touching. Without breaking eye contact, he takes my hand and presses it to his chest. His heart. His skin is warm through the thin barrier of his shirt and his heart is beating frantically. He doesn't blink as he slides my hand down, down over the ridges of muscle over his belly, down to the thick hardness of his cock.

I swallow. I don't pull back. He rubs his length with my hand and all I feel is want. Need. Heat.

Heat between my legs.

"Take it out," he says, releasing my hand, placing both of his on either side of my head.

He watches me as my fingers fumble with his belt, undoing it, then the button, then the zipper of his pants. I push them down and I can feel him through the cotton boxer briefs. I look down. I want to see him, see him naked. Touch him. Hold his hardness in my hands.

Swallowing, I shift my eyes up to his.

He nods.

I slide one hand inside and he sucks in a breath when I grip him, sliding his boxer briefs and pants down.

Fingers intertwine with the hair on my head and he's pushing me to my knees.

I kneel and his cock is at my face, brushing against my cheek, my lips. I lick the tip, lick the moisture there, and his hand becomes a fist as he turns my face up. Looking at him, I open my mouth and I take him in and watch his face, watch his eyes close as he bites his lip and flexes his fingers in my hair. He's hurting me, but I don't care. I want this. I want him.

I want him.

When he opens his eyes, the pupils have dilated so they appear almost black. Holding me, he moves his length deeper, in and out slowly, and I can hear him breathe. It's a moan of pleasure as I take him in, tasting him, his salty sweetness, breathe in his scent.

But when he moves too deep, too fast, he cuts off my breath and panic has me pressing my hands against his thick thighs. He draws out a little, but he's still got my hair and his cock is still inside my mouth.

"Easy," he says in a low growl. "I won't hurt you."

I've never done this before. I've never even seen a man like this.

"Just a little more." He's moving again, pumping in and out, deeper, then more shallow, then deeper yet, and all I can do take him. All I want to do is take him.

My vision blurs from tears. He moans and I look up to find him watching me.

"I'm going to come down your throat," he says, pumping faster.

I make a sound. I don't know why—don't know if it's panic or arousal or what.

"Shh. Just relax. All you have to do is swallow."

He's thrusting harder, faster and I'm not sure how long I can take this, but just then, his grip in my hair tightens. He settles himself deep inside me and I feel the first spurts of cum, feel them hit the back of my throat, slide down, feel him shudder, hear him let out a moan and hold still as he empties, and I feel like I can't take any more, I'm so full, too full. But then he releases my hair and he's pulling out of my mouth and when I open my eyes, he's looking down at me, coming to a crouch so he's almost at eye level.

My mouth is closed. I'm holding his cum inside it. He leans close, wipes the corner of my lips.

"Swallow," he says, sliding his hand down between my legs, pushing the crotch of my panties aside to tickle my clit, rub it. "Swallow my cum, Eve."

He doesn't release me from his gaze until I do, then nods his approval.

"Your cunt is dripping."

He's manipulating my clit but his eyes are locked on mine. With his thumb on the hard nub, he presses a finger inside me and I gasp. He smiles, then closes his mouth over mine and kisses me deeply.

"I like my taste on you," he mumbles against me, and when I gasp, he draws back to watch me.

He adds a second finger and there's a moment of discomfort, but then pleasure again. When he pushes deeper, I make a sound and he pauses. His eyes narrow a little. He tests the barrier again. It doesn't give and he draws his fingers out, concentrating on my clit. When he touches me there, it's like I can't think. Can't speak. Can't do anything but feel.

"Look at me," he says. "I want to see your eyes when you come."

I'm so close, all I can do is grip his shoulders. He likes it, likes me like this. I can see it on his face.

"Come, *habibi*."

I do.

I do, despite his use of that word, despite the wicked grin on his face. I come hard, so hard that I fall into his chest with a moan, my fingernails digging into his arms as I climax, my breathing ragged, my body too hot, too sweaty. And when it's over, when the wave passes and I'm left limp, he pulls his hand away, watching my face as he does, smearing his fingers along my thigh.

He rises to his feet while I'm left kneeling. When I look up at him, he's still looking down at me. He pulls his boxer briefs and pants back up, zips and buttons them then buckles his belt.

"Still a virgin," he says.

I feel my face heat up. Why aren't I getting up off the floor?

"First time sucking cock too, wasn't it?"

Is he making fun of me? I can't tell, but I feel ashamed. Humiliated.

But it's when he lifts his fingers to his nose, those fingers that were just inside me, before licking them, that I'm vanquished.

"Get cleaned up. We have work to do," he says and walks out of the room.

I listen as Eve scurries up the stairs to, I assume, the bathroom. I'm a dick. I know it. But I don't like what she does to me. Don't like what happens to me when I'm around her. Like this thing now, I can't even think about that. When she made that comment about the graveyard, I got fucking pissed. But then she was there—so close—trapped. Trapped between me and the wall. Small and scared and at my mercy.

And all I could do was touch her. Kiss her.

Kiss her to shut her up? No. That's a lie. I kissed her because I wanted to.

I shake my head and pick up a folder. I spent the whole of the morning at a fucking copy shop printing shit out. Now I'm taping all those photos up on the wall opposite the one with my men.

The doctor who saved me, Anthony Hassan, was

a good guy. Is a good guy. His son—I called him Ace, never did get his real name—he's my connection in the Middle East. If I need anything, he usually knows where to find me the answer. They risked their lives for me and although I know by contacting Ace, I'm breaking my promise to Anthony, I need his help. I'll know in a few minutes if Ace delivered.

I hear her come into the room even though she's trying to be quiet. I turn to her. She flushes pink and can't hold my gaze, and all I can see is how she looked on her knees before me. Sucking my cock. Her little virgin tongue so wet, her mouth so hot.

But I can't think about that now. I won't be able to do what I came to do if I go down that road, and I already fucked up today. Because in a way, she's right. This is a graveyard. And what I just did, I did before the dead.

"What are these?" she asks, walking over to the new photos I've just put up. Three are of the same man in various disguises. The others are different. I want to know if she recognizes anyone in particular. I hope she does because that will be my first lead.

"Is one of these men the one who gave you your passport?"

She shakes her head no, but I see her pause at each of the three images which are of the same person.

"Sit down."

She obeys.

"Tell me what happened that last day."

She studies me for a few minutes, and the look on her face is sad. Not pitiful, just sad.

"My brother came home that morning as usual, but he was irritable. Irritated with me. And maybe I was anxious, considering. He went to his bedroom to sleep. He always did that after being out for the night with Malik. He was always tired." Her forehead creases and she's looking off in the distance like she's seeing it all.

"Stay with me, Eve."

She startles and shifts her eyes to mine. "He asked me that afternoon why I was nervous. Said he was going to take care of everything. When I went to cook dinner, some men came over. It wasn't that unusual for his friends to eat with us, but these men were...different. I didn't know them. And they carried weapons into the house. In front of me. He didn't usually allow that. That's when Armen told me to sit down. When he..." she trails off.

"When he called you a whore?" I see that word upsets her and I'm not sure why I use it.

"I already told you all this."

"Tell me again."

"He said it was time for me to be punished. He injected me with something that knocked me out, and when I woke up, I was at that place. Where the auction was. My wrists were bound and I was gagged, but I could hear everything. It was a little while before Armen came though, and he didn't come to me right away. He was talking just outside the room where I was being held. I remember he was speaking in English. I didn't understand why."

"English?"

She nods.

"Then the door opened and he dragged me out. I still remember how his eyes looked. The dark circles around them. The look inside them that for a second told me he didn't want to do what he was about to do."

"Put you up there to sell you?"

"Yes. The rest you know."

"Tell me about passing out."

She shakes her head. "There isn't much to tell. I heard that explosion and my head hurt so badly I thought I'd been shot or hit by something else, shrapnel maybe. That's all I remember. After that, I woke up in that room with that man waiting for me."

"Passport man."

She nods.

"He never mentioned his name?"

She shakes her head.

"You didn't feel the need to ask?"

"I did ask. He said he was there on behalf of the US military. That was all he said. You have to understand, I was confused. In shock. He showed me photos of the place after the explosion. I saw bodies, Zach..." she closes her eyes and covers her face.

"*Parts* of so many bodies. No one could have survived that."

"Yet you and I both did. I told you this already."

"You don't know the state I was in. I'd just lost everything and it was my fault."

I guess we had that in common.

Silence stretches out. I watch her. She's seeing it all again. I know the look of someone losing themselves in memory. In guilt.

Slowly, she raises her eyes to mine, then drags them to the photo of the man I'm hoping she'll recognize. When she gets to her feet, I don't stop her. She moves to stand in front of it again.

"It's him." She touches it, covers his beard with her hand. "He didn't look like that when I met him. He was clean-shaven. Wearing a suit. Hair lighter."

In the photo, he's got a full beard and he's looking a little worse for wear.

She turns to me. "He told me the passport was in thanks for my part, even though the mission failed. He said they'd found me alive and rescued me and that I needed to get out of the country because if Malik found out I'd survived, he'd have me killed. I asked him about Armen, and he told me he'd died. I also asked him about you. He said you had cost them the mission."

I can't let myself linger on that. I can't think about it. I take the photograph and look at it. Then I take out my phone and scroll through to an image I didn't print. I hold up my phone to show her.

"Is this the man?"

She nods.

"His name is David Beos. He was supposed to have died almost four years ago."

"What?"

"Car bomb exploded during his transfer to a military prison. The vehicle Beos was riding in was hit. The bodies were unidentifiable."

"What had he done that he was going to prison?"

"Informant to Malik. He was a traitor."

Color drains from her face. She's putting it together now. I'm only one step ahead of her.

"Malik saved my life?"

I'm studying her, trying to make sense of this. "It's the only thing I can think of. Your passport is a fake, Eve."

"I don't understand."

"It wasn't issued by the United States government. What I want to know is why in hell would Malik save your life? What value could you hold for him?"

"Do you think...could it mean Armen survived? Made a deal? Maybe Seth and Rafi—"

I shake my head. Most likely, they're all dead, and she shouldn't get her hopes up. "I don't know. What I do know is that Malik's associates rarely last more than a couple of months. He's a burn the bridge kind of guy."

"What do you mean?"

"He covers his tracks. Very well. It's how he's managed to stay ahead of the US and other enemies who have hunted him for years. We don't have a single photo of his face. Not one. And that's unusual. There's always something, but he's like a fucking ghost. Disappears just when you think you have him."

"You want to find him, don't you?"

Her question triggers something that's been niggling at my brain for a long time.

Something's wrong with this, with all of this. It stinks of a setup. All this while, I've thought she was part of it, but my gut is screaming no. It's telling me she's innocent.

And that maybe I don't have to try to find him.

Maybe he's found me.

She doesn't wait for me to answer. "If he thinks you're dead, why won't you leave it alone? Live your life."

"I'm not a coward, and I know the debt I owe to those who are dead."

"You survived. There's nothing you can do for the men who died. Revenge won't bring them back."

"Don't you think I know that? The people or person responsible for their deaths deserves to pay."

"You're on a suicide mission."

I chuckle and shake my head. "You still don't get it." I begin collecting the photographs hanging on the walls.

"Don't get what?" she asks in a quiet voice.

I turn to her. "I was meant to find you. He knew I'd come looking for you."

"What?"

"You're a trap, Eve. You've been set up, and so have I. Again."

She shakes her head, then drops down in the chair. I can see from the crease in her forehead, the intensity in her eyes, that she's trying to make sense of what I'm saying.

"Get yourself together. We have to go. *You* have to go."

"Where? Why?" she asks. She rises to her feet, rubs her face. "I don't understand."

I put the photos down and go to her, take her by the arms. "He expected me to find you. Make contact with you."

"What do you mean?"

"You were the bait. Malik somehow knew I survived. And I guess he knew I'd come looking for you once I learned you had too. I made it pretty obvious when I bid on you at the auction. It's why he kept you alive."

She's processing slowly. Panic is rising, I can see it in her eyes. I squeeze my hands around her arms, shake her once.

"You need to keep it together. I have a contact, I'll get you a new passport. A new name. You'll have to leave Denver behind, but—"

"What are you talking about?" She shoves her hands against my chest, but I hold tight. "Let me go."

"No."

"This makes no sense, Zach. It's crazy." She squares her shoulders and looks at me. "*You're* crazy. Paranoid and delusional."

I snort. "I wish you were right."

"Let me go. I'm leaving."

"Yes, we are. You'll drive home and get packed. I'll get you settled—"

"You aren't hearing me! *I* am leaving. Alone."

I give her one hard shake. She's wasting time now. She doesn't believe she's in danger, but if what I'm thinking is right and she's worn out her usefulness, Malik will burn this bridge too.

"I can't add one more name to the graveyard on my back, Eve. And I won't add yours."

She stops fighting, stills completely and looks up at me. I'm not sure whom I've surprised more by what I've said—her or me.

"Do you understand now?" I ask.

"I need to think. Make sense of it."

Problem is, I'm not sure we have the time. I need to get her hidden before I leave to find Beos. I know he's my link to Malik.

"Okay, take this afternoon. Go back to work. I'll

pick you up there at five to take you home to get your things." And that will give me time to set up a hiding place for her.

She nods her head. "Okay."

This is too easy. She agreed too easily. But I release her.

She takes a step and rubs her arms.

"You really shouldn't stay here, you know," she says.

"I can't stay with you." I wonder if she understands what I'm not saying. That for a while last night, I lost control. That with her, I need to be careful.

I can't lose control with her.

My mind is full of so much information that I drive into Denver on autopilot. What he's saying, it's got me confused. I realize if it's true, if he's right, that I'm in danger. But it also gives me hope. Hope that my brother maybe isn't dead. Maybe he survived too. If Malik arranged the explosion, why wouldn't he save Armen's life too? Armen was loyal to him.

But then Zach's words come back to me: *"Malik's associates rarely last more than a couple of months. He's a burn the bridge kind of guy."*

But maybe he's wrong this time.

I need to go back. If there's a chance my brother is alive, I need to know. He's all I have left. Even after what happened, he's it. At a traffic light, I reach over to my purse to pull out my cell phone. My passport is beside it. I took it when Zach left the room after telling me to go clean up. It was in the duffel bag. He didn't realize it was missing then, but I know it's naïve to think he won't notice soon.

Zach thinks he's going to hide me away while he goes after the man who destroyed my family. I know if he does find him, and if Armen is alive and with him, he won't be for long. Zach will kill him. I can't allow that to happen.

I dial the office and am grateful when Miranda tells me Devon's at lunch. I ask her to take a message for me and let him know something's come up, a family emergency, and I'll be gone for a few days. When I hang up, I'm already turning onto my street. I park the car and head inside to look up flights to Beirut and pack my bag. By the time Zach gets to the office at five o'clock, I'll be long gone.

The first thing I do when I get inside is start my laptop to check availability on flights. I should be able to get on one that leaves at quarter to midnight tonight. I get a suitcase out of the closet and begin to empty my drawers, filling it with as much as I can, not sure how long I'll be staying. Not sure if I'll be returning at all.

The whole time I'm packing, I'm trying really hard not to think about what happened with Zach. Trying not to remember what it felt like to have him kiss me. To touch him. Taste him.

To have him touch me.

I almost feel guilty about what I'm doing, but then I make myself remember what happened afterward. How he humiliated me. Dismissed me.

I need to remember that to him, I'm a pawn. A means to an end.

He doesn't care about me.

Christ, where did that come from? I don't expect him to *care* about me. That's ridiculous.

He needs me. That's all this is.

Or at least he did. I'm of no use to him anymore. I gave him information. Named a man. He has the next link in this chain that will ultimately hang him.

I shake off those thoughts and even consider a shower before leaving the house, but I should get out of here. I can't trust that he'll go to the office at five, like he said. What's to stop him from coming straight here? I decide to head to the airport and get a hotel room there while waiting for the flight.

Once I've stuffed the suitcase and changed into an outfit more suitable for traveling, I glance around the small house like it's the last time I'll see it. And it might be. I can't think about that now though. It'll zap any courage I have if I let it. So I turn and walk out the door, dragging my suitcase behind me and holding on to my purse, which contains my laptop and passport. I place the case in the trunk and get into the driver's seat, taking an extra moment to look around me. Wondering if Zach's right. That I am a trap. That I'm being watched.

That I'm expendable because Zach is what they wanted.

With a shudder, I start the car and head to the airport.

I should have known she wouldn't do as she was told.

I'm standing in the real estate office while the receptionist—whose voice grates on my nerves —won't stop talking. I stopped listening once she told me Eve had called to let them know that she wouldn't be back in the office for a few days due to a family emergency.

Family emergency.

Of course. I should have known she'd stop thinking about anything else the moment she thought that maybe, just maybe, her brother had survived that night.

What she can't see is that he's the one who betrayed her in the first place.

"She got a package too," the girl says. "Never

picked it up. Brought by a special courier and everything."

"Give it to me. I'll swing by her house. She has some paperwork I forgot to sign."

"Oh, she's not there. I got a call to approve a company credit card charge a little while ago. She's at the Marriott at the airport. Room 402. Devon asked me to drive it out to her, but the airport's a pain in the ass to get to."

I'll take one guess as to where Eve thinks she's going.

"I'll meet her out there then. Easier for me, since I'm heading out of town too."

The girl looks at me like that's quite the coincidence.

"It may be time sensitive if it was special couriered. I can take it with me."

She looks down at the envelope. It's not big, but it only has Eve's information on it. No sender info. That worries me.

I lean into the desk and give her my best smile. "I really don't mind taking it, and I won't mention it to your boss."

"Okay," she says. "I guess if you're going to see her anyway."

"Thanks." I take it and turn on my heel. I don't bother with a goodbye before heading out to the truck. Once inside, I carefully tear the package open.

I don't know what I'm expecting, maybe some sort of bomb to go off. But white powder can kill as easily as an explosive, and I know the people I'm dealing with.

No powder in this envelope though. Only two things. A Lebanese passport and an airline ticket.

I open the front page of the passport. Eve El-Amin's pretty face is smiling back at me. I check the issue and expiration dates. She's had this since before I met her. It expires in three months. The airline ticket is for tonight, and it's a one-way ticket to Beirut.

I pocket both things. I'll give her the passport, but no way in hell she'll be on that flight tonight.

That receptionist is right about one thing: the drive to Denver International Airport is a pain in the ass. When I get to the Marriott, I spot her car easily and park beside it. I climb out and head inside, straight to the elevator and to her room. I knock on the door and step to the side, out of view of the peephole.

When the door opens, I'm looking into Eve's shocked face. It takes her a moment to react. To try and slam the door shut. But before she can, I have the toe of my shoe inside so it bounces off and knocks her backward.

"I told you I'd pick you up."

She scurries around the bed. "I'll scream!"

I close the door. "Go ahead. Make my fucking day." I don't wait for her to make a move. Instead, I lunge for her, catching her as she picks up the phone, and toss her onto the bed. She bounces once, then scrambles onto all fours, but before she can get away, I capture her ankle and drag her back so she's flat on her stomach. I flip her over and climb on top of her. "I'm getting the feeling you like this."

"Let me go!"

"No."

She's struggling beneath me and this is so not the time, but my dick's getting hard. I draw her arms over her head. "You listen like shit." Looking at her like this, flushed, trapped beneath me, feeling the contours of her soft body against mine, it makes me hungry. Then there's her mouth... lips parted, swollen...

I kiss her. I can't help it. She's surprised, there's a momentary halt of all activity, a sound she makes, but then she starts again, like she knows she should fight it. Fight me.

"I like your mouth." I transfer both wrists into one hand and with my face an inch from hers, slide the other down along the curve of her body and between us to grip the waistband of her jeans.

"What are you doing?"

I grin and undo one button, my hand slips inside, my fingers are beneath her panties. "Touching you."

"Zach—"

But my fingers close over her sex and her expression changes, her pupils dilate and she bites her lip, thrusting her pelvis upward—at least for a moment.

"Stop." It's a squeak.

"You're wet."

She can't deny it. The evidence is on my fingers.

"Stop," she tries again.

"No."

I release her wrists and slide down over her body, keeping eye contact as I do. She makes some sad attempt to free herself, but I know what she wants.

Dropping off the bed, I drag her down so her legs are dangling.

"Stop!"

I undo her jeans and drag them down. She sits up, trying to shove me away, but it's halfhearted at best. I hold her off with one hand. Her panties are askew and I pull them down, then shove them and her jeans off so she's only wearing a tank top. I take my time looking at her, then with my hands on either thigh, I spread her legs wider.

"You're fucking soaking, Eve."

"I'm not." She tries to shove my hands away, to close her legs.

I dip my head down and inhale deeply before taking a long, slow lick of her sex, her glistening, wet pussy, then take her clit into my mouth and suck.

"You taste fucking amazing."

Her hands are in my hair, fingers entwined there, but she's also moaning, pressing herself into my face.

"God. Stop." She's practically grinding against me.

"You don't want me to stop," I say, then resume sucking.

She's pulling my hair now, holding me tight. She's up on one elbow, watching me, her breathing coming in short gasps. And when I slide one finger into her tight virgin pussy, she lets go, squeezing her thighs around my neck, her fingernails digging into my head as she moans, her eyes squeezed shut, coming gloriously on my tongue.

After an eternity of panting, her legs loosen and she falls backward, swallowing hard, blinking, her face burning as she refuses to look at me.

I stand up and wipe the back of my hand across my lips, watching her. She keeps her face averted.

"Look at me, Eve."

She shakes her head.

"Look at me."

She does, although reluctantly.

"I like watching you come."

I know it's taking all she has to keep her gaze on mine while her face burns red.

"And there's nothing I'd like more than to slide my cock into that tight little cunt of yours."

Shock registers on her face. I'm going to guess it's my word choice. It makes me smile.

I adjust myself. No time for release now, this has already delayed us and we need to get out of here.

"But sadly, we don't have time. We need to go."

I toss her jeans and underwear in her direction and go to the window, draw the curtains back to look outside. I can see my truck and her car but not much else going on in the parking lot.

"Go?"

When I turn around, she's zipping her jeans.

"Yes, go."

"I'm not going anywhere with you."

"I know what you think you're doing, but you can't go back to Beirut. No fucking way."

"This has nothing to do with you," she says.

"Where are your things?"

She almost steps right up to me, but stops herself. Red is flushing her cheeks again and if there's anything I've ever wanted, it's time. Right now. Time to make her blush some more. Make her come some more.

"You can't just walk in here and...and—"

"Eat your pussy?"

That gets me the desired result: shocked silence.

"Get your purse, let's go."

"No."

"You're wearing on my nerves, Eve." I take her arm to move her along. "Let's fucking go."

She tries to free herself. "You didn't have to come here. I'm not your problem."

"Well, you are, actually. Like I said earlier, I'm not planning on getting your name tattooed on my back."

"I'm not planning on dying!"

"You're sure as hell giving it a good effort!"

A knock comes on the door then. I pull her into my chest and close one hand over her mouth.

"Room service," a man's voice calls.

I look down at her. Her eyes have gone wide.

"Let me guess, you haven't ordered room service," I whisper.

She shakes her head.

I release her and get up, putting a finger to my lips. "Get on the floor. Don't move, and don't make a sound."

She slides down to crouch behind the bed. I make my way to the door as "room service" knocks again. I don't have a weapon, but I'll have the element of surprise.

I look through the little peephole to see a man dressed in a uniform looking up and down the hall-way. The tray he's holding is covered by a napkin and one hand is underneath it. I open the door, using it as a shield between us. He's obviously expecting her to be right there, and it takes him a moment to step into the room. As soon as he does, I slam the tray out of his hand and shove him into the wall by the back of his neck. A shot goes off and even though the gun has a silencer, it makes enough sound that Eve lets out a scream. I grab the hand with the gun and slam it hard against the wall once, twice, three times, until he drops it. After kicking it away, I spin him around and punch him across his jaw.

He's a big guy, but I'm bigger. And he's surprised by my presence here. We were obviously being watched at the house, and she was being followed.

"Who sent you?" I ask, punching him again.

Nothing. He's struggling to focus on me.

"Who the fuck sent you?"

He gives me a grin. One of his teeth has come loose and I decide to knock out a few more. I don't realize I'm still hitting him until I hear her.

"Stop. Zach, stop. It's enough. Zach."

She's pulling at my arm, her weight on my back. The guy's on the floor beneath me and he's not moving. His head is resting at a funny angle.

"Zach?"

I look at her, then at him. Then at my bloodied fist. My bloodied shirt.

"You okay?" I ask. She stares at the dead man. She's just watching him. This can't be the first time she's seen a dead body.

"You—" her face crumples and she begins to cry quietly—giant teardrops sliding down her face.

Fuck.

I stand up. I don't know how much noise there was. Don't know how long I was beating the shit out of him. All I can think is that we have to get out of here. "Where's your stuff, Eve?"

She looks up at me like I'm speaking Chinese.

"Your things. Where are they?"

She just keeps staring at me. I look around the room and guess they're in her car.

"Stay there." I go into the bathroom to wash my hands and face, glad the black of my T-shirt hides the blood. I dry my hands and return to drag the dead man into the bathroom. I close the door. Her purse and computer are on the desk so I take them, and shove the dead man's Glock into the waistband of my pants.

"Let's go," I tell her.

She's still exactly where I left her. Her face is white, her eyes wide. Her hair's a mess.

"We need to go. Now. And you need to keep your shit together until we're in the truck, understand?"

She's staring straight ahead.

I squat down to make her look at me. "Eve?"

Nothing.

I pat my hand to her face. "Eve, look at me."

Nothing. She's in shock.

I don't want to do this, but I slap her once. Twice.

She blinks rapidly, pushing me away, finally meeting my gaze.

"We have to go *now*."

She nods, touches a hand to her cheek. I didn't hit her hard, but it's already turning red.

"I'm sorry about that," I say as I open the door and make sure the hallway's empty. It is. Wrapping an arm around her waist, I lead us toward the stairs. They're empty too. I guess he'd come alone, expecting only to find one unarmed, unsuspecting target. I don't want to think about what would have happened if I hadn't come when I had.

Somehow, she manages to keep her shit together as we walk through the lobby. Outside, I get her into my truck before finding her keys and moving her things from her car to mine. I then get into the truck and start it.

"No. No, what are you doing?" All of a sudden she's animated, trying to grab the steering wheel.

"We have to get out of here."

"I can't. I have to—"

"I know, catch a flight home."

She stops, looks up at me, then nods.

"It's not safe, not for you."

"What do you mean, not for me?"

"You can't go back."

"My brother may be alive!"

"You can't go back, Eve."

"Why not?"

"Because they're fucking expecting you!"

"What?"

I reach into my pocket and pull out her passport. The real one.

She takes it. Opens it. "Where did you get this?"

"You received a package at the office."

"I forgot about that. From who?"

"No return address."

"I don't understand."

I'm reluctant, but decide to tell her. "That's not all. There was a ticket included."

"Ticket?"

"One way. To Beirut."

"It's my brother."

"It's Malik."

"I have to go, Zach."

I'm thinking. This isn't adding up. She may be right. Why send her a ticket home then send someone to kill her?

"Zach." My name is a whisper on her tongue. Her hand falls to my arm and it makes me turn to look at her. "I can't hide, not if there's a chance my brothers are alive. I owe it to them."

11

I'm watching the black sky of nighttime as we fly toward Beirut. I wonder if it should feel familiar. I guess I'm too far out for it to. I don't remember the last time I flew in the opposite direction. That day was a blur. That year was a blur.

"Here. It'll help you sleep."

I look up. Zach's settling back into his seat. He's in the aisle and I'm sardined in the window seat. He hands over a plastic cup and a little bottle of whiskey. I take both.

He doesn't pour his out, but drinks it from the tiny bottle and every time I look at him, I feel my face burn as heat rushes through my veins always ending up in the same spot. It's like my body is separate of my mind.

He gets that wicked grin on his face and leans in close. "You're thinking about it, aren't you?"

I turn away, bring all my attention to twisting the cap off the bottle. "No."

He's closer now, he's lifted the armrest between us so his body is pressed against mine. "You're a bad liar."

"Stop."

"Last time you said that, you were squeezing your thighs around my neck so hard I thought you'd snap it."

I look around us to see if anyone's heard, but everyone's asleep and all I hear is the soft hum of the airplane.

"Was that the first time a man licked your pussy?"

"Shut up!"

He shrugs, finishes his drink and opens his second bottle.

I take a sip of mine and wince.

"Force it down. You need to get some sleep."

"You're not sleeping."

"Suit yourself."

"What are we going to do once we get there?"

"We aren't going to do anything. You are going to sit in the hotel room I put you in and I am going to meet with my contact and hope he's got a location on Beos."

"I'm coming with you."

"No, Eve, you're not. You agreed to my terms when I agreed to bring you with me."

His terms were more like one command: do as you're told.

I roll my eyes.

He lets it go, finishes his drink and closes his eyes.

He's right, I need to get some rest, but I can't. Once we're in Beirut, I need to look for Armen.

I know Zach's not sleeping either. And all I can do is sit here and watch him. He's so big, powerful, and his face...it's beautiful. Thick, dark hair that's grown out since he left the military, tanned olive skin, features sharp, his jaw as if carved with a chisel. I remember what the scruff on it felt like when he had his face buried between my legs, tongue soft, stubble hard and scratchy.

I can't think about that now. It can't happen again. I don't know how I could have let it happen then.

Two flight attendants come down the aisle. They're staring at Zach, one whispering to the other, and it's pissing me off. One catches my eye. Her expression changes, and she nudges her friend. The whole flight they've been falling all over themselves to serve him. Or more like *service* him.

I snort, and he opens his eyes.

"What?"

"Nothing."

The look on his face tells me he knows I'm lying.

"It's nothing."

He shakes his head and picks up a magazine from the seat pocket.

Leaning away from him because I guess during my staredown with the flight attendants I'd scooted closer, I shut my eyes, certain I won't sleep, but the next time I open them is when we're flying over the city, close enough that I recognize it. I stare out the window, mesmerized, oddly happy. This is home. I may not live here anymore, but it's where I belong.

But a knot of foreboding twists my belly.

I keep watching as the plane lands smoothly. We're taxiing to the airport when Zach touches my arm.

"Here," he says.

I turn to find him watching me. In his hand, is my passport. The Lebanese one.

I take it.

"Anyone asks questions, we just got married. We're coming back here to celebrate with your family. You miss them so damn much."

"Married?"

"Don't get excited, *habibi*. It'll just be easier."

"Don't call me that."

The bell goes off to say we can get up, and he's on his feet. He opens the overhead compartment and hands me my purse, then wraps an arm around my waist and tugs me close, almost making me bounce off his chest. "Last time I called you that, you came," he whispers in my ear.

"This way, Mr. Beckham," a flight attendant says, her smile flirtatious.

I want to smack her.

"Thanks, Bonnie."

"Bonnie?" I ask once we deplane. "When did you have time to get her name?"

"Careful, you sound jealous."

"You don't have to hold me so tight."

"Too hard being so close to me?" He gives me a flirty wink.

I try to pull away, but he tightens his grip as we approach immigration.

"We have to talk about what happened," I say as we get into the line, wanting badly to change the subject. Maybe hoping to get him off kilter.

His face hardens and he turns to me. "Which part? The part when you lied to me? Or the part where I made you come?"

"You know perfectly well which part."

"Now isn't the time. If you want to find your brother, then do as I say."

He's right. I know it.

When it's our turn, Zach smiles at the female agent. He's charming. I'd forgotten how charming he could be. About half an hour later, we've claimed my suitcase and his duffel bag and are getting into the back of a taxi. Zach hasn't let go of me once, but he also hasn't spoken a word since we got through customs and immigration. I've seen how he looks around at everything though. At everyone.

At the rental car counter, he speaks with the agent in Arabic. When I open my mouth to say something, he gives me a shake of his head.

"You have trust issues," I say.

"You *should* have trust issues," he replies.

We ride in silence to the hotel while I watch the city I grew up in whiz by. So much has changed in two years. After the civil war, the city's slowly been building itself up. But it seems every time it does, something happens to set us back twenty years. I just hope we're not at that point in the cycle now.

No, that's not all. I hope that cycle has ended.

It's midday and I'm more tired than hungry. When we get out of the cab at the hotel, I let Zach lead me inside and he asks for a room with a king-size bed. When I give him a glare, he only winks at me and tells the man behind the desk I'm a shy bride. I'm fuming, but I know he's doing this to get under my skin and I won't let him do it.

When we get into our room, he still hasn't let go of my hand, even as he's texting with his other.

"What are you doing?"

He ignores me, finishes his text, then turns to me.

"You can let go of my hand, you know," I say.

"Why don't you go have a shower?" He's distracted, I can hear it. Besides, if he wasn't, I'm sure he'd make some comment about showering together.

His phone buzzes and he shifts his body to read it, holding the phone at an angle so I can't see the screen.

"Why don't you tell me what we're doing? What our plan is?"

"*Habibi*," he tucks his phone into his pocket, takes both my wrists, and walks me backward until the backs of my knees hit the bed. He looks at me, then with the flat of his hand on my chest, he pushes lightly, making me sit. When he leans down to place his hands on the mattress on either side of me and leans in close, I can't help but draw back. Up close like this, the difference between us in size is remarkable. Scary, actually.

But it's not fear I feel. No. It's something else. Something I don't want to admit.

I know I'm licking my lips when his gaze falls to my mouth. It takes him a long time to drag it back to my eyes. I don't know if he's doing it on purpose or not. If he knows how it makes me feel. Thing is, I can't think about that right now. My body's physical reactions to him seem to be out of my control. I don't understand it. All I know is when he's this close to me, when he's in control like this, all I want to do is give in. All I want is him, his hands, his mouth. Him.

And he knows it.

I see it in the glint in his wicked eyes.

In the way one side of his mouth curves upward.

"*We* don't have a plan. You're going to be a good girl and have a shower, then lie down and rest, order room service. Whatever you want, as long as you stay in this hotel room. Understand?"

He's so close, I can hardly breathe. I don't answer and he doesn't move. Not at first. And when he does, it's not what I'm expecting. He slides his face by mine, the scruff on his jaw scratching my skin, making my entire body come alive as his mouth reaches my ear. I feel his lips there. Soft. Barely touching. His breath is warm and it makes me shudder.

"Do you understand, *habibi*?"

The hair on the back of my neck stands on end. I swallow and when I inhale, I smell him. Aftershave mixed with his own unique masculine scent. I feel it deep inside me. Feel everything.

I want it. I want *him*.

"I smell you, Eve," he whispers, his tone low and dark and dangerous. "And I bet if I slide my hand into your panties, you'd be wet."

I draw my arm back and slap him, or intend to, but he catches my wrist and pulls me up to stand. He's holding me to him, and one hand snakes down my arm and to my other hand and presses it against him, against the length straining his jeans.

"Nothing to be ashamed of, *habibi*. I want you too," he says, but this time there's a taunt in his tone.

"I hate you."

"No, you don't."

"I do."

"You hate that I'm right."

"Fuck you."

"Is that an invitation?"

I open my mouth, but I'm at a loss and instead, struggle for him to release me. But he holds fast, switching the grip on my hand, the one that's cupping his dick, to my wrist, and twisting it back.

"I asked you a question."

"No, it's not an invi—"

"Not that question, sweetheart." He winks. He actually winks. And I feel my face go red. "You have a dirty mind, don't you?"

I hate that he gets under my skin. Hate that he's right.

"This isn't the military. You can't order me around," I manage.

"I can cuff you to the bed. Gag you. Do all kinds of things to you that you can't bring yourself to admit you want."

"Is that why you brought me? So you could mess with me?"

"I tried not to bring you at all, if you recall." He's dead serious suddenly.

I try again to free myself one last time.

"Eve, I need to take care of something. Get some information. And I need to know you'll stay here while I'm gone. That you'll be here when I get back. I can't keep you safe if I don't know where you are and you being here, you being in jeopardy, that's on me."

"I can keep myself safe," I try.

"Like you did at the hotel?"

I stop. He killed a man. He beat a man to death in front of my eyes.

I look to his hands and it's like he understands. Like he knows what I'm thinking.

"Let me go," I say.

"I won't hurt *you*, Eve. What happened at the hotel—"

"Just let me go."

He does.

"What did happen at the hotel?" I start. "It's like you were...gone or something. Like you weren't there at all."

He takes a step backward, his eyebrows knit together and he runs a hand over the back of his neck and rubs. It takes him a long time to look at me. "Nothing."

It's not nothing. Not even close.

He checks his watch. "I have to go. I'm meeting someone who may have some information about

Malik or maybe even your brother. I need to know you'll be here when I get back. I'm serious."

I know I need him if I hope to find Armen, so I acquiesce. "I'm tired anyway. I'll just take a shower and lie down."

He studies me, like he's trying to figure out if I'm lying.

"I promise."

His phone buzzes and he checks the screen, then nods. "I'll be back as soon as I can. Don't let anyone in."

"Okay."

I ONLY LAY DOWN TO CLOSE MY EYES FOR FIVE minutes. I thought I was too excited to sleep. Too anxious, but it's dark when I hear someone enter then close the door. My eyelids fly open, but I'm lying on my side and my back is to the door and for some reason, I'm afraid to turn around. Afraid to see who'll be standing there.

But a moment later, when footsteps retreat to the bathroom and I hear the shower go on, I realize it's Zach. I sit up and check the time. Two in the morning. I've been asleep for hours, and he's been gone all this time.

After Zach had left, I'd had a shower, then gone to one of my favorite falafel places to get some food.

It'd been two years since I'd been back. Surely no one would recognize me. And I made certain before walking up to the counter that I didn't know the man standing behind it. I'd taken my sandwich and brought it back to the hotel and that first bite had tasted like heaven.

I miss being here. Living here. Miss the excitement of life in Beirut. The fashion. The food. The people. The energy.

It took all I had not to go to the beaches where I used to go as a child. Not to swim in the waters I grew up in. Not to stare up at Suicide Rock in awe of its beauty. Of the power of the earth and the water. But I'd been a good girl. Done as I'd been told. I'd come back to the hotel room and taken a nap, intending it to be a short one.

The shower switches off and I find myself touching my hair, wondering what I look like. Chastising myself for caring. I'm sitting in the dim red light of the alarm clock when he opens the bathroom door and exits, a cloud of steam behind him. I can't drag my eyes away from him, his hips wrapped in that too small towel, his chest and arms bare and wet, his hair sticking up in all directions.

When I meet his eyes, I see he hasn't missed the fact that I'm looking at him like he's food.

I shift my gaze away. "It's two in the morning. Where have you been?"

Even in the dim light, I can see his eyes narrow.

"Why don't you ask me what you really want to ask me?"

"What?"

He walks to the table where he must have placed his phone when he came in because he picks it up, reads a message and types something before setting it back down. "You know what," he says, heading toward the bed.

"I don't know what you're talking about."

He raises his eyebrows and pulls the covers back, but I stop him. "Your bed's there." I point to the couch.

Zach grins. "I much prefer this one."

I'm about to argue, but he drops his towel, rendering me mute with shock. I've seen him before, but still, I react. He's huge and he's not even erect.

Placing one knee on the bed, he leans down toward me. "Move over."

Again, I find myself clearing my throat, blinking and dragging my eyes up to his.

"Zach, you—"

He draws the covers back and climbs into the bed, lying down on his side, facing me. He moves too fast for me to realize what he's doing when he wraps his arm around my middle and draws me down, hugging my back to his front, just like he did at my house.

His fingers brush the hair away from my ear and I'm staring straight ahead, unable to move. My heart is racing, and his big hand is splayed across my belly, his fingers too close to...everything.

"Ask me what you want to ask me, *habibi*." His voice is a drawl, low and taunting and seductive.

"I don't know what you mean."

"Liar."

His mouth is too close to me, to the tender flesh of my ear, my cheek, and his breath makes me shiver involuntarily.

"Don't you want to know if I was with a woman?"

"No," I say sharply, but even I can hear my own lie.

He snorts. "I wasn't." He pulls me closer. "But it's been a long day. Good night."

I'm surprised and honestly, a little disappointed when I hear his breathing level out.

I don't sleep, not for what seems like hours, but I guess I do eventually doze off because I'm awakened by someone talking. The speech is agitated, and it takes me a minute to remember where I am. Who I'm sleeping next to.

It's Zach who's talking. He's on his back when I turn to him. His eyes are closed and his face is tight. I watch him for a long time, watch him twitch, reach out to grab something, catch air instead. He's calling out to someone, but it's not a name I recognize. Not one of the ones tattooed on his back, at least I don't think so.

"Zach, wake up," I say. He's becoming more and

more restless. "Zach?" I touch his arm, try to shake him.

He blinks several times, but starts talking again, and I make out only one word. *Trap.* And this time when I touch his shoulder, he turns on me. He pins me to the bed, grabbing me by my shoulders, his full weight on top of me.

"Zach! Stop!"

His eyes are open and they're almost black in this light, and although he's staring at me, I don't think he sees me, and I realize it's like it was at that other hotel. When he beat that man to death. His eyes had gone black then too. It had been one of the most frightening things I'd ever seen.

He shakes me hard. "Why did you do it?"

"Zach, please!" I'm trying to free my arms, but I can't. I fight him, try to kick him, but he's got me trapped. He knows how to fight. I don't. And he's twice my size.

"Why?" he roars.

"Wake up, Zach. It's me. It's Eve. Wake up!"

When he releases one arm to wrap his hand around my throat, I scratch at his face, slap him, desperate to wake him as his grip tightens. I can't talk. I can't get in enough air to. And just when I think he's going to kill me, he blinks once, then again. He's still looking at me. A line forms between his eyebrows and his grip loosens a little, but he doesn't release me, not yet. He looks around the room, then back at me and only then removes his hand from my throat.

"Zach?" I'm crying.

He's staring at me, eyes so intense it's like they're boring into me, reading what's inside my head.

Instead of rolling off me, saying he's sorry, instead of any of that, he kisses me. He smashes his mouth against mine and kisses me. And all I can do is kiss him back. There's an urgency between us. He's devouring me, taking my will from me, kissing me so hard it hurts. One hand slides down and I open my eyes to find his are watching me. I know what he wants. This is the moment. I have to tell him no. That I don't want this.

He's tugging down the shorts I was sleeping in, and I should tell him to stop. I should tell him to get off me, and he's waiting for me to. I know he will if I say it. I just have to say the word.

But I don't.

And when he pushes my panties off and spreads my legs open with one knee, I still don't.

"Eve." His breathing is tight and I feel his hardness against my thigh. "Tell me to stop."

I don't. I can't. And when the head of his cock is at my entrance, I brace myself, opening my legs wider, wanting this. Wanting him.

"You need to tell me to stop now," his voice is a growl.

I know he's trying to control himself. I know he's

struggling to. And I know he doesn't want me to tell him to stop.

He presses into me, just the thick head, and I can see it's taking all he has for him not to plunge into me. Not yet. He knows I'm a virgin. He felt it when he finger-fucked me.

He's stretching me slowly and I close my eyes wanting only to feel, even the pain, at least for a moment. Feel him inside me. I know he'll be brutal. I know he needs to be. And I want it. I want him brutal. Rough. Savage.

His elbows are on either side of my head and when I open my eyes again, his are locked on mine. His breathing comes harder as he thrusts slowly in and out, shallow thrusts because he's hit my barrier.

He pauses then and I brace myself and I'm afraid now. More afraid than I've ever been with him. He's volatile and even though he hasn't hurt me yet, I know what he's capable of.

"This belongs to me. Always did."

I hear a sound, realize it's me, realize it's me trying to pull back a little. But he won't let me.

"This is going to hurt," he says. "It's going to hurt so good."

He's moving again, and I want it. Want him deeper. He dips his head down to kiss me and I open to him as he bites my lower lip. I taste blood simultaneously as I feel myself tear when he thrusts past my barrier. I gasp into his mouth and he groans, seating himself deeply, painfully, inside me. His eyes close for an instant, and when he opens them, he's watching me again. His eyes are intense. Dark.

He licks my lip, licks the blood there, as he pulls back and thrusts in hard.

He's hurting me. He knows he is. He wants it this way.

And so do I.

"I wanted to take this from you that night." His voice is low. Deep. Sweat from his forehead drops onto my face. "I wanted you then too. It fucked with me that night."

I barely hear the last part. I'm too far gone. Pain gives way to something else, a raw pleasure, a hot, bleeding sort of pleasure. I'm breathing in shallow gasps of air.

"Look at me," he says.

I do, and I don't know what I feel when I do it. He's inside me, but this, looking at him, our eyes locked, him seeing me like this, when he's taking this from me, it's intense. It's like I've just become this physical thing. Like every nerve ending is alive and pulsing with sensation and I'm lost.

"Your blood is warm, little virgin *habibi*."

I bite my lip, taste iron. I shudder.

"You're going to come on my dick and I'm going to watch," he says.

I reach up to kiss him, bite his lip, but not to

break skin. He likes it, I can see it, but he pulls his face away and shakes his head.

"No. I want to see you come. See your eyes."

He draws all the way out and thrusts in hard and I squeeze my eyes shut for a moment, gasping loudly. Too many sensations all mixing together: pain and need and in the distance, an agonizing pleasure, everything magnified.

He shifts his hips and thrusts again and hits just that right spot. I cry out. I've never felt like this before. Never felt this intensely before.

"You like it hard, don't you?"

I realize my nails are digging into his shoulders, realize I've broken skin there. I'm so close, I can't even answer. "I…"

"I knew you would." The savage inside him is freed and he's thrusting, relentlessly spearing me again and again, his arms keeping me pinned at my shoulders as he has me, takes me. Owns me.

"Zach." I'm breathless. "God."

His smile widens at that and when he reaches one hand down to pinch my clit between two fingers, I come. I come so hard that my vision blurs.

"Fuck, Eve," he says, and I know he's close. He's moments from letting go. "Your tight little cunt is squeezing my cock so fucking hard."

I'm coming. I can't make sense of his words. All I can do is feel, feel him inside me, feel him holding back. Feel the tightly coiled tension in his body.

As my orgasm slowly subsides and he comes back into focus, he's still watching me, his face tight, and I realize he's waiting for me, waiting to pull out of me. Because in the next instant, he does and he's lying on top of me, his cock pressed to my belly, and he's coming. Ropes of cum wet my stomach, my breasts and he groans and all I can do is watch him. Watch his beautiful face, watch his eyes brighten as waves and waves of pleasure take hold of him, and don't release him for an eternity.

He blinks several times then, and leans his face down to mine, sweat-covered forehead touching mine. He doesn't kiss me though, just stays like that for another eternity. We're breathing hard. Our eyes are locked.

And when he rolls off me, I feel cold. Empty. No longer whole.

He gets out of the bed. I look down. His stuff is smeared all over me, belly and chest. I don't know if I should get up. Have a shower. I don't know what I'm supposed to do, but he returns before I have to decide, holding a wet washcloth. Without speaking, he sits down and wipes me clean gently, softly. And when he's done, he wipes my thighs and I realize they're bloody. The bed is bloody. It's smeared across his thighs.

I move, embarrassed, but he shakes his head, places the cloth between my legs and presses it there.

"Okay?"

I study his face, his eyes. No teasing. No laughter. He wants to know if I'm okay. That's all. And some part of me wants to cry. Wants to have him wrap his arms around me and press my face into his chest so I can disappear there. I don't know what this is. What I'm feeling. Can he see the confusion on my face?

I don't answer his question. I can't.

The warm cloth feels good and he keeps it there a little longer before taking it away and sliding back into the bed.

"It's dirty," I say, still embarrassed.

"No. Not dirty." He resumes his position on his side and pulls me to him, again holding me with his hand flat on my belly, arm heavy around me. I know I'm trapped until he allows me to get up. And a moment later, I hear his breathing level out and he sleeps.

I'm not tired anymore, but I lie there in his arms and I think I cry a little. What we did, what happened, it was always going to happen.

Fate and time and destiny, they don't forget.

He's meant to break me, just as I'm meant to break him.

I fulfilled my part. This is his. This is him breaking me. I realize it was naïve to think I could survive this. This vendetta, it's bigger than him. Than us. But it belongs to both of us.

And something very bad is coming. Or maybe

we're walking right toward it. I know it. I know it with every bone in my body. I know I owe the souls of the dead men inked on his back, same as him. He betrayed them to save me. They died because of us, and we'll both have to pay. Together. The difference between us is that Zach has known this all along.

12

ZACH

She thinks I'm still sleeping when she slips out of the bed. I keep my eyes closed and let her go. Let her slide out from beneath my arm. At the memory of last night, of her face when I reached her barrier, when I broke through, the tearing—I'll never forget the look of it, the feel of it. The gush of warm virgin blood. The squeeze of her tight little cunt. It makes my dick hard now.

I don't know if I intended to fuck her all along. Although I was just messing with her until last night. Until she woke me up—finally, and thank goodness for her—from that nightmare. But I don't want to think about that part right now.

The shower switches on and I throw the covers back and get out of the bed. There's a slight smear of blood on me and I like it there. Like knowing what I took from her. What she gave me. Her virginity belongs to me now and no matter what, no one can take that away.

I walk into the bathroom and hear her gasp when she sees me from behind the glass barrier of the shower.

"Morning." I walk to the toilet, lift the lid and piss.

She's watching me, I can tell. I imagine her little virgin eyes are in shock, but there's something dirty about Eve. She doesn't want to admit it, but she likes the dark. And I plan on doing all kinds of dirty to that sweet, innocent, and very willing body of hers.

I flush the toilet and face her. Steam obstructs my view, but not so much so that I can't make her out. I haven't actually seen her tits yet. I've always been more of an ass man, but still. I pull the shower door open and step inside.

"What are you doing?"

I like this hotel. Enough room for four in this shower.

"What does it look like I'm doing?" Even though there's a second showerhead, I decide to share hers. Get in her space.

She backs up. I like this cat and mouse game we're playing so I get closer, back her into the corner. My face is inches from hers and her golden brown eyes have gone huge. "Hand me the soap," I say. I don't hide the fact that my gaze is moving along her body, down to her tiny tits with those big, hard nipples. Hard even in the heat of the shower. My dick's hard too.

"Zach, this...we—"

I push the wet hair off her face, then lift her chin up. "We what?"

It takes her a minute to reply. "We can't...what happened last night, it can't..."

"What happened last night?"

Nothing. She's blushing again and I know she hates being made to say it. She's so fucking easy to read.

"We fucked," I say, helping her out. "I fucked your virgin pussy and you came on my dick."

She's staring at me like I've lost my mind.

"And," I let go of her chin and lean in close, lips to her ear. "We determined you like it rough."

"We did not!"

I laugh and take the bar of soap from behind her, give her some space as I lather up my hands.

"Let me get a look at you."

"No. Get out." But she's trying to get past me to the door to get out herself.

I block her way. "Eve, you have to know last night wasn't a one-off."

She's staring up at me now and I like the physical differences between us. She's soft and small, and I'm the opposite. I can make her do whatever I want and I know it makes me a dick, but I like it.

"What do you mean?" she asks, but she's not stupid.

I take a step forward and she takes one back. Water is splashing off of us. It's kind of irritating, but I have plans for our morning shower so I deal with it.

"What do I mean?" I ask, and I can't help smiling a little when I see her eyes bounce from my dick to my face and back.

I set the bar of soap down on the little bench against the wall and decide to make very clear what I mean. So I grip her pussy with my soapy hand, curling my fingers into her, rubbing a little.

She stops breathing after her initial gasp of shock.

"I mean I want more of this. More of your pussy." I'm circling her clit with my thumb, watching her eyes dilate. I reach back with my other hand and slide it between her ass cheeks to find her other hole. She makes a sound and her hands are flat against my chest, pushing. But not really. "I want this too. I bet your little ass is tight."

I think she's going white but am not sure with the steam, and I'm trying hard not to laugh outright at her expressions as I rub her clit and her asshole and she tries to pretend she doesn't like it.

"And this," I say, kissing her mouth. It's open, but she isn't kissing me back. It doesn't matter though, she's not fighting me and her little tongue tastes good when I suck it.

Her knees buckle and I press her up to the wall to hold her upright between myself and it.

"Virgin here too?" I ask, pressing against her asshole. I know she is. If she's never had vaginal sex, no way she's had anal. But I can tell from the look in her eyes she'll be open to it, and that thought makes it imperative I get inside her before I blow right here, right now.

I cup both her ass cheeks and lift her up, leaning down a little myself to rub my cock against her slick pussy. I slide inside her and she lets out a long moan and closes her eyes.

"I'm clean and I know you are, but are you protected?"

I'm rubbing her asshole again and watching her face, watching her bite her lip, her hands gripping my shoulders rather than shoving at my chest.

"Focus, Eve," I say, but it takes me pressing the tip of one finger into her tight little hole to get her attention.

She tightens up immediately, and her nails are digging into my shoulders.

"Relax. I won't fuck your ass today."

"Let me go."

"Let you go where?"

"It hurts."

"Don't tense up and it'll feel good."

"Zach, I don't think we should—"

I pull my finger out of her ass, and, still keeping her impaled on my dick, cup her chin and force her to look at me.

"Not only should we, but we are. You're mine, Eve. You belong to me. That night at the auction, I was buying you for this. I wanted to fuck you then too, but there's a difference between then and now. Then, I was good. Now, I'm not. I want what I want and you can't tell me you don't want it too."

I bring my thumb to her clit and circle it.

"What did you see last night?" she asks quietly. "The nightmare."

I move inside her, she's not pushing me away, but I'm not expecting that question. Not right now.

"You want to talk about that now?"

She nods.

I reach to switch off the water but I've still got her trapped between the wall and me, still speared on my dick.

"I saw you up there," I say, pulling out and thrusting hard once.

She lets out a grunt with the force of it, and I hope for her sake, she's prepared for what's coming.

"On that stage. Almost naked."

I thrust again.

"I saw your fear."

Is it sick I'm still hard? Getting harder.

"Some part of me, it wanted the auction.

Wanted to take you home. Strip you myself. Bed you." I slide her off my dick and put her down. She's confused, disappointed. I give her a grin and turn her around, put her arms up, hands flat on the wall. I look down at her sweet little ass, grip it with both hands, draw her backward, splay her open.

She's being a good girl, keeping her hands where I put them. I'm looking at her, her tiny asshole, her gaping pink pussy. I slide back inside slowly, taking my time, sucking in air as I do. I keep her spread and fuck her, watching my cock slide in and out of her, watch her little pussy stretch to take me. She's meeting my thrusts now.

"That's good," I say moving deeper. I let go of her ass and slide one hand around to her clit.

"What else?" she asks, breathless.

I lean against her, bringing my other hand to her breast, her nipple. I pinch it and her body tightens, making me groan as her cunt squeezes my cock.

"I wanted this. This pussy." I slap her hip. "This ass." The sound of fucking, flesh on flesh, her wet cunt taking me, fills the room.

"You saved my life."

I pinch her clit hard and she lets out a moan.

"I don't want to talk about this, not now. I just want to fuck you, Eve."

She nods, thrusting her hips back. I pull her to me, one arm like a metal bar across her middle, the other working her clit. I kiss the side of her face, half her mouth.

"You can't come inside me."

Fuck. I should be using a condom. I will. Next time. If she weren't a virgin, I'd come inside her ass, but can't do that now. I'd hurt her, she's so tight. And I like her warm, slippery cunt right now.

I groan.

"Zach." Her breathing is heavy. She's close, I can feel it. And so am I.

"Come. And when you're finished, you're going to suck me off." I move the arm that's around her middle to grip a handful of hair and fuck her harder, thrusting deep. I twist her head around so I can watch her. I like it, watching her come. She's so vulnerable in that moment, it drives me mad.

"Come, Eve, so I can shoot down your throat. Watch you swallow my cum."

It takes one more thrust before I feel her pulsing around me. Her eyes squeeze shut and it takes all I have not to let her tight cunt milk me dry, but I hold back, and when she's finished, I turn her to face me and push her to her knees.

"Open," I order, my dick bouncing at her face, still glistening with her cum.

Eve looks up at me and opens to take me in and —fuck me—she's sucking hard, and as much as I want to enjoy this, her on her knees, her eyes wet from taking me deep, it only takes a few thrusts and once I hit the back of her throat, I come. Fuck. I come. She's gagging but I hold her steady, watching her eyes, her panic and it makes me come that much harder, emptying down her throat, pulling out slowly once I'm finished, watching her struggle to swallow it all.

I keep her on her knees for a few minutes, my hand in her hair forcing her to look up at me as she wipes her mouth.

"Admit it," I say, slowly drawing her to stand. "You like it dirty."

She doesn't have time to answer as I cover her mouth with mine and kiss her, and reaching behind her, switch the shower on.

I'M SITTING IN THE HOTEL ROOM WAITING FOR EVE TO get ready. After what just happened, she still took her things into the bathroom to get dressed. I'm scrolling through my phone, not paying attention to it really. My mind is on her.

I don't know what it is with this girl. I'm obsessed or something. When I came looking for her, I hated her. Or I thought I did. But the thing that happened that night two years ago, it wasn't her fault. It was mine. I know that. I've always known that. Even if she betrayed me, no matter her reasons, I made the call that got my men killed. That part belongs to me, and only to me.

She wanted to know what my nightmare was, but I'm trying to make sense of it myself. Because what I saw, it doesn't make sense.

The bathroom door opens and I look up. Why am I stunned when I see her? She doesn't look any different. I've just seen her naked. Seen all there is to see of her. Yet, her standing there in a knee-length skirt and a tank top, wearing no makeup apart from lip gloss, and her wet hair pulled into a long ponytail fucking stuns me.

I don't know if she feels it or not, but she keeps her eyes level with mine. I know she's struggling to do it. She's so skittish. But I won't make it easy on her. I'm all for owning who you are. She needs to take an honest look at herself and take responsibility. She could have said no anytime, both last night and today, but she didn't. And I want her to own that.

She clears her throat and takes a step into the bedroom, dropping some things into her suitcase and slipping on her sandals. They have a two-inch heel but when I stand up, I still tower over her.

"You'll need different shoes. Walking shoes."

She doesn't ask me where we're going. I have a feeling she knows, but doesn't want to admit it just yet. She slips out of her sandals and puts on a pair of sneakers.

"Tell me the rest," she says. Her voice is strange, like her mind was somewhere else.

I take the keys of the car I rented last night and those of the hotel and shove them into the pocket of my jeans. Before opening the door, I grab my duffel bag.

"Are we checking out?" she asks, looking confused.

"No. We'll be back."

"Why do you have your things then?"

"I need them."

She studies me, but I point to the door. "We have a lot to do."

"What's in there that's so valuable?"

Smart girl. Thing is, she'd almost seen them that first day. I'd planned on showing them to her. Making her look at them. It was part of my punishment for her.

But then I'd changed my mind.

"Nothing."

She studies me a moment longer, then decides to let it go and walks out the door. I follow close behind and we don't speak until we're in the car and I'm driving out of the city.

"Where are we going?"

I don't answer. I'm not sure she wants to know, and I haven't been back there since that night.

"Zach?"

"Baskinta."

I feel her tense up beside me, but pretend I don't. Neither one of us wants this, but we both need it.

"I just need to make one stop." I pull into the parking lot of a drugstore. "Stay in the car." I want condoms. I realize how ridiculous it is my brain has room for that, but I know myself. I know what I need. And she's it.

She doesn't argue and I'm in and out in a few minutes with some bottles of water, snacks, and a package of condoms. We're soon on our way to Baskinta.

"Tell me the rest of the nightmare," she says.

"It was that night again. That's all."

"That's not all. You were saying something. Trying to grab something. Or someone."

Someone. But it couldn't be. I've been getting bits and pieces of that night back for two years now. I remembered everything before the blast, but afterward, it's a blur. This nightmare had been the most vivid yet. But what it had to tell, it made me doubt everything because it couldn't be.

"I spent five months in a coma," I say, not ready to talk about that dream just yet. Still needing time to process it myself. It's easier to talk about what happened after that night.

"What?"

"After that night. I should have died, but I didn't. I was in bad shape though. A local doctor and his son found me. Took me to their home and kept me hidden there."

"Hidden?"

"He had the sense to know if word got out of a survivor, whoever did the job would be back to finish it. Seeing as how I was flat on my back and unconscious, I'd be as good as dead if that happened."

"What happened after the five months? There's a year and seven months between that and now."

"Recovery. You don't just get up and walk away from injuries like I sustained. I'm indebted to Dr. Hassan and his family."

"How did they find you?"

I shake my head. That's a question I've asked too. "They were nearby. They heard the blast."

She nods, but she's distracted. She's looking at the road. "Do we have to go back to that place?"

"I need to see it. I owe it to the dead."

"What if—"

We hit a pothole and she jumps, catching herself on the handle above the door. I reach out and cover her other hand with mine.

"I won't let anything happen to you."

"That man at the hotel in Denver, he tried to kill me. Someone sent him to kill me. Do you think it was Malik?"

"I don't know but I do find it strange that on the same day, someone sent you your old passport and a one-way ticket home."

"What if that was Armen? It has to be him. Who else?"

"Don't get your hopes up, Eve." She gives me a sideways glance. "Dr. Hassan healed me," I continue with my story, wanting to distract her. I don't have answers to her questions just yet, but I do know one thing. I meant it when I said I wouldn't let anyone hurt her.

"He told me what happened to me. Told me that everyone else had died." I glance at her. "Everyone but you."

She only studies me, and I'm not sure I expect any sort of answer.

"Once I woke from the coma, my skin was... healed, I guess you could say. I still had pain, but I shouldn't have. I think that was my mind fucking with me. The doctor and his son helped me through the hardest times. They stayed with me during nightmares. Taught me how to work around the limitations of my injuries. Helped me get strong again. It took me a couple of months, but I realized my own government turned their backs on us. Deserted my men. Me. For all I know, they set us up."

"You believe that?"

"I don't know what I believe anymore, Eve. I'm here to find answers though. This ends here. One way or another, this ends."

"Did it occur to you this could be a suicide

mission?"

"Some things are worth dying for."

She swallows as I turn off the road. I drive as far as I can into the dense forest before parking the car and killing the engine. I'd need an SUV to go farther.

"We walk from here."

When I reach to unzip the duffel, she takes hold of my arm. "The dead are dead. Nothing you do can bring them back."

I laugh. "I'm not here to resurrect them. I'm here for revenge. I'm here to *take* more life."

All color drains from her face. I pull my arm away, unzip the duffel and take out the Glock I took from the assailant of the other night.

"What are you doing with that?"

"Keeping us safe."

"Maybe we shouldn't be here."

"We have to be. We owe it to the dead."

I get out of the car. Emotions are high. I'm anxious to get to the site, hoping it will jog that final memory into place.

The hike in is about two miles through thick forest. She's mostly quiet, we both are. I remember this path, know this forest like the back of my hand. Hiking through it was something I did with my men in the cover of night. With Eve, I'm slower. She wants to rest, but I'm not sure it's physical rest she needs or if she's trying to put off the inevitable. I give her a few minutes now and again, but we push through.

The names of the dead on my back burn as we near the spot of their massacre. We're quiet, and the only sounds are those of the forest. I touch Eve's hand and put a finger to my lips, signaling for silence as we near the clearing of the old building. I stop, look, and more importantly, listen. I'm not expecting company, but no way I'm walking into an ambush.

But we're alone. There's no one here.

My heart is calm although I feel the hair on the back of my neck stand on end as I close the space between me and the rubble that was once a small stone building. I look at the boundary of walls, step inside it. Eve follows close behind me and although I've got one eye on her, my attention is on the space. On the single wall that remains half erect. The rotting wood where the glass for the window was blown out even before that night. Where the first grenade was hurled in. The elevated area where Armen had dragged her onto the stage. Had stripped her naked.

I look back at her. Her eyes are riveted to that spot. She glances at me, but neither of us speak. Instead, I take a turn along the perimeter of the wall. It's bigger than I remember.

There's an energy to this place. Unfinished business. Blood unavenged. I'm here to finish it though. I'm here to honor my men.

I walk the room again and again, trying to remember. I can hear the sounds of that night. Men shouting as weapons were sold. Remember thinking it was a good thing most of these men didn't drink. They were armed and dangerous. Fucking insane, some of them.

I also remember the stench of the night. Too many unwashed bodies in one place.

I glance at Eve who's walked out of the perimeter and is sitting on a tree stump, her eyes on me. How could he have brought her here? She didn't belong here. Didn't belong in the company of those men. I wonder if they wouldn't have torn her limb from limb in their savage lust if hell hadn't broken loose. She'd been terrified. Trembling. Desperately trying to cling to the scraps of clothing left on her as her brother tore them off to display her.

When I called out the number doubling the last bid, the room fell silent. It was a silence that didn't belong there. Didn't belong to men so violent.

It's in that memory of silence that I remember him. The piece of the puzzle that's been fucking with me ever since I woke from the coma. Eyes I recognized. Eyes that once had looked at me with kindness.

Or what I perceived to be kindness.

Eve stands and takes a step toward me. She's a blur though. I think she calls out my name, but I'm gone. I'm back there. Back in that space. The screaming, then the silence just before the utter and complete hell. That instant when I see him. Commander Maliki Remi. A man who took me under his wing when I first joined the military at eighteen. The man who mentored me through the darkness that was my past: my mother turned to ash; my father dead. One brother imprisoned for his murder. Another going insane within the remains of our family home.

Kids are resilient. Kids block the pain. The past. But thing is, it comes back. Nothing is ever forgotten. What you bury deep within fucking eats at you from the inside out. It's like a cancer. You can't unsee things. Can't unfeel them. It's stupid to think you can. Stupid to think you can ever run away.

Maliki was the only person I told about it. And I remember feeling proud when he'd told me of the potential he saw in me. He recruited me, made me a part of his team. I was its youngest member. I trusted him. And he trusted me. But I'd been wrong about him. His betrayal had almost cost me my life. And it did cost him his.

Now though...the memory of that night two years ago is flooding back. And it's knocking my legs out from under me.

It takes everything I have to drag myself out from

the past. I blink hard, sounds of the forest slowly waking me. Bringing me into the present.

Commander Maliki Remi isn't dead. Had they ever said he was, or did I just assume that? It didn't matter though, what they said. Maliki wasn't dead at all. He'd been here that night. Standing there, wearing the same scarf to cover his face as the others. And when I went down, I saw them. I saw him stand by and watch as hell broke loose on earth. As screams and gunfire competed, as bodies hit the ground, hit me. But when I blinked, he was gone.

"Zach?"

I turn to find Eve at my side. I rub my face trying to make sense of this, but I can't. I can't reconcile this memory. Could it be my mind making up memory? Filling in the empty spaces? Because if it's true—if Malik is who I think he is—it changes everything.

13

We drive back into the city in silence. Eve leaves me alone, and I need to be alone. I need to figure this out because it doesn't make sense.

Maliki Remi can't be Malik. He's dead. I know. I'm the one who put a bullet in his chest.

When we pull into the parking lot of the hotel, I switch off the engine and rub my face.

"Zach?" Eve's hand is on my arm. "You need to tell me what's going on. What happened back there?"

I look at her and I know I shouldn't have brought her here. I should have hidden her away. Maybe sent her to Italy. To my brothers, Raphael and Damon, to hide her. They'd know what to do. They'd know how to keep her alive.

Me? I'm no good for her. Being with me is going to get her killed. Because I'm a dead man walking.

"You need to get out of here, Eve." As I say it, I'm already thinking how I can do this. Italy isn't too far away. I can get her on a flight today. I'll send word to my brothers. It doesn't matter anymore if I do. I'm not in hiding anymore. I have no doubt Malik knows exactly where I am.

"What?"

I look around the parking lot, taking note of every single car, every shadow a threat. I face her. I know she'll fight me, but she has no choice.

"I know who Malik is."

She processes the words slowly. "I don't understand."

"It's me he wants. This has nothing to do with you. Remember when I told you he's a bridge burner?" She shudders. I know she remembers. "Your part's done. You can't stay here. You can't be with me."

"I'm going to find Armen," she says. "Maybe Rafi and Seth too."

I ignore her. "I'm going to put you on a plane to Italy. My brothers are there. I'll arrange for Raphael to pick you up. He'll get you somewhere safe until this is over. Until Malik is dead." This time, for real.

I get out of the car and grab my duffel from the backseat.

She gets out and slams her door shut. "This won't ever be over. Don't you get it?"

I walk to her side and take her arm. "Don't make a scene." We're walking into the lobby and she has the sense to stop talking. I bypass the elevator and we walk up to our room on the fourth floor.

"I'm not going anywhere. I'm too close," she says.

"You'll do as you're told. Period."

"Fuck you."

A door opens, and a woman steps into the hallway. She stops short. She must feel the tension. It's fucking crackling between us. Eve's fuming. And I'm a fucking time bomb.

"I said don't make a scene," I say through clenched teeth, squeezing her wrist in warning. The woman passes hurriedly as I get our door open. Eve slips free the moment I let her.

"I don't know what the hell is wrong with you, but I'm not leaving. You're not sending me anywhere."

"Get packed." I start shoving shit into her bag.

She's pulling it out as I'm putting it in.

"No."

She grabs one end of a dress and tugs it back out of the case, but I take hold of the other end and pull so hard, she slams against my chest before bouncing off.

"This is over, Eve!"

"No, Zach!" she's loud. Louder than I've heard

her before. And her eyes are on fire. "The only way this is over is when you die!"

I blink at the abruptness of her statement.

She sounds as surprised by her words as I am, but when she continues, her tone is quieter. Like she's just realized what she's said herself. How very true it is.

"That's what you want. It's what you've always wanted."

I can't look at her. Not at her face. Not at her eyes.

"You say you want to avenge the deaths of your men," she continues, "but I think what you want is to join them. You have so much fucking guilt that you'd rather be dead than alive. Dead like them."

I wrap my hand around her throat and in two strides, I have her pinned to the wall. Her hands close around my forearm and she's trying to pull me off.

"Maybe I do have a death wish. Maybe you're right. Maybe it's what I've wanted all along."

"Coward," she spits.

I squeeze harder, and she makes a gurgling sound.

"Zach." She can't breathe. And I watch her. Watch her face redden. Watch her eyes widen. Feel again how fragile she is. How easily her neck can be snapped.

I let up a little and she wheezes.

"I won't tattoo your name on my back," I say. It's a

low growl. I'm not even sure she can make out my words. I keep my hand around her neck, but I'm not squeezing anymore.

"You won't have to if you're dead."

Our eyes lock, hers are a deep amber flame. Her breath comes in shorter heaves and my gaze drops to her chest. She's wearing a lace bra. I see it through the fine cotton of her tank top. How did I miss it before?

Her nipples are hard.

I slide one hand beneath the tank, over her belly and cup her breast, flicking that nipple once before capturing it between thumb and forefinger. I return my eyes to hers before I squeeze.

"I need to fuck you. Be inside you." I smash my mouth into hers and she moans, urgent fingers moving to the hem of my shirt, drawing it up and over my head. Our lips lock again as I tear her tank off, walking her backward to the bed. Dropping her down on it when the backs of her knees hit, leaning into her as she undoes my jeans and pulls them open, cupping my cock. I draw her hand away and straighten, push my jeans and boxer briefs down and fist myself, begin to pump my length while she watches.

She's greedy, licking her lips, so I cup the back of her head and slide my cock into her mouth. She'll appreciate the lubrication in a minute because I'm not planning on using a condom and I can't pull out again. I need to be inside her when I come and there can't be anything between us, and since I can't come in her pussy, she'll take me in her ass.

Her lips make a smacking sound when I pull her hair to tug her off me.

"Up on all fours, Eve. Ass to me," I say, looking at the array of lotions the hotel left on the nightstand. I take one.

When I turn to her, she's watching me. She hasn't moved yet. I lean down and get in her face. "Ass to me so I can fuck it."

Her eyes are dark, pupils dilated and she's breathing in gasps. She bites her lip, then moves slowly up to her hands and knees. I flip her skirt up and drag her panties down and just look at her for a long minute, her knees wide, ass cheeks splayed open, all of her displayed, offered.

Mine.

I lean my head down and lick her tight little asshole and am gratified with her shocked, aroused gasp.

When I straighten, she's craning her neck to watch me and I press one hand between her shoulder blades to push her down onto her elbows, her face in the bed. I slide my cock into her pussy and she sucks in a sharp, audible breath. I don't move inside her. I don't want to come yet and with her, my control always slips away.

I empty the contents of the little bottle of lotion

onto her back. She lifts her hips, and it makes me smile seeing her like this. All mine. I've claimed her mouth and her pussy. Now, I'll claim her ass too.

Dipping my fingers into the lotion, I smear it down toward her asshole. I pump my cock a little as I began to circle that tight little bud.

"It's going to be a tight squeeze, Eve." I groan and can hardly fucking wait to have her snug little ass milk my dick. "Think you can take me?"

I meet her eyes as I slide all the way out of her pussy, then back in slowly, making sure she knows how many thick inches she'll be taking.

She moans and I press a finger into her tight hole.

Her eyes squeeze shut and her muscles tighten around my finger, but then relax again and I can slowly pump in and out, in and out. I add a second finger and spread more lotion inside her and when she slips her hand between her legs and begins rubbing her clit, I know she's almost ready.

"Make yourself come." I pull my cock out, but leave my fingers inside her. "Make yourself come with my fingers in your ass, Eve."

She's so fucking obedient. I hook two fingers inside her and hold her hips up and watch her cunt drip down her thighs as she closes her eyes and comes and—fuck me, I'm going to blow right now if I don't get inside her.

I pull my fingers out, smear her cum all over my

dick and bring it to her tight little virgin asshole. She's filled up with lotion, lubricated inside and out, and I take her cheeks into my hands and pull her wide and penetrate her.

"Too big!"

She's gone still, her hands are fisted.

"Shh. I'll go slow. Put your fingers back on your pussy. Rub your clit. Get ready to come harder than you've ever come in your life."

She's a good girl and obeys, begins to rub herself again. I know she's nervous, I can see it on her face, I rub her back, then grip her hips again, slide in a little more, take a few more inches.

"I can't wait to come in your tight little ass. I'm going fill you up and when I'm done, I'm going watch my cum drip out of you."

"I'm going to come again," she manages, just as the waves of her orgasm begin to squeeze my dick. I press in deeper, pumping in and out slowly, claiming more of her, all while she comes beneath me, and when I'm fully seated, our eyes lock and she's so fucking beautiful and so far gone, my dirty little virgin, that I know I don't have long.

"One more time, *habibi*. One more time for me." And when I say it, I begin to fuck her. I fuck her like I want to, like I need to, and she's whimpering beneath me. She's fisting the blankets— she's ultra-sensitive now after those orgasms—and as tight as she is, as slippery as she is with all that lotion inside her, it doesn't take long for me to come. For me to blow inside her with a sound every room on this floor must hear. I grip her hips hard and I come, and she's coming with me, one more time.

We're sweating by the time I fall on top of her, spent. I hold her close, my dick still inside her, and she's got her hand over my wrist and is holding tight.

I want to ask her if she's okay. I should. But I can't speak. And I know she is. She's more than fine. She came three times.

"I like fucking you, Eve. I like fucking you every which way."

"I like you fucking me every which way."

"Dirty little virgin."

She cranes her neck and looks at me, gives me a wicked grin.

I give her a nasty one back and slide my dick out of her, then get up and go into the bathroom. When I return with a damp washcloth, I draw her over my lap so her ass is elevated.

"What are you doing?"

I spread her ass cheeks open. "I told you. I'm watching my cum drip out."

"Zach!" she tries to pull away but I smack her ass once and grip her ponytail, which is falling apart after the sex.

She twists her head back.

"You're dirty, Eve. You like it as dirty as I do. You

want to show me. Don't deny it, the innocent act isn't you, *habibi*."

I don't mean *habibi* like I did in the beginning. Then, it was a taunt. A degradation. Now, she's just *habibi*. Baby.

My baby.

She stops fighting me and I spread her wide and I watch, almost hard again at the sight.

Afterward, we sit in the tub together, and I know she remembers our conversation from before.

"Eve," I start. We need to do this.

She shakes her head. "I won't leave."

"You're not safe here."

"You're wrong." She turns to me, her eyes searching mine for a long moment before she finally speaks. "I'm safest with you."

14

I'm still wrapped in a towel when Zach's phone buzzes with a message. He walks across the room naked and I can't take my eyes off him. Being with him, it's intense. Insane.

And fleeting.

That last one, it scares me. The feeling sits like a brick in my stomach.

"What is it?" I ask when he tosses the phone on the bed and pulls on his jeans.

He glances at me while searching for a clean T-shirt in his duffel. "I have to go. Beos is at the market."

"He's the one who made my passport."

Zach nods. He's sitting on the bed putting his shoes on.

"I'll be ready in a sec," I say, picking up a dress that's still lying on the floor after our earlier battle.

"Eve." His hands are on my shoulders, warm and strong. He squeezes gently, then turns me to face him.

I know what he's going to say.

"Zach—"

"No." His answer is final, I know it.

"Please."

"It's too dangerous." He's shaking his head. "Stay here until I'm back. I promise we'll make a plan together when I'm back."

I'm looking up at him, his gaze is heavy, dark.

"This is about me too."

"If he sees you, he'll run. We're too close to lose him and he can get us to Malik. To your brother, maybe. I have to go, okay?"

Reluctantly, I nod. He's right. I know it.

"Good." Setting me aside, he reaches into his duffel bag and takes out my pistol, the one he'd confiscated a few nights ago. He loads it with ammunition. "Do you know how to use this?"

I look at it. I don't want to use it. I suck in a breath, steeling my spine. "Aim and shoot," I say.

He puts it in my hand and closes my fingers around it. "Don't let anyone in."

"You think someone's going to come?" I'm scared. I hate feeling like this, but I am.

"No one knows we're here. You've been inside the hotel or with me the whole time. I just want you prepared."

I remember my trip to the falafel stand the day before, but I don't mention it. He needs to focus on getting information out of Beos.

"Okay, Eve?"

I nod. I have to get better at hiding my thoughts. He reads me like a book. "Go. I'll be fine."

He wraps his hands around my upper arms and pulls me in tight, his eyes intense on mine, like he's trying to memorize me. Like it's the last time he'll see me. I shudder at the thought because I wonder if it is. If he's walking into a trap.

"When you're back, you'll tell me who Malik is." It's not a question.

He nods. Then leans down to kiss me hard on the lips. When he's done, he looks at me for another long minute before tucking the Glock into the waistband of his jeans then slipping on a jacket to hide it. "Lock the door behind me. Don't let anyone in but me, understand?"

"I understand."

The moment he's out the door, the room feels empty, too big. And I feel too alone. I look at the pistol in my hand, set it on the nightstand and sit down on the edge of the bed. What am I doing? What am I thinking? Feeling?

I've been alone for the last two years, yet I've never felt as lonely as I do right now. It's like when he walked out the door, he took something with him. Some part of me. I get up and walk to the window and see him just as he circles to the car. He glances up, but I don't think he can see me. The windows are tinted so I can see out but from the outside, no one can see in. I stand there until he's driven away then begin to pick up my things from the floor, begin to neatly fold the clothes he'd randomly thrown into my suitcase.

I put on a pair of panties and bra, then choose a dress. That's when I glance at his duffel bag. My eyes drift to the locked door, then back to the bag. I know it's wrong, but I go to it. Unzip it. Pull it open.

He carries this thing around like it's some part of him. To me, it's like a rope around his neck, the anchor dragging him under, and it's only a matter of time before he sinks. I want to know what's inside it. What's got this hold on him. I should ask him, I know, but I don't. Instead, I shove the few pieces of clothing aside. The thing I'm looking for is at the bottom. It's inside those worn-out folders that look to be a hundred years old.

My hands are shaking as I lift them out and I can't drag my eyes away as I carry them to the bed and sit with them on my lap.

I open the first one and there's Armen's face. This photo I've already seen. I touch it, touch my brother's face. He's not smiling. He's in the middle of what I can tell is a heated conversation. The person he's talking to isn't in the shot, but Armen looks fierce. Not quite angry, but intense.

I place the picture face down on the bed beside me. I wish I had another one of him. One where he's smiling. He had the best smile. At least he did before Malik stole it away.

The others in this file are also ones I've already seen, back at the McKinney property. My brothers, and Zach's men. They're smiling, some of them at least. I make myself look at each one. See each man who died that night. Remember each of their names. Say them out loud. It feels right, even if it makes tears stream down my face. Zach was right this morning. I didn't want to go to Baskinta, but we needed to. We owed it to them.

I take a tissue from the nightstand and wipe my nose. My eyes are locked on the pistol and something makes me pick it up, put it beside me on the bed. I look at the next folder. I should get dressed. I should wait until Zach's back and ask him to show me himself. But I don't. I open it instead.

And I regret the moment I do. Because what greets me, well, I'm not expecting *that*. I'm not ready for it. I don't think I ever could be ready for it.

One hand covers my mouth as bile rises up my throat. He's carrying these around with him? The massacre, the scene of the bloodbath, the bodies, body parts. Walls, the ones that are still standing, leak blood and flesh and insides. I can't count the number of bodies. I can't count how many lives were lost. It's impossible. A severed head here, a foot there, someone I recognize in the corner, captured as he's dying, blood smearing the wall as he slides down, a corpse. Beos showed me some photos before I left Beirut, but they were nothing like these.

I'm going to vomit.

I stand so fast, the photographs scatter to the floor at my feet and I run into the bathroom and lift the toilet seat just in time as the first wave sends the little I've eaten today up and out. Wet hair sticks to my face, I can't pull it away fast enough before I throw up, tears clogging my eyes. I feel like I'm going to die. Like nothing is left inside me. One clammy, trembling hand fumbles up to flush the toilet as I lean back, but only for a moment, because it's not finished yet. The images are burned onto my brain now and it's like they're running on a slideshow I can't stop and I'm puking again. I don't know how long this goes on, but it feels like forever before the dry heaves end and I'm leaning my back against the cool tub, weeping. Filthy. Covered in my own vomit.

That's when I hear him.

He's back. Zach's back.

I hear the sound of the lock disengaging, the doorknob turning.

The chain breaking.

I'm breathing hard and I can't get up. I can't make my legs work. My eyes are locked on the open bathroom door and my fingers move of their own accord and I only half acknowledge I've brought my pistol with me. I must have picked it up when I ran in here.

Because I'm going to need it.

It's not Zach.

Heavy boots walk through the bedroom. The bed strains with the burden of weight and someone makes a tsk-tsk sound.

"Someone's made a mess."

He hears my intake of breath. He must. It's so loud. He knows I'm here. In here puking my guts out.

I force myself to stand, the gun in my hand.

He stands too. I hear the bed creak. Hear papers crunch beneath his boots. My fingers are working involuntarily and the gun at my side is cocked and when the man steps into view, he takes up the entire doorway. He's huge, his face scarred, his black eyes hard. Cruel. He's wearing black from head to toe and it's like he's blocked out any sunlight.

A smile breaks across his face but it doesn't touch his eyes. No. They're roaming over my body and I realize I'm still naked, or almost so.

Slowly, ever so slowly, he drags his eyes back up to meet mine. "Well, well, if it isn't Eve El-Amin, all grown up."

I recognize him then. It's his voice that does it, that triggers something deep inside me. And without thinking, without hesitating, the arm that's holding the pistol rises to his chest and there's a moment of shock on his face, and it looks so strange there. So human.

But he's not human. He's one of the men who came that last day. One of the ones Armen brought into our house. The one he had words with. The one who dragged me up by my hair as Armen injected me.

I wait until his eyes meet mine and he gives me that grin again. That grin that says he'll hurt me now, like he did then. And then it's done. I pull the trigger, and it's finished.

This man, this giant, stumbles backward one step, two. He still has that look on his face. That surprise. But then that's gone too and I watch him the whole time, follow him into the bedroom, memorize every flash of anything that crosses his face. And when he falls, it's like slow motion and as he's falling on those photographs of death, it's like history repeating itself. Death on death. Blood on the walls. Blood on me. In my hair. In my mouth. I can taste it. I taste his blood in my mouth.

It's me who stumbles this time. Me who falls backward against the wall. Slides down it, the pistol falling to the luxurious, ruined carpet beneath my feet. And all I can see all around me is death.

Death.

Past and present colliding.

Death.

"What do you mean change of plans, Ace?" I'm making my way through the market and trying not to yell into the phone, but I'm pissed.

"He sent a text message. Didn't exactly explain himself."

"What the fuck is going on?" My phone beeps. It's another call. I ignore it.

"Maybe he got spooked."

"Maybe."

"Relax, okay? I'll arrange another meeting."

The caller won't stop. "Soon." I hang up. I know it's not Ace's fault, but I was counting on this. On today. Beos is the next step to finding Malik. He's the next link. Without him, I've got nothing.

I pick up the call just before it goes to voicemail. "Zach?"

"Eve?" I know something's wrong the instant I hear her voice. "Eve?"

A loud sob.

"Eve? What's happening?" I'm running to the car now.

"I killed him."

"What?"

"There's...it's...Zach?"

"Where are you?" I've reached the car and start the engine before the door even closes.

"I stayed in the room."

"I'm on my way. I'm fifteen minutes away. What happened?"

Someone honks the horn. Fucking Beirut traffic. I don't know why they bother with traffic lights.

She starts sobbing so hard I can't understand her.

"Eve, are you hurt?" Fuck. Fuck. Fuck.

"I killed him."

"Killed who?"

"I don't know."

I keep her on the phone as I race to the hotel, swerving through traffic so I make it back in ten minutes. When I scan the parking lot and lobby, I don't see anything out of the ordinary and take the steps three at a time to our room. When I get there, the door's locked.

"Eve?" I'm fumbling for my key, and finally find it, slide it into the lock. I push the door open and stop short because I need a few minutes to take it all in.

She's sitting against the far wall and is aiming the pistol at me. Blood's splattered on her face, on her body but it's not hers. It's the big guy's.

"Put the gun down, Eve."

She blinks twice, as if just recognizing me. The phone is still in her other hand. Slowly, she lowers both. I step inside, close the door and get a look around as I bend to check the guy's pulse. It's faint, but he's got one.

When I look at her, she starts to cry again.

"I killed him," she mutters.

"No. You didn't." But he is going to die.

I turn back to the man, squat down, take hold of his face, close his nose, his mouth. He doesn't struggle. He can't. I give it another few minutes, and this time, when I check his pulse, it's gone. I turn to her.

"I killed him," she says again.

"No, you didn't. I did."

She's confused, but there's relief in her eyes.

I stand and go to her, noticing the photographs that litter the floor. My photographs.

She saw them.

She wasn't meant to see them.

I take the pistol from her hand and wipe her face, smearing blood across her cheek as I push her hair back and cup her head. Her eyes are puffy and red and she's trembling and cold. I pull her into my chest and she lets me, tucking her arms between us and letting me hold her.

"I shouldn't have left you here alone."

She says something, but I can't make out the words. When I draw back to look at her, I see her eyes bouncing from the body to me and back. I have to get her out of here, but how the hell did anyone know we were here? Who is this guy? Who sent him? And what the hell did he want?

"Let's get you cleaned up," I say, lifting her in my arms as I stand and carry her into the bathroom.

I set her down in the shower and start it, not caring that I'm still dressed and getting soaked as water splashes off my back. A steady rust-colored stream comes off her as I strip off her bra and panties, let them drop to the floor.

"He had a key," she says. She's mumbling. "He broke the chain. I was…"

She looks up at me.

"You were what?"

She shakes her head. "I thought it was you."

"I'm sorry. Christ, I'm sorry. I shouldn't have left you alone here."

"He worked for Malik. I've seen him before. The night of the auction."

I search her eyes. I know it's true. I know Malik knows we're here. It's stupid for me to think otherwise. He has eyes and ears everywhere. I know it.

"What are we going to do?" she asks.

"I'm going to get you out of here."

When I let her go, she sinks down onto the small bench in the shower. We don't talk as I wash her hair, her body. I'm scrubbing her like I can scrub away the stain of a killing. "I almost murdered someone."

"Self-defense is different than murder, and besides, you didn't kill him. I told you. I did."

She's not hearing me. She's stuck in her head. "I shot him."

"Look at me." She doesn't. I force her face up. "He's not worth your guilt. He was here to hurt you. If you hadn't shot him, he would have killed you."

Her face scrunches up, and I can see she's trying hard to hold herself together.

"Eve. You did the right thing. Okay?"

She blinks, wipes her nose with the back of her hand. Nods. It's not very convincing, but we'll deal with this later. Right now, I have to get her out of here. I switch off the water and stand back to look at her. She's looking straight ahead but her eyes tell me she's far, far away.

"Come on, let me get you dressed." I grab a towel and wrap her in it, then lift her back up in my arms. Instead of taking her into the bedroom though, I put the lid of the toilet down and set her on it. I then go into the bedroom myself to get her something to wear. There isn't much to choose from. Blood's splattered on everything. But I find her a dress and some underthings and get myself a change of clothes too. After changing out of my wet outfit, I dry and dress her, even brush her hair into a ponytail.

"I'll get what I can salvage. Stay here for a minute."

She grabs my arm when I turn. "Don't leave me here. Don't leave me alone."

"I won't. I promise."

She releases me, eventually, and I go into the bedroom. I want to pack my photographs, moving the dead body to get them all, even those splattered with his death. I set them in my duffel, then put any clean things of hers inside it too. After that, I search the man and take his pistol which is still in its holster. He knew she'd be alone. They must have been watching us. Waiting for a vulnerable moment. But was he here to kill her? Kidnap her? Use her to get to me? Malik had kept her alive for two years, knowing I'd go after her. But why? He knew I saw him that night. Did he know I recognized him? Why not kill me? Or did he think I'd died?

No. Makes no sense.

He had to know I survived. And he had to know I'd go after her once I learned she too had survived. But why? Why all the trouble? Was I truly so well protected at Hassan's that he didn't know where I was? Couldn't find me?

I check the dead man's pockets but don't find any ID. I do find a cell phone, though. I take it and the pistol, tuck both into my duffel bag and return to the bathroom to collect Eve. No way to clean this up, no time.

"Come on, Eve. We have to go." I pick her up, but she stands on her own.

"I can walk. I'm okay."

"Look at me. Just keep looking at me when we walk through the room."

She nods and turns her face into my chest. I wrap an arm around her and walk her out of the hotel room, closing the door behind us, hanging the Do Not Disturb sign on the doorknob. I make eye contact with every single person on our way out to the car, and I hope if they are spies, they carry back a warning to Malik. I'm coming for him. And this time, I'm going to get it right. This time, I'll be sure to put the bullet between his eyes.

I take her to the only place I can. It takes us over an hour to get to it, and I'm not sure we'll be welcome, but I have no choice. I pull through the overgrowth of trees that hang over the long road leading to Dr. Hassan's ancient home. The stone walls come into view after about another mile, but it's almost night and the property is modestly lit. A truck and two cars, all older models, are parked outside. Those I recognize. It's the stroller sitting beside the front door that takes me by surprise.

The headlights of my car shine into the downstairs window. I slow to a stop, hearing the hum of insects once the crunching of gravel beneath the tires ceases.

"Whose house is this?" Eve asks from beside me.

"Dr. Anthony Hassan and his family."

"He's the man who saved your life. And his son, the one you've had contact with."

"Yes. And his daughter." I don't look at Eve. I haven't mentioned Julia before. It wasn't that I was hiding it, just wasn't important.

"Daughter?"

"Julia." My eyes are still on the house and I see movement inside. "Stay here until I tell you," I say to Eve as the front door opens.

I get out of the car and walk toward the dark entryway, wondering if Hassan's recognized me. He steps outside a moment later, still no smile on his face, eyes intent on mine.

"Doctor," I say.

His glance shifts momentarily to the car. He won't be able to make out Eve's face, but he'll see her outline there.

"Who is it?" I hear Julia's voice. When she comes around the corner, I see she's holding a baby on her hip. I'm taken aback.

She stops too, and surprise registers on her face.

Hassan puts an arm out to stop her from coming farther.

"Zach?" she asks.

I look at the older man's face. I'm trying to read

what's in his eyes. "Go inside," Hassan says to her without ever taking his eyes from mine.

I'm confused. I've kept in touch with Ace. Why didn't he mention the baby? And why this cool reception? I drag my eyes from the baby.

"But—" Julia starts.

"Go." His word is final. I know it, and so does she. Julia gives me one last glance and retreats into the house.

"What are you doing here?" Hassan asks.

"I need your help."

He looks to the car again. "It's not safe here. Not for you. Not for my family."

"You helped me once. I hope you'll help me again."

I hear the car door open and close and Eve's footsteps as she approaches. But I don't turn to her. It's Hassan I'm watching as she comes into view.

He recognizes her.

The baby's cry breaks into whatever it is that's going on out here, and Hassan steps to me. "You weren't followed?"

"No."

He casts a wary glance at Eve.

"Get her inside."

Eve looks to me for the okay. I nod, and with a hand at her back, walk her into the house.

I look around, remembering the place, although it feels smaller now. I realize I'd forgotten the smell.

Old. But the house *is* old. Ancient. Hassan and Ace had built onto the existing structure. I touch the original, rough stone wall of the hallway as we make our way to the kitchen situated at the back of the house. The light is on and I can see Julia. Her back is to us, and the baby is at her breast. A woman I don't know is pouring hot water into a teapot. Hassan goes to her and says something in a near whisper, taking the pot out of her hands. She glances at us, nods, then leaves the room. Once she's gone, Hassan invites us to sit down. We do.

"Who was that?" I ask, realizing how widely I mistrust people. Even the man who saved my life. But something is wrong. Off.

"Housekeeper. She doesn't need to know our business."

"Suzanna's trustworthy," Julia mutters to him, unlatching the now-sleeping baby and adjusting her dress before facing me. "You've recovered well." She smiles, but there's something in it that's strange. That I don't understand.

"Thanks to your family." I can feel Eve's eyes on me. On us. "Congratulations," I say, gesturing to the child.

She smiles and brushes her fingertips over the wisps of dark hair on the baby's head. "This is Hope. The new boss of the house."

I can see from the corner of my eye that Hassan is tense. I think Julia was trying to make a joke of it, but there's an awkwardness to it. Hope opens big caramel-colored eyes that catch mine. A moment later, they're closed again.

"She's beautiful," Eve says.

Julia looks up at her, no emotion passing over her features as she studies Eve. "Thank you."

"This is Eve El-Amin." I turn to Hassan. "But I think you know that."

He doesn't deny it. "Julia, take the child to bed," he says without looking at her.

"Father—"

He turns to her and the tenderness with which he looked at her before has changed. Hardened. "I said go."

She rises, gives me a look, ignores Eve and kisses her father's cheek before leaving the room. We listen to her footsteps as she climbs the stairs, and Hassan doesn't speak until the door closes.

"It's dangerous for my family for you to have come. To have brought *her*." Hassan's eyes are on me when he speaks and I feel the hostility he feels for Eve. He's the one who had told me she'd survived. That she was the only one who had. But now I'm wondering how he had known.

"I had no choice. We had an intruder in our hotel room today. They came while Eve was alone."

He glances at her, but returns his gaze to mine quickly. "I told you when you left, you couldn't come back, Zach."

"Like I said, I had no choice. I owe you and your family my life, and I don't mean you any harm." It's like there's an elephant in the room, but no one will mention it. "We just need a safe place tonight." I choose my words carefully. "I'll be gone tomorrow."

He's studying me, and I know he has as many questions as me.

"Have you been in touch with my son?"

I nod once. I'm not going to lie to him.

He sighs deeply and rises to stand. From one of the kitchen drawers, he returns with a key in his hand. "Take the girl to the cottage. You remember where it is?"

"Yes." I stand, relieved.

He nods, then sits back down. I know he'll be waiting here for me to come back.

Eve's watching us when I turn to her. "Let's go," I say. She rises and follows me out the front door. I lead the way around the property to the small cottage. It looks like a shed, a ruined shed, but it's not. It's where I slept for five months in a coma. Where I healed after that. I unlock the door and switch on the light. It's a bare lightbulb hanging from the middle of the ceiling. Eve walks in, looks around.

"It's basic, but we'll have everything we need and it's clean."

"Why didn't you ever mention Julia?" she asks when I come back out.

I meet her eyes. "There wasn't anything to mention."

She studies me. "How long ago did you leave here?"

She's doing the math. I am too.

"You feeling better?" I ask, ignoring her question.

She nods.

"Good." I draw her to me, pull the dress off her, kiss her mouth. I walk her backward to the bed, but when her hands reach for the hem of my T-shirt, I catch them. Drag them to the sides. "Why don't you lie down?" I say.

"You're not staying, are you?"

"Lie down, Eve."

"Are you going to see her?"

I'm halfway across the room, but stop and turn. "Her?" I know full well who she means, but honestly, this isn't any of her business.

She folds her arms across her chest and thrusts one hip to the side. "Julia."

I walk back toward her, stand close enough that our bodies touch. My chest to hers. "Do I need to tie you to the bed?"

"The handcuffs are in your duffel bag."

"I can be creative."

"I bet."

I reach behind her and unhook her bra, slowly slide it off her arms. Then, locking my gaze on hers, I

reach for her panties and drag them off her hips.
They drop to the floor.

Her eyes have gone darker. I see it even in the
dim light. She's aroused. Exactly how I want her. I
push her to sit on the bed, then lean down, forcing
her to lie down. Her legs are spread. I'm standing
between them. She watches me as I look to her
pussy. I dip my head down and inhale deeply, then
lick the length of her slit.

Eve's breath hitches and I lean up on one arm
while hooking two fingers in her cunt and my thumb
over her clit.

"Be a good girl. Stay wet for me. And when I get
back, I'll let you sit on my face and I'll lick your
pussy until you come."

She swallows, tries to kiss me, but I pull back and
quickly flip her over on her belly and smack her ass.
"Be a bad girl and I'll spank your ass, then have you
suck my cock until you choke on my cum. All while
your tight little pussy aches for it."

I tear my eyes away from her perfect ass blem-
ished only by the pink print of my hand, and look up
to meet her eyes.

"Got it?" I ask.

"Got it," she says.

"Good."

I walk to the door and don't turn around. "Do I
need to lock it?" I ask.

"No."

With a nod, I walk out, and enter the house through the back door. Hassan is waiting for me in the kitchen. He's got a bottle of whiskey and two glasses, one of which he drains before pouring another.

"Exactly how old is Hope?"

"Sit down," Hassan says.

I sit.

He studies my face for a long minute. I study him back. Hassan was always intense. He had to be. I always thought it was because he was taking a chance with me. Saving my life put him in danger. Put his family in danger.

I pick up my glass and drain it. It's good. I need this.

"Three months," Hassan answers my earlier question and keeps his eyes on me as I do the math.

Relief floods through me. If she's three months old, it means she was conceived after I left.

Hope isn't mine.

"But I know you disrespected me with my daughter in my own house."

At that, I look at the ground and it takes me a

moment before I can look at him. "I'm sorry." I am. He's right. He took me in, saved my life, and I fucked his daughter right here on this kitchen table.

He nods. An acknowledgment. Nothing more.

"How did you know about the blast? You said you'd heard it, but Malik would have made sure no one was around for miles." How hadn't I asked this question before?

"I knew because I was told."

I'm surprised by his response, his honesty. "Told?"

He nods again. Drinks. Pours another.

"Tell me about your history with Malik," he says.

"He used to be the commander of my battalion. Special ops. US military. His name was Maliki Remi. Commander Maliki Remi. When I first met him, he was a sort of mentor to me. Helped me when I needed help. Gave me purpose. Distraction from my own troubles. I've told you about my family."

"Go on."

"There was an informant in our ranks though. A small group of us were tasked with finding the traitor. Commander Remi led that operation himself." Hassan fades from my vision as I travel back in time to that night, hearing myself retell the story as if it isn't me speaking at all.

"I was there that night. I'd found evidence on one of our men. A friend of mine. Robert Hastings. Commander Remi wanted to question him alone. I knew it would get ugly. We'd been questioning him for two days and he hadn't cracked. But it wasn't protocol that he be in there alone, and it didn't sit right with me. Not when the screams started."

I blink, my eyes warm. Hassan comes back into view.

"If I hadn't gone in there, he would have gotten away with it. He must not have heard me over Hastings' screams, but I heard him. Heard what he said as he touched the cattle prod to an open wound. I just stood there at first. Like a fucking idiot. Hastings was naked. Bleeding. Covered in bruises. He'd pissed himself. Remi had left him to stand in his own piss."

I rub my mouth with my hand, my chin. My vision is blurring again. I take the bottle of whiskey and drink three long swallows directly from it.

"I understood what was happening too late. Too late to save my friend. And Remi just stood over him with a look of indifference. This man who had been loyal to him—with whom I'd seen him laugh—Remi killed him. Slowly. Painfully. If I hadn't been so shocked, I may have killed the commander that night." I look at Hassan. "I thought I did, but the bullet obviously didn't hit its mark. Something hit me on the back of the head and when I woke up two weeks later at a military hospital, they said I was lucky to have survived the attack. That Commander Remi and Hastings had been killed by assassins. I was so confused, I didn't understand. Both Remi and

Hastings were decorated as heroes postmortem. And when I asked questions about what I'd seen, I was shut down. It made no sense, and I knew something was wrong. I got it, that something was being covered up. And I was a coward because I remembered Hastings' body, what it looked like, and I just shut the fuck up."

I rub my face again, shake my head, then meet Hassan's eyes.

"They kept you down. Drugged," Hassan injects.

I didn't have to ask how he knew. It would be the same source who told him about the blast. Told him to keep me alive. And I already knew who that was, didn't I?

"I guess I didn't kill him that night though, because he's alive. I saw him the night of the blast. Maliki Remi. A.K.A. Malik the Butcher."

"My half-brother."

I stop.

I'm staring at Hassan, the man who saved my life. The gentle man who saved my fucking life. And as much as I expected Malik or one of his men was his contact, this revelation, it floors me.

"What did you just say?"

"Malik...Maliki Remi, he's my half-brother."

I'm on him before I can think. Off my chair, the sound of it crashing to the floor behind me background noise as I wrap a hand around Hassan's throat, taking him down.

"What did you just fucking say?"

He's choking, his eyes are bulging, red. I shake him.

"What did you fucking say?"

But he doesn't answer. Instead, I hear the cocking of a pistol and feel its cold barrel at my throat. He had a gun on him all along.

It takes me a minute, but I loosen my hold, release him. He uncocks the gun and sits up, rubbing his throat. He's not aiming the pistol at me anymore, but he is watching me.

Hassan holds out his free hand, palm up.

I reach down and help him up. He straightens his chair and sets the gun on the table between us, then pours himself a healthy glass of whiskey. He doesn't speak until he's drained it.

"He's my blood. It doesn't mean he has my loyalty."

I sit. Drink. "Why didn't you tell me before?"

"You didn't remember before."

"Why did you save my life? How did you know about the blast?" I'm thinking. "How did you know Eve had survived? You tell me you're not loyal to him, but everything points to the opposite."

"Getting information and being loyal are two different things. He told me about the blast. Told me to get you out. Keep you alive. Told me some months later about the El-Amin girl. He knew you had a weakness for her, so he used her. You saved her life because of it."

"Why? Why did he want me alive?"

Hassan shakes his head. "I don't know."

"And Ace?" I realize in that moment that my contact is my enemy's nephew.

Hassan ages about twenty years before my eyes. "His loyalties are...different."

"Fuck. I can't fucking believe this. He knows exactly where we are, doesn't he?"

"Malik? He hasn't been in touch with me in months. Does Ace know where you are?"

"No. He knows we're in Beirut, that's all. He's setting up a meeting with me with Beos, the man who—"

Hassan's eyebrows knit together. "Beos is dead. He turned up dead several months ago, his body half decomposed."

"Ace set me up. He's been playing me all along." I stand. "I need to fix this. And I need to know Eve will be safe with you when I go."

"You can't leave her here."

"I can't take her with me. She's dead the second Malik has me."

"Sit down, Zach."

"I don't have time to sit."

"There's more you should know."

I feel my forehead crease. How much more can there be?

He stands up and walks to me, standing inches from me. "You're not going to hurt my son. You can kill that son of a bitch Malik, but you're not touching my son."

"And you're going to stop me?"

"He wasn't always loyal to Malik. He hated him for a long time. But my half-brother has a way of charming people. Of making people do what he wants. I mean, take me for example." Hassan shakes his head, looking away as if disgusted with himself. He sits. "I did his bidding with you, didn't I? Saving your life? I'm a doctor. It's my oath. But I told you about the girl when Malik wanted me to. He knew you'd go after her. It's what he wanted, was banking on. I knew it would set Malik's plan in motion."

"What plan?"

"There's a reason he hasn't killed her. A reason apart from baiting you. That was...secondary."

"Enlighten me, but make it fast." Because I want to wrap my hands around Ace's throat and squeeze until blood pours from his eyes.

"Her brother."

"Her brother?" I assumed Armen died. Assumed they were all dead.

I realize something then. Hope's eyes. When she'd opened them, they'd looked almost familiar.

They're the same color as Eve's. As her brother's.

"Armen El-Amin is the father of Julia's baby." It's like he's reading my mind. "Which, to Malik's twisted mind, makes him family. He doesn't hurt family. Well, mostly."

Now I'm confused. I drop into the chair. "Her brother is alive?"

"And loyal to Malik, still. You see what's happened to my family?"

I look up at Hassan. His eyes are red with unshed tears.

But I don't care about his family. Not anymore. That comment he made about family and Malik's twisted mind, well, I have a feeling that illness runs in their entire fucking family.

"What about the others? Rafi and Seth?"

"I know Malik was using them as leverage before. Forcing Armen's loyalty with a promise of keeping them alive. But I don't know if they are. Where they are. Nothing."

The sound of a door has us both looking toward the stairs. But Hassan only shakes his head and turns back to me. "She knows all of this." He's talking about Julia. I know. "Maybe more."

"What about Julia? Is she with Armen?"

He nods. "Thing is, I think he loves her, but he's Malik's soldier. His right-hand man. And Ace his left. But Armen, since the baby...he's different. Just trust me and keep the girl hidden if you want to keep her alive."

"What do you mean Ace is his left-hand man?"

"I mean Armen and Ace are mortal enemies. The

only reason they're both alive is because Malik forbids the killing of either one. He likes having this control. It's a game to him. Everything is a fucking game to him. He's sick. Mentally ill."

"Why did he keep me alive?"

He shrugs. "Like I said, he likes playing games."

17

I'm drifting off to sleep when the door opens. I know it's Zach even without the light. He closes it behind him, locks it, then walks to the bed, stripping off his clothes as he comes toward me.

He draws the covers off me slowly. "I know you're awake."

I stupidly cover myself as I sit up. He goes to the window and opens it, letting in the silvery light of the moon. He turns to me. He's naked and hard and I see the savage glint he gets in his eye when he's aroused. In one swift move, he's on the bed, lying down on top of me, his weight pushing the breath from my lungs. He kisses me with an urgency that catches me off guard. That makes me want.

"Were you a good girl?" he asks, flipping us over so he's on his back and I'm on top of him. "Are you wet for me?"

I don't have a chance to answer though because he's lifting me up, gripping my hips and drawing me to him, to his face.

"Zach—"

His response is a growl as he crushes my pussy to his face. His mouth is soft, his stubble scratchy, and when he moans low in his chest, I grip the headboard and arch my back, biting my lip as he takes my clit into his mouth and sucks.

"Nice and wet," he says. I can barely make out his words, I'm smothering him, his tongue is on me, licking my pussy, dipping inside me, lips closing around my clit and sucking. I slap a hand across my mouth when I realize the moaning is coming from me. Zach's grip on my hips is so tight, I think he'll leave bruises, but I don't care. Somehow, it feels better this way. The hurt, the pleasure, all mixing up into pure sensation.

"I'm going to come."

When I say the words, he slides a finger into my pussy and closes his mouth over my clit and I let out a scream as I come, as he works his tongue over me, his fingers inside me. When my breathing finally slows, I try to pull off him, needing him to stop touching, stop licking my sensitized clit. But he's holding me tight and just when I think I can't take another second, he flips me onto my back and he's on top of me. I feel precum on my belly and spread my legs wide. He's kissing me and his face is wet and all I can taste is myself on him.

He pulls away, stands up.

"What are you doing?"

He's rooting through the duffel bag and a moment later returns, unwraps a condom, rolls it over his dick. He doesn't speak, but the look in his eyes is predatory as he pushes my legs wide, pressing them down with his hands on my thighs. His eyes lock on mine when he thrusts into me.

I gasp. He draws back and does it again. And again. When he pulls out, I'm confused. This time though, he stands and grips my ankle, drawing me to the foot of the bed. He flips me over so my legs are hanging off, and he stands between them, hands on my ass, splaying me open, lifting my hips to the angle he wants.

"Your pussy's mine, Eve." His finger dips into my pussy before circling my asshole. He thrusts his cock into my dripping pussy. "It's always wet for me." He pumps in and out twice. "Your ass is mine too," he says, making me tighten everything as he presses two fingers into me, lifting my hips higher, using his fingers like a hook.

My knees are on the bed and I turn to look back at him. He's watching his cock disappear in and out of me, and as hot as that is, it's when his eyes meet mine that I'm done for. And he knows it, because he gives me that lopsided grin just as the first wave of orgasm claims me, making me fist the sheets, making me bury my face in the bed to muffle my cries.

"You like it hard like this? Like my fingers in your ass while I fuck your dirty little cunt?"

Fuck. I'm going to come again. I feel myself dripping down my thighs, hear the wet sounds of his cock thrusting in and out of me.

He's still hard, still moving inside me when the waves pass and I can see again. He's still grinning. He pulls his fingers out of my ass and leans down close, flattening me to the bed.

"You're a dirty little virgin, aren't you?"

He squeezes his hand between my belly and the bed and his fingers close around my clit. I squeeze my eyes shut and nod my head.

"My filthy little virgin."

His thrusts come deeper and I feel him thicken inside me and when he stills, I open my eyes to watch him come and his blue eyes are dark and watching me, like they did before. I can't get enough of it. Of him. Like this. For all his rough edges, there's a softness, a vulnerability I see only in moments like this. Only when he's lost in pleasure. And all I can think is I want more of it. More of him. Hard and soft, and any way I can have him.

I want him.

I'm surprised when Zach gets up to shower and I slip on his discarded T-shirt and turn over onto my side, face to the open window, taking in the cool mountain breeze, not quite believing I'm back. I want to be up early tomorrow. With the sun. I remember how beautiful sunrises are here. How otherworldly they make everything look. Soft and beautiful. Almost as good as the sunsets. More beautiful than the human eye, the human heart, can stand.

The shower switches off and I turn to the closed bathroom door. Zach emerges a few moments later wearing a towel slung low at his hips.

"You should sleep," he says, his eyes keen on me.

"I was waiting for you." He puts on a pair of boxer briefs, then his jeans and a clean T-shirt and I sit up. "What's going on? Why are you getting dressed?"

"Go to sleep, Eve."

"You're leaving?"

He rifles through the bag, searching for something.

"What happened?" I ask, getting up out of the bed.

He finds whatever he's looking for but tucks it into his pocket before turning to me. He takes a moment to think, gives a brief shake of his head. "It's fucked up, Eve." He comes toward me, takes my hands, kisses my mouth.

"How fucked up?"

He hesitates.

"Just tell me."

"Malik is Hassan's half-brother."

I drop down onto the edge of the bed. "What?"

"He says he's not loyal to Malik, and I believe him. He had no reason to tell me at all."

"What does he want then? Why tell you?"

"I think he wants his family safe."

"Does that mean his son—"

"Ace, unlike Hassan, *is* loyal to Malik."

"Oh my God."

"Beos, the man I was supposed to meet with, the one who made your passport, is dead. Has been for months. Which makes me wonder if he set me up so he could set you up."

"You mean he sent that man to kill me?"

"I don't know if he was there to kill you or kidnap you, Eve. Take you to Malik, maybe."

"Why?"

He sits down beside me.

"I've been remembering who Malik is slowly ever since I woke up from the coma. Bits of pieces of that night coming back. It's when I have the nightmares. I remember a little more every time."

He looks at me, almost ashamed. I don't blame him for that night. I touch his hand. "Go on."

"Every time I have one of those episodes, I remember a little more of what happened. See another scene. It could be my brain fucking with me, but it doesn't matter because for months, I haven't been able to get one thing out of my mind. I understood why that day we went to the site. Malik is—or was—Maliki Remi. Commander Maliki Remi. My commanding officer in the military."

"What?"

"He's supposed to be dead though. I killed him. Or I thought I did."

"Are you sure, Zach?"

"About which part?" He snorts. "Obviously, not about having killed him. But the rest, yes."

"What does he want? You dead?"

Zach shakes his head. "I'd be dead if that's what he wanted. He knew where I was while I lay unconscious in a coma. Knew when I woke. Orchestrated the day Hassan told me you'd survived. That you'd literally walked away, walked into a brand new life. Led me to believe you were in on it. Malik is the one who made sure Hassan found me, brought me here. Kept me alive."

"I don't understand."

He looks up at me. "He was a traitor. But before that, he was a friend. A mentor. You don't know about my past, Eve. My family. And it doesn't matter anymore, but back then, when I first joined the military, it did. He was the only one who could get me out of my head. Make me feel like I was worth something. But then I learned the truth. Saw with my own two eyes what he was capable of. And I shot him point blank. He shouldn't have survived."

"Are you sure he did? Is Dr. Hassan lying?"

"Why would he? And besides, I saw him there that night."

"What about Julia's baby?" I ask, unsure I want to hear the answer. I'm not angry, it's something else I feel and I can't quite put my finger on the strange emotion.

Zach studies me for a long time and I know he's contemplating something, but I don't know why he hesitated when he answers. "Julia and I had a brief affair. It was inevitable, really. But the baby isn't mine."

"How can you be sure?"

"Hassan knows who the father is," he says, his eyes steady on mine.

I get the feeling there's more to tell, but before I can ask, he's up on his feet and talking again.

"I made a deal with Hassan."

"What deal?"

"That I won't hurt Ace."

"In exchange for?"

"Him keeping you safe."

"What do you mean?"

He reaches into his pocket and takes out what looks to be a syringe.

"What is that?"

"I'm going to Malik, and I need you to stay here while I do it."

I'm up on my feet and walk around the bed, away from him. "No. No way."

"Now that I know everything, I'm prepared to confront him. Understand what he's thinking. What he wants. You can't be involved in that."

I'm shaking my head as he approaches. "I'm going with you. He could have my brothers!"

"I don't know what his plan for you is, but if I know Maliki Remi, he has one. And I'll be damned if I let him get his hands on you."

"So, what's the plan then?" He's stalking closer and I'm running out of space. "Is that to knock me out?" I ask, pointing to the syringe. "Keep me here while you go get yourself killed?"

"Eve."

"No, Zach. You can't. You can't go alone, and I need to know if my brothers are dead or alive. I *need* to know."

"One is alive. I can tell you that." There's venom in his words. "I don't know about the others, but I do know you'll be staying here."

"What do you mean?" I'm backed against a corner, but wrap a hand around the lamp on the nearby table and pick it up.

"Put that down, Eve." He uncaps the syringe.

"You put that down." I gesture to the needle. "I don't want to hurt you."

He gives me an "are you for real" grin when I

raise the lamp up. It's so heavy that I have to grip it with both hands, like a baseball bat.

"I mean it!" I say.

"All right," he sets the syringe down and puts his hands up as if in surrender. "Put the lamp down."

I look at the needle, then at him. "Is it Armen? He's alive?" I ask, tears filling my eyes as I lower my makeshift weapon. My arms hurt from the weight, and my brain is whirling with the knowledge that my brother is alive. That he has been for two years. That he hasn't contacted me in those years.

"Yes," Zach says, stepping closer, a cautious look in his eyes. He closes one hand over the lamp and takes my arm with the other, his blue eyes searching mine as he sets the lamp down and pulls me in for a hug.

"Did he know where I was? Maybe he thought I'd died."

"He knew," Zach says. "I have no doubt he knew." He's holding me so tight.

"Maybe he sent that plane ticket?" I ask, drawing back. Looking up at him. "Maybe he wanted to protect me from Malik."

"Maybe. Maybe not." He smiles down at me. "You're sweet, Eve. And naïve. And you want to deal with people who are capable of monstrous things. Things you can't imagine."

I shake my head. "Armen isn't like that."

"I'm really sorry to do this."

While one arm locks me to him, the other reaches for the syringe.

"No!"

"It's the only way to keep you safe."

"Let me go!" I'm pushing against him, but it's like trying to move a freaking bulldozer. "Zach, please." In my periphery, I see him squeeze a small amount of liquid out. I stop fighting, wrap my hands around his face. Make him look at me. "Please, Zach. Please don't do this to me."

"I'm sorry."

I feel the prick in my hip in the next instant. Watch his face, his eyes, as he empties the barrel. The effect is almost immediate. My knees go weak, arms slide slowly down his chest.

"I trusted you," I manage, my eyes closing as I feel myself fall. He catches me in his strong arms, lifts me up. He's blurring though, my vision fading. I try to reach up, scratch at him. Fight him. But my arm drops to my side and my eyes close.

"I'll be back for you, Eve. I promise."

18

ZACH

I feel like a jerk, but this is the right thing to do. It's the only way to keep her safe. I tuck Eve into the bed, then brush the hair from her face. Her lips are parted slightly but she doesn't move when I touch her, when I draw the blanket up over her.

There's a knock on the door, then it opens. I know it's Hassan. I look at Eve for one more minute before I turn.

"You have six hours. Eight at most," Hassan says.

This is my deal with him. He keeps Eve safe. I don't kill his son. We're not friends, he and I. But we do have the same goal. Kill Malik the Butcher. Because that's the only way any of us will be free.

I walk toward him, stopping close enough that I'm towering over him. "If anything happens to her—"

"I promised I'd keep the girl safe. Now you keep your promise to me."

The fact that his son's life hangs in the balance is the only reason I can trust him.

"Truck's ready." He holds out a set of keys.

I take them, fish out the Glock from my duffel, and follow Hassan out the door. I look back once before closing it behind me, locking it as if I were locking away a treasure. I then get into the truck and pick up the map with the highlighted route. I look at the destination, confused.

"He's at a monastery?"

"He hasn't found God, if that's what you're thinking. This is my brother's modus operandi. Thinks he won't be attacked if he's surrounded by two dozen monks."

"He's in for a surprise then." I start the engine, glance once more at the cottage where Eve is sleeping, and drive off in the direction of Deir el Ahmar.

19

I blink, my eyelids feeling heavy. My head throbbing. The room comes into view, then fades again. Moving my arm feels impossible and I'm not sure if I fade out again or for how long, but the next time I open my eyes, I see the blurry vision of someone in the room with me.

Which room? I'm not in Denver anymore. I'm in Beirut. I'm at the cottage outside Dr. Hassan's house. This is the room where Zach recovered.

Zach.

I sit up, and immediately fall back down, eyes closing against the ache in my head.

Zach did this to me. He tricked me. I trusted him, and he fooled me.

"Sleeping beauty finally up?" a woman asks.

I don't recognize the voice right away.

"Leave her alone. Get out of here."

Now this voice I know. This one I know well.

I force my eyelids to open and stare up at the ceiling for a long time, long enough for the spinning to slow. I turn my head to find Julia leaning against the wall with her arms folded across her chest, hate in her eyes. But I shift my gaze a little from her to him.

He's got his back to me, but it's him. His black hair, now spotted with gray, is cut so close to his head, I know it will prickle like little thorns if I touch it. He's wearing a black T-shirt. Like Zach. His shoulders are broad, but not as wide as Zach's. And he's a few inches shorter. The skin on his arms is tanned a golden brown and, unlike Zach, it's not marred. Not tattooed. He bears the scars of a soldier, but he didn't nearly die.

Armen turns to look at me. Golden eyes meet mine. We all have them, every one of my brothers. They're from my mom's side. My dad had black eyes.

"I thought you were dead," I manage, smiling a little as a warm tear slips from my eye. I sit up, push through the dizzy spell until I'm leaning my back against the bed.

His eyes sweep my face, but I can't read the emotion inside them. It's not what I expect at our reunion though.

"You should have died," he says.

I'm taken aback.

Julia snorts from her corner as I process what my

brother just said. Armen closes the folder he's holding—Zach's folder—and sets it down, then comes toward me. Why do I shrink away when he does? He's my brother. He won't hurt me.

But he already has, hasn't he?

I shake away the memories.

"Armen?"

He reaches out and grabs my arm hard, yanking me from the bed. When I stumble, he lets me fall. My knees hit the hard, cracked tiles. I look up at him.

"Everything would have been easier if you'd just died."

His stare takes me in, and disgust curls his lip. "Get her dressed. I don't want to see her like this. Nearly naked in his bed."

Then, to my horror and shock, he turns his back and walks out the door. I just sit there staring at it, in utter disbelief at his actions. His words. Because I know he doesn't mean it. He can't. I know what I saw that night two years ago. I know he didn't want to do what he did. He was made to.

Wasn't he?

Tears warm my eyes.

Julia tosses my dress, bra and panties at me. "You heard him. Get dressed. Let's go."

"Where? Why?"

The sneer she gives me chills me through. She squats down close and I back away. "You don't know how this is killing him. He's right. If you'd died that night, he'd be free. We both would be. But you just don't die, do you?" She grips a handful of hair and stands, drawing me painfully to my feet. "Get dressed."

"Where's Zach?"

She snorts again, shaking her head once, then raises her right arm and slaps me so hard across the face that I fall onto the bed.

"Because of you, he's on his way to getting himself killed."

Holding my hand to my hot, stinging cheek, I sit on the edge of the bed to stare up at her.

"If you want to see him before Malik puts a bullet in him, I suggest you get fucking dressed." She turns and walks out the door, but doesn't close it behind her and I hear them talk outside.

They've zip tied my wrists together too tight. So tight, my skin's rubbed raw. My brother won't look at me as the car bumps along the road heading farther and farther away from the city. He's driving the car and Julia is beside him, and I'm putting two and two together.

"Hope is your baby."

Armen finally glances at me in the rearview mirror. He looks older than his thirty years and this close, I see more gray in his dark hair and deep lines around his eyes.

"I thought you died that night, Armen." Neither of them react. "For two years, I've lived thinking you were blown to bits, but you've been here all this time. And you have a baby."

Nothing.

"Did you know I survived?"

"Yeah, sis, I knew."

I think that hurts worse than anything else. Worse than how he looked at me earlier. Worse than Julia's hand across my cheek.

"What about Rafi and Seth?"

I see the exchange between Armen and Julia.

"Are they alive? I have a right to know."

"You have no rights," Julia says.

"Why do you hate me?" I ask her. "I don't even know you. I didn't know you existed up until last night."

She turns, gives me a smirk. "Well, sadly, I've known of your existence for far longer."

"Stop," Armen tells her.

"Why? She's been living it up the last two years. What have you been doing? What have I been doing?"

"I haven't exactly been living it up. I thought I'd lost my entire family, you bitch."

"Stop it," Armen says again.

"You're the bitch. Bitch-whore."

Armen slams on the brakes, stops in the middle of the road. If I wasn't wearing my seatbelt, my face would be smashed up against the front seats.

My heart thunders in my chest, but he turns to Julia. "I said stop," he commands, his rage barely controlled. I watch her, am stunned that she obeys. He then turns to me. "You too. Just be quiet."

"Tell me about Seth and Rafi, and I'll be quiet. Tell me how you could do what you did to me, and I'll be quiet. All I wanted was to save you, Armen. Save you from becoming like him. Like Malik."

"But there wasn't any need because I wasn't becoming like him. I was *already* like him."

"I don't believe that, and neither do you. We grew up together. I remember how you took care of us. All of us. How after mom and dad died, you stepped into the role of both parents. How you went hungry to feed us. How you did whatever it took to take care of us."

His eyes are like lasers, slicing right through me. "And after all that, I failed, didn't I?"

"You're not a monster."

"You can say that after what I did to you?" He shakes his head and turns his attention back to the road, picking up speed. "You're stupid, Eve. Now shut the fuck up."

I sink back in the seat. I'm confused, relieved he's alive, yet afraid of the man he's become. And I have a bad feeling—like the worst is yet to come.

My head hurts from the drug Zach injected me with, and my heart hurts when I think about what Julia said. That Zach is on his way to getting himself killed. I think about Zach's deal with Hassan and wonder if Hassan knows what's happened. Where I am. That his daughter and my brother have kidnapped me. And they're taking me to Malik.

What use am I to Malik? I still don't understand. I know he used me to get to Zach, to lure him. Play with him, maybe. But what can he want with me now?

A cell phone rings and I watch as Julia fishes it out of her pocket and looks down at the screen. She answers at the fourth ring.

"Father." She's so cold. Last night, I'd thought it was because he dismissed her, but now I'm getting the impression that's just her.

Hassan is talking loud enough that I can hear him, but I can't make out his words.

"I left milk in the refrigerator. Hope will be fine. You just take care of her and don't worry about anything else."

So Hassan didn't know what they did.

"No, I don't care about that. I'm fixing this. Today. I want this done. We both do." A pause. "Don't worry, I'll take care of my big brother. Like always. When we're done, he'll get exactly what he deserves."

Hassan is still talking when she disconnects the call and switches off her phone.

It's another hour before we pass through a set of gates where two armed soldiers stand sentry. And it's another ten minutes after that before the large building comes into view. A monastery.

"You ready?" Julia asks once Armen waves to the guards and drives through the gates to park the car.

"Yeah," Armen answers.

"It's almost over," she says.

Her words are ominous and I can't think about what she means. He smiles at her and I can see alongside the anxiety in his eyes something else. Something like tenderness.

"Give us a minute," he says to her.

"I'll go let my uncle know we're here."

Julia gets out of the car with barely a glance in my direction. Once she's out of view, Armen turns to me. He's quiet at first, and he looks...resigned. "I did it to buy them back. That's how it started."

"How what started?"

"Seth and Rafi, when they disappeared, I went to Malik. I made a deal with him. I'd work for him and he'd get our brothers back."

"Back from where?"

"The group holding them prisoner. A group loyal to him." He shakes his head, and I see guilt in his eyes.

"Where are they now?"

"I don't know."

"Are they—" I can't say it.

He doesn't answer. Just looks down.

"What's going to happen to me?"

"You should have come on the flight I arranged for you. I could have hidden you."

"It was you who sent that ticket?"

He nods. "Now it's too late." He can't hold my gaze and when he speaks, any tenderness I saw earlier is gone, replaced by the cold, impenetrable man I remember from my last days here two years ago. "Now, I'm going to have to prove my loyalty."

That's all he says before climbing out of the car and opening the back door. He reaches in and takes hold of one arm, dragging me out. Forcing me, as I stumble and fight, toward the front door of the huge estate.

I'm not sure what I expected when I found him.
It's certainly not this. I'm sitting on thick cush-
ions with a low table before me. My wrists are
handcuffed to a D-ring beneath the table and there's
a small, chipped cup of Turkish coffee a few inches
from me. The girl who brought it, her hands shook
so badly that she spilled some of the thick black
liquid onto the saucer. I haven't touched it yet for the
obvious reason that I'm bound. I don't expect it to be
drugged. I know Maliki Remi. He'll want me alert to
fuck with me. Besides, I'm still in shock at the girl's
punishment administered by the guard, wondering
how she didn't cry out as the cane sliced into her ass
with a sound that made me flinch.

The monastery wasn't even in sight before three
SUVs drove out to greet me. Surrounding my car,
one man held out a rifle, signaling for me to stop. I

did. I knew them to be my welcoming committee. I never expected to get inside undetected, but the drive from where I left Hassan's truck to the guarded gates of the monastery was another two miles, which made me wonder if they'd seen me coming or if Hassan had tipped them off.

It doesn't much matter now though. I only hope I'd made the right decision to leave Eve behind. I wish I hadn't drugged her, but she wasn't going to let me go alone otherwise, and I couldn't be sure she wouldn't follow me if she did.

But this is between me and Maliki. Eve is a toy to him. Something to play with as long as it's fun. Something to crush beneath his filthy boot when she loses her shine.

And I guess he's finished playing his game when I hear his laughter coming from outside the door. I remember the sound, but this time, it chills me.

When that door opens, the girl clears out and the guard stands at attention. I watch as first another guard enters, followed by Ace, followed by Maliki Remi.

He stops once he sees me, as if surprised by my presence. As if he didn't know I was here.

I study him. He's older, but it's not that he's aged. Not in that way. He looks strange, more feral. More unpredictable. More insane.

"I'd stand, Commander, but..." I trail off, gesturing to the cuffs that bind me to the table.

When the guards met me a few miles out, I was searched, weapons confiscated. All I have now are my two hands, which are useless at the moment.

He studies me. I wonder if he's thrown off by my use of his title. His old title, that is. His expression is strange, it changes infinitesimally as he takes me in, my face, my neck, the edge of ink there, my arms. One tattooed, the other marred by fire.

Ace stands by his side, and I see him in my periphery. My eyes are locked on Malik. I'm not afraid. My heart isn't pounding. I'm not sure what I feel, actually. All I know is that the names on my back are burning again. Like they're here with me, the lost souls of the men who shouldn't have died that night.

Like they're here for their revenge.

Malik barks an order in Arabic. I'm rusty, but considering how quickly one of the guards comes to uncuff me, I figure out what he said. Once free, I make to stand. A hand falls heavy on my shoulder. It's the soldier at my back.

"Sit, Zachary." He always used my full name, and today, I hear a slight accent in his voice. I wonder if it was absent before or if I just never noticed it.

I remain seated. Malik walks toward the table, takes a seat where his back is to the wall and he's facing the door. He's relaxed again. He's fully in command. I lock eyes with Ace, whose black eyes appear not to recognize me. There's no hostility, but there's no warmth either. Nothing of the man I'd come to know. To trust.

Trust. Christ, what the fuck is wrong with me? When will I learn?

Malik snaps his fingers. A door opens and the same girl who got her ass caned for spilling my coffee carries in a tray containing two more small cups and a plate of sweets. I guess she knows better than to spill this time because the saucers are clean as she sets everything down and exits the room.

Ace sits waiting at Malik's side and I give a little shake of my head. He's like a fucking lapdog.

"You liked Turkish coffee before," Malik says, his English perfect, his tone like I remember before. "Drink."

I pick mine up and drink it. It's almost cold now, but it's good.

Malik nods, then sips his and picks up a pastry. He pushes the plate toward me, but I decline. He doesn't offer Ace one. Ace, who is watching me intently as Malik and I take each other's measure.

"I shot you. Point blank," I say.

"With blanks," he responds. "And I was wearing a bulletproof vest."

"It was a setup?"

He shrugs. "It wasn't you who was supposed to do it, but I'm flexible. I just needed to be dead."

"What the hell's going on, Malik or Maliki or

whatever the fuck your name is? Or is multiple personality among your disorders?"

He smiles and sips. "Malik is my given name."

"Malik. Tell me what the hell is going on. Why this charade?"

"Uncle," Ace starts after checking his phone. He leans in to Malik and whispers something.

Malik nods. Ace rises and walks out of the room using the same door the girl had. Malik returns his attention to me.

"I really would love to know why you're doing all this before I kill you," I say.

"So confident." His face twists into something dark. "So arrogant."

"I trusted you."

"That's not your fault, Zachary. I'm an excellent liar."

"What am I doing here? Why am I not dead?"

"You're too useful to be dead. It'd be a waste to kill you." There's a sound in the hallway, a scuffle of some kind. We both glance toward the door, and Malik smiles, rising as he finishes his sentence. "Although, I will if I have to."

The door opens and once again, when I begin to rise, that hand falls on my shoulder. But when I see Eve being brought inside, instinct kicks in and in two moves, the soldier is on his back on the floor, my boot crushing his windpipe, my hand closed over his gun, ready to take it. Use it.

"No, no, no," Malik says calmly, and when I turn my head, Armen's holding Eve against him, a blade at her neck.

I stop. Take my hand from the weapon. Move my foot.

"Let her go," I command.

Armen's icy eyes lock on mine, but he doesn't do what I say. Not that I expect him to.

Malik moves toward us, looks down at the guard who is slowly making his way up to his feet. Malik shakes his head, a smile on his lips. One that could be tender if it wasn't lethal.

"Zachary," he says, eyes still on the fallen soldier. "I changed my mind. Take the weapon and put a bullet between his eyes."

I look at Malik and realize in that moment that this is a different man than I knew. This one, he's ruthless. Evil.

When I don't move, he meets my stare. "Her life or his. Your choice."

I look at Eve, who's staring at me with big, frightened eyes.

"Armen," Malik says, still watching me. "Motivate Zachary."

A dark streak of red mars the otherwise perfect skin of Eve's neck. He's cut into her. It's shallow, but he's still cutting. She makes a sound, tears spilling down her face now, and before I can think, I've got the gun in my hand, I take aim between the soldier's eyes and pull the trigger.

Except nothing happens.

The soldier stares back at me, dumbfounded, and from the quickly darkening circle on his pants, I know he's pissed himself.

Malik laughs, gestures for Armen to stop, which he does. I look at Eve, at the line of red at her throat. Shallow. Armen knows how to kill. How to hurt. He was careful not to do the former. But is this a game? Is it planned? Rehearsed, even?

I open the chamber of the gun. It's empty.

Malik walks toward us, still laughing, although it's fading now. But when he takes a look at the piss-darkened pants, the smile disappears and this time when a gun is fired, it's his, and it's real. Eve screams. No one else makes a sound. The man lies flat on the floor, a bullet between his still-open eyes, blood pooling behind his head.

"Coward," Malik says, holstering his weapon. He gestures to two soldiers who come to take the body away. "I have a great distaste for cowards."

I'm watching Eve. Tears still pour down her face and she can't stop staring at the dead man, at the blood where he lay just moments ago. But she doesn't know Malik. The moment Malik told me to shoot him, he pronounced his death sentence. It's why he's so powerful.

In the next instant, Julia enters the room and

shoves at Eve, which forces Armen to release his death grip on her. She strides toward Malik. "Uncle," she says, kissing his cheek. If she's noticed the blood on the floor, she isn't moved.

He smiles at her, studies her for a long minute before kissing her cheek. I wonder to myself if this is a different girl than the one I knew two years ago, because that Julia, she wouldn't have kissed the cheek of a man who had just murdered a defenseless man. Would she?

"Let's move to the veranda," Malik says. A girl walks in with a mop as our group makes its way out. Malik waits to walk beside me. "They're not all empty," he whispers to me as if we're in cahoots. "It makes things interesting." I realize he's referring to the guns.

"Let her go, Malik. She has nothing to do with this."

He shrugs and gestures to a guard when I don't move. The man joins us. This one has a rifle slung across his shoulder and he's nudging me forward. I walk out the door and through the outside hall, taking in the view of mountains and sea in the distance, the calm, quiet surroundings. The two monks walking across the otherwise empty courtyard.

"It's nice here," he says to me once we reach the veranda. "Peaceful."

It's large, with beautiful pillars for support, and

set with comfortable furniture. Armen sits Eve on one. Julia sits beside her, taking her hand. I know she's squeezing it, digging her nails into Eve's skin from the look on Eve's face. But Eve's doesn't pull away. She's only watching me.

I take a step toward Eve. Julia releases her hand and I'm not sure if I'll be stopped along the way, but I'm not. I crouch down before her, take her bound hands in mine. "You okay?" I ask her.

She shakes her head no.

"You will be. I promise."

"Aww. So tender," Malik says from behind me. "But you really shouldn't make promises you can't keep."

The hair on the back of my neck stands on end and I rise to face him.

He takes a stroll around the room, giving me a chance to count guards. Two at the door, one at either end. Two more on a sort of watchtower. All have machine guns slung over their shoulders and I have a feeling these are not empty of bullets.

"I knew it the day of the auction. Saw it in your eyes when her brother brought her up on that stage." Malik smiles wide as if he's talking of some fond memory. "Such a pretty girl," he says, looking at Eve's face. He turns to me. "It saved her life, that look. That love." The way he says that last word, it's meant to taunt.

But it doesn't. It has a different effect.

It makes my heart stop for just a moment.

"That look saved her life," Malik repeats. His tone is suddenly sharp when he next speaks, calling out Julia's name. With a gesture, he tells her to move. She does.

"Sit, Zachary."

"Fuck you, Malik."

His face hardens. I guess he's not used to people talking to him that way. "I said sit."

I step toward him. "I don't much feel like sitting. Tell me what the hell you want. You could have killed me a hundred times over by now. Clearly, you don't want me dead. So what is it you do want?"

When he comes to stand closer, I see how empty his eyes look. Soulless. I wonder if it's how mine look. He stops when we're inches from each other, but I guess he didn't take into consideration the fact that I'm taller. And I like the advantage, so I step even nearer.

"You want to know what I want?" he asks.

From my periphery, I see a guard step up. Malik gives a nod and a hand lands on my shoulder, pushing me down. Down until I'm on my knees.

"I want to have a little fun," he says, nodding. That's the last thing I see before a sharp pain at my temple makes my vision go black, and Eve's scream is the last thing I hear when I crash down onto the unforgiving marble, everything fading from consciousness.

21

Three military vehicles drive us over rough, bumpy unpaved roads. I know where we're going. My wrists are still bound and Julia sits beside me in the backseat of one vehicle. Whenever I look at her, she's looking out the window, holding onto the bar over the window as we bounce along. At one point, she takes out her cell phone, switches it on. I see her scroll through the contacts, but when she catches me watching, she pockets it and turns her face away.

One armed guard sits in the front seat beside the driver, and the glances he gives me make my skin crawl.

Armen and Ace are riding in the same vehicle as Malik. Zach's unconscious body was dumped into the trunk area of the third Jeep. I touch my neck, grateful Malik ordered someone to bandage it up. I can still feel my brother's grip as he held me, hear his uneven breath at my ear as he sliced into my flesh. The memory makes me shudder.

I wonder how far he's willing to go to prove his loyalty.

Will he kill me if he's ordered to?

And what about Zach? What will happen to Zach?

Night has fallen by the time we get to the site of the auction. The three vehicles stop in a sort of semi-circle, their headlights illuminating the ruins of the building. I can't open my door from the inside so I have to wait until the soldier opens it. He takes my arm, but I shove it away, stumbling out on my own. The trucks cast an eerie glow over the space, almost making me think I can see the ghosts of the dead, like they still haunt this place. And maybe they do. They will, until they've been avenged. The wrong righted.

But a moment later, a thud to my right catches my attention. It's Zach. They've dumped him on the ground, but he's moving. He's waking up. The skin at his temple is blue and swollen, and blood has dried and created a crust on his cheek. His hands are bound with rope and he blinks hard, looking around. I know the reality of where we are is coming back to him. I can see recognition dawning on his

face. I think about his back, the names tattooed
there. I wonder if he feels them now, burning onto
his flesh. Reminding him why he's here. Reminding
him that he lived and they died and that he needs to
be strong for himself, for them. The pain on his face
tells me he's remembering just that and I think back
to when he'd brought me here just a day ago.

Was it only a day? It feels like an eternity has
passed since then.

In that moment, Zach catches my eye. My heart
thuds against my chest when I look at him, and I
know we're going to die here. We're both going to die
tonight in the very place where maybe we both
should have died two years ago. Maybe the last two
years were borrowed time for us both.

My throat closes up but I bite back the tears
when two men haul Zach to his feet. He grunts, but
stands straight and tall. Taller than the others.
Bigger. Stronger.

But unarmed.

I take a step toward him, drawn to him, but Julia's
hand wraps around my arm and drags me backward.
When I look at her, she doesn't speak. Just sneers.

"Here we are," Malik says, stepping over a barrier
and into what would have been the interior of the
building. Ace is close behind him. "Back again. The
spirits of the dead haunt this place," he says casually,
picking up a strip of cloth from the ground. For all

292

the dirt, I recognize the pattern. It was a piece of the dress I'd worn that day. The one Armen tore from me.

"Did you orchestrate the auction just to kill the men you once led?" Zach asks, his voice powerful, proud. The men walk him into the building's perimeter as Malik watches. "Men who mourned your death."

"You know, strange thing. Guilt isn't something I've ever felt."

"Makes sense. Psychopaths typically don't feel remorse."

Malik's grin falters, just for an instant, but it's long enough for me to see it. He turns to Julia. "Bring the girl."

The men holding Zach stand taller, and I know he's just tried to break free.

I stumble as Julia shoves me forward. In my periphery, I see Armen. See him stand by and watch.

"How did it go?" Malik asks when I'm a few feet from him. He turns to Armen. "Do you remember?"

Armen's forehead is creased and he won't look at me. It's so strange to see him like this. His eyes so gentle, yet him so...not.

"You want me, Malik. She has nothing to do with this. Let her go. I'll do what you want." It's Zach. A moment after he speaks, one of the soldiers jabs the butt of his machine gun into Zach's ribs. Zach grunts, hunches over, and I see the effort it takes him to straighten. To keep his face hard, impassable.

"But you don't even know what it is I want," Malik says.

He grabs my arm roughly and throws me to Armen, who catches me, holds me, keeps me facing away from him so I can watch the interaction between Zach and Malik.

Malik looks to one of the soldiers, the one who drove the vehicle Julia and I rode in. "Take my niece home."

"Uncle!"

"This isn't something for a woman to see," he tells her.

"But—"

"Go home to Hope."

"Please—"

Malik nods to the driver who opens the passenger side door for her. "I said go, Julia."

She takes in a deep breath, turns her attention to Armen. I glance at him, find his eyes locked on hers, their gaze intense. Maybe they're not sure who will walk away tonight either.

Armen nods, and, without a word, Julia turns, takes the few steps toward the Jeep and disappears inside. The driver pulls away, crunching branches and leaves beneath the heavy tires. With one set of headlights gone, the space is even more eerie.

"Where were we?" Malik asks, turning to me.

I know what he's going to do. He's planned this. He's been waiting for this moment for two years.

"Yes, the girl. Armen, do you remember? I want it done exactly the same. It was such a sight, that I want to see it again."

"Why are you doing this?" Zach asks.

He knows what's coming too. I can hear it in his voice.

Malik looks at him, but doesn't respond. Not right away. Instead, he shifts his eyes to Armen. "What are you waiting for? Now's your chance to prove your loyalty."

I swear I can hear Armen swallow and with my back against him, I feel his heart thudding against his chest. But then he obeys, walking me toward the platform, or the remaining part of it, where he'd stood me before. Where he'd stripped me.

"Walk," he says quietly when we get to the stone steps. There are three of them. That night two years ago, I hadn't had to climb them. I'd been backstage, so to speak. Hidden behind a curtain, knocked unconscious and bound, awaiting my debut.

The sound of a vehicle approaching, radio loud, makes us both stop. When I look at the company collected, the only man unsurprised by the approach is Malik. I know why a moment later.

A truck takes the place of the one that drove Julia away. This one has a back covered by camouflage material that blows in the slight breeze. I watch dust and dirt settle in the headlights as the engine is shut off, plunging us into near silence, at least momentarily. Armen's hand tightens around my arm as soldiers unload from the back.

"Malik," Zach says over the sound of it, of a dozen men in military fatigues crunching ground beneath their boots, piling into the perimeter of the building and I only realize I'm crying when I taste the salt of my own tears.

Zach's fighting. He's fighting so hard, two more men have come to help the soldiers holding him back.

"Armen," I start, turning my head. "What's going to happen?" I know though. I know.

Armen's eyes are wide. Locked on the men whose heads and faces are covered with scarves, the same pattern as those most of the men wore that night. I wonder if he recognizes them. If he knew they'd be here, or if Malik planned this part himself.

"Don't look at them," he says in a voice low enough that only I hear it. "Don't think." Our eyes lock and in the glistening tears I glimpse inside, I see his apology.

"Malik!" Zach's voice is louder than that of the truck when it approached, than that of a dozen sets of boots marching to take their places in this sick reenactment of that terrible night.

"Armen," Malik says, smiling, sitting on the edge of the stone wall, his stance casual. "Begin."

A roar breaks into the night. It's Zach. But no one pays any attention to him. Not when Armen releases my arm and comes to stand in front of me. That tenderness, the vulnerability I saw in his eyes a moment ago is gone, but his hand trembles when he grips the front of my dress.

I think he mouths the words *I'm sorry*. But maybe that's just in my own head.

"Don't do this," I say, tears falling down my face, onto the back of his arm. "Don't."

He looks at me. He just stands there looking at me. And I know he's not going to do it.

But I also know what it will cost him.

"Armen." It's a sob.

Can you hear a bullet rip through air? Hear it tear flesh?

I think I scream as blood splatters across my face, against my open mouth, as my brother falls away from me, falls backward off the stage, onto the dirt, at the feet of all those men. All those men, none of whom help him.

I scream again when I see them kick at him and for a single moment, his eyes catch mine and that's when I drop to my knees, the jagged stone stage tearing my flesh as they beat his body, breaking him. They only stop when he goes limp like a ragdoll, and no more sound comes from him.

When I try to get up, to go to him, hands grip me hard, and I look up. Ace stands behind me. His grin is chilling as he tucks his pistol into the waistband of his jeans and grips my shoulder with one hand, bracing me as the other tears my dress apart.

I gasp, look down at myself, see my brother there, bleeding out on the ground, choke on a scream as Ace's hands rip my bra in two, tear it away, leave me naked but for my panties. The men scream and cheer and I stumble backward, nearly falling off the broken stage.

But Ace raises me to my feet, holds me there, laughs as he calls out another number.

Like two years ago, once I'm fully naked, I search for Zach. I find him. His eyes are wide, locked on mine. Just like that night, but different too.

Wild.

Feral.

Savage.

Ace leans in to say something in my ear but all I feel is his hot breath, his wet mouth. He turns back to the crowd, but it's all muted now, muted and blurred. Men are screaming out numbers. Ridiculous numbers. And Zach, he's screaming too. I can't hear what he's saying though. Can't hear his warning. It's all happening so fast.

Air rushes past me, the sound drawing my gaze from Zach's to Ace's. His expression changes. He stops. Blinks. Stumbles. I look behind me and see

Hassan stepping out of the woods, his face strange, hands somehow steady. He fires another shot and this time when I stumble, I fall. I fall backward off the stage with a thud onto the ground. That's when all hell breaks loose around me, an exact reenactment of that deadly night two years ago.

22

ZACH

I saw Hassan before anyone else did. Watched him step out from the thick cover of trees. Screamed for Eve to drop to the ground. To take cover. But she wasn't hearing me.

A second bullet sends Ace to the ground. Sends Eve falling off the stage. Hassan is still approaching but guards have seen him now, not the crazed men bidding on Eve's naked body, but the men beside me. The men by Malik. It's the moment I need. They should have tied my hands behind my back, not in front of me. Now they'll pay.

The soldier who raises his machine gun first has my attention. I lunge, throwing my weight against the length of it. He's not expecting this, not expecting me, and I use surprise to my advantage, relieving him of the weapon, knocking him out with the butt of it before whirling around, using the gun like a baseball bat to knock the knees out from under the second soldier by my side. He screams in pain, falling as I shatter one of his kneecaps. I don't care about him though.

I stand. Eve's still on the ground, but she's moving, watching me. She's not hurt. Hassan's been hit, but he's still walking, and I turn the weapon on the room and open fire and it's like that night is happening all over again. The sounds, the screams, the tearing flesh and the blood. The past grabs hold of me, ink burning into my back, but I can't let it have me. Not yet. Not now. I have to stay here for her.

My body vibrates in time to the machine gun I'm emptying. Men drop before they've reached for weapons, but bullets are flying toward me as I walk, making my way through the downed men, stepping on bodies, feeling flesh beneath my boots.

I have one target in my sights. One man who, two years ago, escaped. Walked away.

Tonight though, things will go differently.

He's not walking away. None of them are.

Pain in my left arm momentarily stops me. I look at the circle of blood forming, and turn in the direction from where the bullet came and I mow down the men standing there. I don't feel a goddamn thing when I do it either. No remorse. Nothing.

Maybe I've become like him too. Like Malik.

Ruthless. Insane.

A monster.

I turn to Malik again, find Hassan standing a few feet from him. Hassan's face is strange. Blood is smeared across it and his pallor is...wrong. But he's standing. And I realize it's quiet. I look around me and see only downed bodies. Only one headlight hasn't been shot out, and that's the one illuminating Hassan and Malik.

"He's mine," I say, my eyes locked on Malik.

Both men turn to me, but Malik is the only one grinning.

I know why in the next second. I know it when he draws the blade out of Hassan's belly and Hassan stumbles backward, catches the half-wall, falls.

"Mine," he says, clutching his gut, his hand searching for the wall, finding it, pulling himself up again.

Malik looks behind him and, realizing he's alone, that grin falters. But only for a moment.

"It's a good night, isn't it?" he asks, and I realize he's holding a pistol in his hand when I hear him cock it. He raises it, but instead of aiming it at me, he aims it behind me to where I know Eve is standing. He returns his gaze to mine. "What do you think, loaded or not?"

But before he can pull the trigger, a shot rings out and Malik stumbles backward, the gun in his hand flying to the ground, lost in the darkness and the overgrowth. I look to find Eve naked, smeared in blood, camouflaged by it almost, and holding a pistol. She takes a step toward us.

"Eve," I say.

Like before, she doesn't hear me. I move, but when I do, she looks to me and aims the weapon at me, blinks, then returns her attention to Malik.

He laughs. Clutching his side, he actually laughs.

"Where are my brothers?" Eve asks, her voice stronger than I expect, even as it trembles.

When he doesn't reply, she fires another bullet, but this one misses him.

"Eve, put the gun down." I'm walking toward her slowly, my weapon pointing to the ground.

"Where are they?" She cocks it again.

It takes three more steps for me to be beside her. "He's not going to tell you," I say, touching her hands, covering them with one of mine, lowering the pistol.

She looks at me, and I see the loss in her eyes. The pain of watching someone you love brutalized before you.

"He's not worth it," I say.

A tear slides down her face.

"He's a monster."

I take the gun from her and tuck it into the waistband of my jeans before hugging her to me. She's shivering, even though it's a warm night. Shock. She's going into shock.

"Armen," she says into my chest. "They shot him in the back like cowards."

"He's still alive." Turning us, I hold her so I'm watching the half-brothers on the ground, one nearly dead, the other not close enough to it. She's looking at Armen. I look at Eve, pull my shirt over my head and slip it over her. "Go to him. Go to Armen," I say. "And whatever you do, don't look back."

She draws away, studies me.

"Understand?"

She nods. She understands. And a moment later, she's walking across this twice-bloodied field to her brother. I go to where Malik and Hassan lie on the ground.

I take the stained blade, the one Hassan has his hand around. He's moments from death and he doesn't fight me for it.

"He destroyed my family," Hassan says. "I never meant—" There's a gurgling sound. A sound of dying.

"Shh. Don't talk now. It's done."

"Julia." It's barely a whisper.

"I'll take care of Julia and the baby. Close your eyes, Hassan."

A chuckle from Malik has me turning, but his wound is worse than I thought. He'll bleed out. I don't have to do this. But I want to.

I shift my full attention to him.

"Why all this?" I ask.

"Because you were always too good to waste."

"You thought I'd come to work for you? After everything you did?"

He tries to shrug.

"You're stupid too, then." I hold up the knife. "I can make it quick," I say. "Tell me where her brothers are."

One corner of his mouth curves upward. "Hell?"

My eyes narrow. I spare one glance behind me, but Eve's good. She's not watching.

When I look back at Malik, it's me who smiles.

"Then don't tell me, bastard."

I tear open his shirt. He grunts, and I glimpse the fear in his eyes now.

"This is for my friends. For the lives you took." And I slice a line from one side of his gut to the other, deep but not too deep. I do this six times, slowly carving each line into him, watching his eyes, seeing his pain as I feel flesh tear beneath my blade. It's not as satisfying as I thought it would be as life drains out of him. But I never thought it would be that. It just needed to be done. And I needed to be the one to do it.

"Fuck you, Malik. Fuck you."

23

Three months later

I've always heard that coming back to your childhood home, you realize it's not as big as you thought it was when you were a kid. But to me, this house, this broken, white-walled house, it's still huge.

And hollow.

I know if I make a sound, my voice will bounce against the walls in an echo. But I don't make a sound. There's nothing to say. No one to say it to. I'm alone as I close the door behind me and stand in the foyer of the house I grew up in. The tiles beneath my sandaled feet are terracotta. My heels click with my steps, even though I'm trying to be quiet. My heart is beating faster too, just a little. It's strange being back here. It's been seven years.

The narrow corridor of the entrance opens into the large living room. At the far end is the kitchen, and next to that, the dining area. No walls to separate the spaces. Most of the furniture is covered by dust cloths. I pick up the one wooden chair that's lying on its side, half exposed, and right it before dragging the yellowed cloth off to expose the table and the rest of the dining chairs. I didn't realize Armen had kept the house as it was.

I walk into the kitchen. Although buried beneath inches of dust, the tea kettle sits in its place on the back burner of the stove. My mom made tea every morning and every evening. She and I were the only ones who drank it. I touch it, smear my finger through the dust. I don't know if I expect memories to flood back, but they don't. I don't know at all what I feel right now.

Wiping off my hands, I turn back around and take in the living room. The carpet with the design I loved now looks old and worn. I look up and what I see makes me smile. My father had a fresco painted on the ceiling like it was the Sistine Chapel. He did it for my mom. I was four then and I remember lying on my back and staring up at it, in awe of it. It's peeling a little now. Time is taking its toll.

The house was built so the second-floor rooms are situated on the outsides of the large living space of the first floor. Six doors total, three on each side.

All the bedroom doors are closed and when I walk to the stairs, I realize I'm holding my breath. My hand closes over the simple metal railing, and I ignore the dust as I climb up. My door is the first one I come to and it takes me a minute to open it.

That's when emotion slams into me. It's when I feel the warmth of tears. It's not even memories. It's just loss.

Light filters in through the slats of the shutters, just enough of it for me to see. My room looks like it did the day we left. My parents had been gone for months by then. I was fifteen. Some of my old posters hang on the walls, but most are on the floor. My bed isn't made. I never bothered back then, not after they died. Nothing was the same after they died.

I walk to the window with its broken glass and push the wooden shutters open. Bright sunlight fills the space. I just stand there for a long time, remembering. I have to force my legs to move, but I make my way to the bed, sit on the edge of it, not caring about the cloud of dust that surrounds me as I shift seven years' worth with my weight. The framed photo of my family is on the nightstand. I pick it up and dust it off. Why didn't I take this with me when I left? I look at it, touch each of their faces. My parents. My brothers. Me. All of us laughing.

My heart hurts.

"You okay?"

Startled, my gaze snaps to the door where Zach is standing.

"Armen told me you'd come here," he says.

Armen survived that terrible night. The bullet had missed his heart, but just barely, and although he was badly bruised with multiple broken ribs and a broken leg, he's healing. And he's home. He and Julia are living in Dr. Hassan's house with Hope.

Zach looks around the room before he steps inside. He's too big for the space and my old bedroom suddenly looks small.

I put the picture frame down and stand up, wiping off the seat of my jeans. "Zach. When did you get back?"

He's been gone for over four weeks. I guess I'm surprised he's back, although he told me he would be.

"You look like you didn't expect to see me." He gives a little laugh, picks up a poster that's lying face down on the floor. "Didn't think I'd come back?" he asks without looking at me.

I shrug. I guess I don't know what I expected.

He looks up when I don't reply. "Hannah Montana?" he asks, one eyebrow lifting along with a corner of his mouth.

That's good. It makes me smile. Helps to turn off the pain, at least for now.

"It's old." I walk to him, make to take the poster, but when my hand touches his, there's a spark of electricity that makes me draw back, gasp. The blue of his eyes are bright, but his gaze is focused, scrutinizing. Being near him, it makes my belly feel like a hundred butterflies take flight at the same instant. It's not just physical attraction, either. Maybe it's circumstances that make me feel the way I do. Make me feel safest when he's near. I don't know. I can't explain it, and I'm not trying to. I know what I want. I just don't know if it's what he wants.

I lick my lips. I'm waiting for him to kiss me, expecting him to, wondering why he hasn't already.

But he doesn't kiss me. Instead, he runs his thumb across my cheek to wipe away a tear. "You okay?" he asks again.

I shake my head, step backward, focus my attention on setting the old poster on the bed. "It's just weird being back here." I'm disappointed he hasn't kissed me. When I straighten, he's still watching me.

"Eve."

I know he's waiting for more, but I'm not sure how to do that without breaking, so instead I just try to keep my eyes on his, even though I know I can't hide from him. He can see inside my soul. I can't even control it, stop it. Not with him.

"Are you okay?"

"How okay should I be?" It's like the floodgates

open then. Years of pain, of loss, of living in limbo, of not living at all.

"Not."

I'm surprised by his answer and have no reply.

"You shouldn't have come here alone. You should have waited for me to bring you."

"You left." He left a few weeks after the night he killed Malik. Once he made sure Armen would be all right, made certain Julia and the baby were safe. That I was safe. He said he needed to take care of old business and disappeared.

"I told you I'd be back."

My gaze falls to the floor and I drop onto the bed. The poster in my hand wrinkles, but I don't drop it. I need to hold onto something, need to keep my hands busy. My gaze on something—anything— other than him.

"I don't know who I am," I start. I know this, have known it for a long time. But to voice it, it's almost frightening. Like it's more real because I do.

The bed strains beneath Zach's weight as he sits beside me. He doesn't speak, but I can feel him watching me.

"I was fifteen when my parents died. That was when my world began to fall apart. It wasn't long after that Rafi and Seth disappeared, and Armen went to work for Malik. I never even graduated high school," I say, glancing at him. I don't think he knew that. "I think I could have survived my parents' deaths, but then Rafi and Seth, and then after that, Armen... Everything changed. That night two years ago was the final straw. The last thing that broke me. For two years I've lived in limbo. Numb. Existing, really, not living." I wipe my eyes on my sleeve and force myself to face him. "Now that I know they're gone, Rafi and Seth, now that I know Armen will be all right, that Malik didn't turn him into a monster. That I have a niece..." That makes me smile. "Hope. It's appropriate, her name, isn't it?"

"Yes, it is." His big hand is at my back, rubbing circles.

"Well, now that I know, I can move on. I just don't really know how." My chest heaves with a deep sigh. These are my cards. It's where I stand.

"The house is in your name," Zach says.

I nod. "Armen did that." He and Julia are together, trying to heal after her losses. She's only just started to meet my gaze when we speak, but I know she has a lot to work through, and in spite of everything, my brother loves her and I'm trying to give her a chance.

"That's a starting point, isn't it? The house?" Zach says.

I look at him.

"Or do you want to go back to Denver?"

"Denver? I have nothing to tie me to Denver. Devon is probably the only person who noticed I left." I chuckle, but it's not really funny. It's sad, actually. That day I was packing to outrun Zach, I realized how little of the things around me were even mine. "I talked to him again yesterday. They sold the McKinney property," I say, teasing.

"That's too bad," he smiles. "But I didn't have any intention of going back to Denver. I only went looking for you in the first place."

His eyes are intense, like he's trying to say a thousand things. And the way he tells me that last part, that he went to Denver for me, it feels strange, makes me feel...hope.

"Where did you go?" I ask. I have no idea where he's been.

"I went to see someone who was in special ops while I was there."

"Who?"

He takes a deep breath and stands, paces to the window before turning back to look at me. "The man who headed up the group searching for Malik. His name is James Jordan. James is the man who had initially questioned me, questioned everything that happened the night I shot my commanding officer. He left abruptly and I never got an answer as to why, where he'd gone. I guess I didn't ask enough questions because I didn't know him and the facts of the night of the shooting were so confused by then. What they told me, what I remembered...it was all mixed up. They had me on drugs and I just couldn't get it right."

I shake my head. "Malik was under your nose the whole time."

Zach nods.

"What happened?"

"Well, after he got over the fact that I was alive, we talked. He lives in the States. Miami."

"You flew to Miami?"

He nods. "I told him everything and it turns out they had figured out the truth at the end. That Malik was Commander Maliki Remi. That the traitor was someone he had trusted. Who had fooled him. When I'd thought there was a cover-up after I shot Malik—my commander back then—I was right. There was. And explaining it would have been problematic, not to mention a huge embarrassment to the military. To Jordan. That's why they covered it up. Decorated Malik as a hero, didn't investigate me for the shooting. Jordan left after that."

"Why did you come back to Beirut?"

He looks confused. "What do you mean, why did I come back?"

I stand. "You didn't have to. It's finished. You killed him. You got your revenge."

"I told you I'd be back, Eve."

"Why? What brought you back?"

He steps to me, sighs, takes hold of my hands. "What do you think brought me back?"

I study him, search his eyes.

"*Who* do you think?" He rubs the back of his

neck and smiles. "You're the only honest, real thing in my life, Eve. You matter to me."

My heart races, my mouth goes dry.

"And when you say you don't know where to start, well, I've been living in limbo too these last years. I don't belong anywhere, I have no ties to anything. My brothers are in Tuscany with their wives, Raphael with a family, Damon I'm sure isn't too far behind. I don't belong there. I guess I could go back, but I don't fit there. Not on my own."

"What are you saying?"

"The States?" He shrugs, continuing as if I haven't spoken at all. "Nothing holds me there. But here, Beirut, it's where my life, the parts that mattered most, were," he pauses for a long time, his eyes never leaving mine. "Where the people that matter most are."

"You're staying?" I feel a huge weight lifted, a relief of sorts. It's the same feeling I've had a few times with him. That feeling of not being alone.

"Did you hear me?"

I nod slowly. I did hear him, am hearing him, but I'm slow to process his meaning because it's too much. Too good. And I haven't had good in too long.

Zach's hands travel up along my arms, circle them, pull me closer so we're just inches apart. He searches my face, and there's a look in his eyes, something strange, different, hopeful?

"I want to stay here. I want to stay here with you. I love you, Eve. I love you. I have for a long time."

I laugh. It's a strange sound, almost manic. I touch his face, take it into my hands and I feel my smile stretching wide. "I love you too, Zach." How haven't I said those words before? "You don't know how happy I am that you came back."

EPILOGUE 1
ZACH

One Year Later

Music is blaring upstairs in the master bedroom when I walk into the house. Eve doesn't hear me and I've told her a hundred times to make sure she locks the door if she's upstairs and essentially deaf to the world. I shake my head, take off my jacket and toss it over the back of a chair, then unbutton and roll up one shirt sleeve, then the other as I make my way up to the second floor.

At least it's music I like. U2. But she listens to some crap too. The scent of paint permeates the house. She's made it her mission to restore it to its former glory. It's a hell of a job, but Armen comes by to help now and again, and it's good for her. Between it and starting college, she keeps herself very busy.

I open the bedroom door and she still doesn't hear me. She's got her back to me and is singing along as she rolls aqua paint over one wall. I must admit, it looks good. Better than I thought it would, but she's got an eye for it. She's finished the living room, restored the fresco, and is working her way through the house. I think she's saving Rafi and Seth's rooms for last. She still doesn't go in there. We still haven't even cleared the dust from those two rooms.

She's singing along and I have to smile. I lean against the far wall, watching her. I've got a good view of her ass from here. She's wearing tiny white shorts and one of my T-shirts and she's got paint smeared pretty much everywhere.

After another minute, I pull the plug on the stereo and watch her jump so high, she practically hits her head on the ceiling.

Eve whirls around, roller in hand, eyes wide, startled, at least for a minute before they narrow on me. "You gave me a heart attack!"

"I told you to lock the front door when you're up here." I go to her, take the wrist holding the roller but keep a few inches between us. I like my suit. But I also like looking at her like this, no makeup, wild hair barely contained with a clip at the top of her head. She's picked up some color in the last year and it looks good on her. She looks relaxed. Pretty. Happy. I lean down to kiss her. It's meant to be a peck—I don't want to ruin my suit—but with her, I can't resist and the kiss turns into something deeper, something more, and when she moans against my mouth, I release her with a groan.

"What?" she asks, all innocent eyes.

"You make me crazy, that's what. Put this down, you're done." I take the roller from her and set it down, then walk her into the bathroom, switch on the shower and pull the shirt over her head. "Why don't you wear your own T-shirts to paint?"

"I like mine," she says with a wink.

I give her a grin, push her shorts down and off, turn her around and smack her ass. "I like mine too. I prefer them without paint splatters, in fact." My cell phone rings. "Get the rest of your things off," I say, pulling the phone out of my pocket and checking the display. I have to take the call. "Get nice and clean so I can dirty you," I say with a wink as I answer the call.

The bathroom's big and we haven't redone it yet so the shower is a tiled area at one corner, no curtain, no door. There's a pedestal sink with a mirror hanging above and in the other corner, a stack of tiles we'll use to replace the old ones.

She sticks her tongue out at me. I give her a shake of my head and listen to Jordan talk while watching her. It's like a striptease when she slides her bra off one arm at a time, cupping her breasts for the slow reveal. My cock's getting hard. She turns around slowly, her ass to me. Her white cotton panties are soaked and see through, and she makes a point of slowly dragging them down her thighs, bending deep, displaying everything.

"Zach, did you hear me?" It's Jordan.

Eve straightens, giggling as she picks up the shampoo. I narrow my eyes, a promise of punishment to come.

She only grins wider.

"I heard you, Jordan." We're not friends, he and I, but we are partners—for now. When he left the military, he had enough contacts in the Middle East to start his own "security" operation. We started to work together half a year ago, when, after our initial meeting, he contacted me about cleaning up Malik's organization. It was much bigger than I'd even realized, but I liked the work. I liked making right what Malik had made wrong and considering the fact I have no problem punishing those who need to be punished, Jordan and I came to an agreement. I needed information, and he needed my help. As for the US military, the Malik cover-up included me so I'm still dead. Which works out fine for me. Michael Beckham is my legal name

"I already took care of it. Your doorbell should be ringing any second with a delivery." The USB drive with the files he wants is on its way. A list of men and women who would prefer to remain anonymous. "Did you get me the information I need?"

When I said Jordan and I aren't friends, I mean I know the man I'm dealing with. See, there is no black or white. No good or evil. Not even me. My hands are in no way clean and sometimes, when I touch Eve with those hands, I wonder if I shouldn't leave her be. Walk away. But I can't. And I guess I still think life owes me, so I don't.

"I know where they were killed. Where they're buried."

I study Eve as I listen, my face betraying nothing. She doesn't know what I'm doing. Why I agreed to work with Jordan. I didn't want to get her hopes up, and I guess I was right.

"You know who did it?" I ask, feeling a disappointment I didn't expect to feel. I wanted to give her different news. Although, she's accepted their deaths. I can leave it alone.

"Yes."

I nod to myself. "I have to go."

"I'll send you the information."

"Good. We're done, then."

"I can always use you, Zach."

"We're done."

I disconnect the call, tuck the phone into my pocket and fold my arms across my chest.

Eve's got her eyes closed and is washing

shampoo out of her hair. Suds cover her naked, flaw-less body and I can't drag my eyes away.

"So, have you always made it a habit to move into someone's home without having an actual conversation about it?" she asks, turning her face into the stream.

I think about this. "Hmm. I guess I do." I unbutton my shirt, strip it off and toss it aside, then do the same with my pants and boxer briefs.

She glances at me and with a grin, I reach to switch off the water.

"Hey! I'm not done."

"Yes, you are." I step onto the wet tiles, push her up against the wall. "You were giving me quite the show, shaking your ass like that." I grip her jaw, kiss her mouth, take one wet breast into my hand and rub the nipple with my thumb before pinching a little. Just until she moans.

"I'm cold," she says, wrapping her arms around my neck, pressing her wet body against mine.

"I'll warm you up." I kiss her harder, hoist her up and carry her out of the bathroom, setting her down near the bed. It's covered in protective cloth which I strip away. She looks up at me, desire darkening her eyes. "Do it again," I say, turning her so she's facing away from me. "Bend over, grab your ankles and show me your ass."

"Zach—"

I grip her hair with one hand, drawing her head

back, making her look at me when I slap her hip. "You like it, Eve. You like it dirty. You want to show me every inch of you. Now be a good girl and bend over."

I release her and take a seat on the bed, legs wide, my dick thick in my hand. Eve turns around, her ass to me, and spreads her legs wide. Slowly she bends over, drawing out every second, driving me insane.

"Good girl," I say when she's in position. My voice is a growl as I take her hips and draw her backward, her ass at eye level. All I have to do to taste her is lean forward, just a little, but I take my time too. She wants me, I can see it on her glistening lips, smell the musky scent of arousal. My hands on her ass cheeks, I open her wider, take in every shaved inch of her before licking her pink pussy, tasting her. I dip my head down to flick my tongue over her clit, sliding it back up along her folds, up to her tiny asshole, tickling it, listening to her moan as I circle it before sliding back down to her pussy, burying my face in her.

"Fuck, Zach."

Her knees give out a moment later, but I grip her, draw her backward onto my lap, sit her on my cock while taking her clit between two fingers.

"Who were you talking to?" she asks, breathless.

I slide her up and down my length. "You have the worst timing." I lift her off, set her on her hands and knees before me, settle myself between her knees and spread her ass cheeks. "The fucking worst." My cock is slippery with her arousal and her pussy stretches to take me. I close my thumb over her asshole and she moans when I press.

"I don't like you working for that man," she pants.

"Shut up," I say, pulling out, flipping her over onto her back and pushing her legs up alongside her torso.

"He's not good," she continues, but the way her eyes are rolling back in her head makes me smile.

"You want to come, Eve?" I take her clit between two fingers.

She nods. "God, yes."

"Then shut the fuck up." I lean down, smash my mouth over hers. It's the only way to shut her up. Drawing my hips back, I thrust in hard.

She gasps into my mouth and I do it again and her tight little cunt is squeezing me and I'm so fucking close.

"Come, *habibi*."

She's such a good girl. She comes on demand, and I don't hold back. I fuck her hard and when her walls pulse around me, with a groan I bury myself deep inside her and she milks my cock and all I can do is watch her face go soft, her eyes dreamlike, and wonder what she sees in me when she watches me come.

We're lying on the floor naked, each of us silently watching the other.

"What did he want?" she asks.

"If you knew who I was talking to, why did you ask?"

She sits up. I follow. "I don't trust Jordan. I don't like him."

"Don't worry, I don't trust him either. We're getting what we need from each other, that's all."

"What do you need from him?" She knows what I do. I've never kept it a secret. But I never give her details either. I've killed men before—in the military and afterward. But I only kill those who deserve to die.

I get to my feet, draw her up with me. "Your niece will be here soon. We should get cleaned up."

She's annoyed, but comes along with me. We shower together, and soon we're sitting out in the back garden, she with a glass of wine, me with a beer. I know we need to talk about what Jordan told me, but it can wait. Her brother will be here soon with Hope and there's something else I need to do first.

EPILOGUE 2
EVE

I mean it when I say I don't trust James Jordan. I've met him exactly once, and I already know he's a bad guy. And as much as I trust Zach, there's something he's keeping from me.

"Let's take a walk," Zach says.

The sun is setting. He likes to go to the edge of the property to watch it. I usually go with him. It's such a beautiful sight.

Zach's quieter than usual when we walk, and I know it has to do with that call, but I also know he needs to tell me when he's ready.

When we get to our spot, we sit against the tree stump, our backs to it, both of us facing the sunset, which has just begun. He takes my hand in his.

"I know where Seth and Rafi are buried," he says.

I turn to him. He's still looking straight ahead. I know they're dead. I've made peace with it. So why does this news make me feel like I'm going to start crying all over again? Because I don't want that. I don't want to cry anymore.

Zach faces me. "Jordan's been working on finding them. Finding out...the truth," he pauses, looks down at our hands, watches his thumb turn a circle over the back of mine before meeting my gaze again. "I don't want to do this to you. I don't want to cause you any more pain."

I smile, but it's sad and my eyes are wet with tears that somehow, I don't shed. "Can we bring them home?" I ask.

He nods. "I'll take care of it."

I wipe my eyes, but it's not the waterfall I dread. There are tears, but they're gone.

"You okay?" he asks.

I nod. "I am. I know they're gone. I've known for a long time."

"I'm sorry, Eve."

"That was the call?"

"Yes. Our business is finished now."

"Good." We slip into silence for a long time, watch the sun set, watch darkness fall like a blanket across the sky. "I feel okay, you know. I do."

"I know."

I look at him, and he's smiling a little, but his eyes are intent on me like maybe he doesn't quite believe me. "What?"

He reaches into his pocket and digs something

out. I know when he finds it because his expression changes. "This." He draws the ring out of his pocket and I look at it, surprised, shocked, maybe? In awe. The moon shines on it, making the diamond sparkle. "I picked it up a few weeks ago."

"Are you...is that..."

"I can't imagine being away from you ever again. I think, actually, that I loved you from the first minute I saw you sitting in that interrogation room. When the others would look at you, it made me fucking crazy. Hell, when men look at you now—"

I put my hand on his. "Shh. Don't spoil it."

He's nervous. I've never seen him like this before. He nods. "I love you and I want you to marry me, Eve. I want to be with you always. I want babies with you. I want...no, I *am* home with you. You're it for me. You're everything."

I drag my eyes from the ring up to his. This is unreal. A dream.

"I love you, Zach. And I can't imagine ever being without you. I mean, you live here already, so..."

"Shh." He slides the ring on my finger and takes my face in his hands. "Don't spoil it."

I giggle, looking at my hand, then at him, and I know I'm grinning like a fool.

Zach kisses me. It's a long, soft kiss. His big arms wrap around me and hold me to him and I feel warm and safe and home and this time, the tears that slide down my cheeks are tears of happiness.

Finally, after so many years, Zach and I, we've come full circle and we're right where we belong.

Together.

The End

Keep reading for a sample from Taken!

SAMPLE FROM TAKEN
HELENA

I'm the oldest of the Willow quadruplets. Four girls. Always girls. Every single quadruplet birth, generation after generation, it's always girls.

This generation's crop yielded the usual, but instead of four perfect, beautiful dolls, there were three.

And me.

And today, our twenty-first birthday, is the day of harvesting.

That's the Scafoni family's choice of words, not ours. At least not mine. My parents seem much more comfortable with it than my sisters and I do, though.

Harvesting is always on the twenty-first birthday of the quads. I don't know if it's written in stone somewhere or what, but it's what I know and what has been on the back of my mind since I learned our history five years ago.

There's an expression: *those who cannot remember the past are condemned to repeat it.* Well, that's bullshit, because we Willows know well our past and look at us now.

The same blocks that have been used for centuries standing in the old library, their surfaces softened by the feet of every other Willow Girl who stood on the same stumps of wood, and all I can think when I see them, the four lined up like they are, is how archaic this is, how fucking unreal. How they can't do this to us.

Yet, here we are.

And they are doing this to us.

But it's not *us*, really.

My shift is marked.

I'm *unclean*.

So it's really my sisters.

Sometimes I'm not sure who I hate more, my own family for allowing this insanity generation after generation, or the Scafoni monsters for demanding the sacrifice.

"It's time," my father says. His voice is grave.

He's aged these last few months. I wonder if that's remorse because it certainly isn't backbone.

I heard he and my mother argue once, exactly once, and then it was over.

He simply accepted it.

Accepted that tonight, his daughters will be made to stand on those horrible blocks while a Scafoni bastard looks us over, prods and pokes us, maybe checks our teeth like you would a horse, before making his choice. Before taking one of my sisters as his for the next three years of her life.

I'm not naive enough to be unsure what that will mean exactly. Maybe my sisters are, but not me.

"Up on the block. Now, Helena."

I look at my sisters who already stand so meekly on their appointed stumps. They're all paler than usual tonight and I swear I can hear their hearts pounding in fear of what's to come.

When I don't move right away, my father painfully takes my arm and lifts me up onto my block and all I can think, the one thing that gives me the slightest hope, is that if Sebastian Scafoni chooses me, I will find some way to end this. I won't condemn my daughters to this fate. My nieces. My granddaughters.

But he won't choose me, and I think that's why my parents are angrier than usual with me.

See, I'm the ugly duckling. At least I'd be considered ugly standing next to my sisters.

And the fact that I'm unclean—not a virgin— means I won't be taken.

The Scafoni bastard will choose one of their precious golden daughters instead.

Golden, to my dark. Golden—quite literally. Sparkling almost, my sisters.

I glance at them as my father attaches the iron shackle to my ankle. He doesn't do this to any of them. They'll do as they're told, even as their gazes bounce from the closed twelve-foot doors to me and back again and again and again.

But I have no protection to offer. Not tonight. Not on this one.

The backs of my eyes burn with tears I refuse to shed.

"How can you do this? How can you allow it?" I ask for the hundredth time. I'm talking to my mother while my father clasps the restraints on my wrists, making sure I won't attack the monsters.

"Better gag her, too."

It's my mother's response to my question and, a moment later, my father does as he's told and ensures my silence.

I hate my mother more, I think. She's a Willow quadruplet. She witnessed a harvesting herself. Witnessed the result of this cruel tradition.

Tradition.

A tradition of kidnapping.

Of breaking.

Of destroying.

I look to my sisters again. Three almost carbon copies of each other, with long blonde hair curling around their shoulders, flowing down their backs, their blue eyes wide with fear.

Well, except in Julia's case.

She's different than the others. She's more... eager. But I don't think she has a clue what they'll do to her.

Me, no one would guess I came from the same batch.

Opposite their gold, my hair is so dark a black, it appears almost blue, with one single, wide streak of silver to relieve the stark shade, a flaw I was born with. And contrasting their cornflower-blue eyes, mine are a midnight sky; there too, the only relief the silver specks that dot them.

They look like my mother. Like perfect dolls.

I look like my great-aunt, also named Helena, down to the silver streak I refuse to dye. She's in her nineties now. I wonder if they had to lock her in her room and steal her wheelchair, so she wouldn't interfere in the ceremony.

Aunt Helena was the chosen girl of her generation. She knows what's in store for us better than anyone.

"They're coming," my mother says.

She has super hearing, I swear, but then, a moment later, I hear them too.

A door slams beyond the library, and the draft blows out a dozen of the thousand candles that light the huge room.

A maid rushes to relight them. No electricity. Tradition, I guess.

If I were Sebastian Scafoni, I'd want to get a good look at the prize I'd be fucking for the next year. And I have no doubt there will be fucking, because what else can break a girl so completely but taking that of all things?

And it's not just the one year. No. We're given for three years. One year for each brother. Oldest to youngest. It used to be four, but now, it's three.

I would pinch my arm to be sure I'm really standing here, that I'm not dreaming, but my hands are bound behind my back, and I can't.

This can't be fucking real. It can't be legal.

And yet here we are, the four of us, naked beneath our translucent, rotting sheaths—I swear I smell the decay on them—standing on our designated blocks, teetering on them. I guess the Willows of the past had smaller feet. And I admit, as I hear their heavy, confident footfalls approaching the ancient wooden doors of the library, I am afraid.

I'm fucking terrified.

One-Click Taken Now!

Benedetti Mafia World

Salvatore: a Dark Mafia Romance

Dominic: a Dark Mafia Romance

Sergio: a Dark Mafia Romance

The Benedetti Brothers Box Set (Contains Salvatore, Dominic and Sergio)

Killian: a Dark Mafia Romance

Giovanni: a Dark Mafia Romance

The Amado Brothers

Dishonorable

Disgraced

Unhinged

Standalone Dark Romance

Descent

Deviant

Beautiful Liar

Retribution

Theirs To Take

Captive, Mine

Alpha

Given to the Savage

Taken by the Beast

Claimed by the Beast

Captive's Desire

Protective Custody

Amy's Strict Doctor

Taming Emma

Taming Megan

Taming Naia

Reclaiming Sophie

The Firefighter's Girl

Dangerous Defiance

Her Rogue Knight

Taught To Kneel

Tamed: the Roark Brothers Trilogy

THANK YOU!

Thanks for reading *Unhinged*. I hope you enjoyed it. Reviews help new readers find books and would make me ever grateful. Please consider leaving a review at the store where you purchased the book.

Click here to sign up for my newsletter to receive new release news and updates!

Like my FB Author Page to keep updated on news and giveaways!

I have a FB Fan Group where I share exclusive teasers, giveaways and just fun stuff. Probably TMI :) It's called The Knight Spot. I'd love for you to join us! Just click here!

ACKNOWLEDGMENTS

Cover Design by CT Cover Creations

Editing by Emma Bancroft

ABOUT THE AUTHOR

USA Today bestselling author of contemporary romance, Natasha Knight specializes in dark, tortured heroes. Happily-Ever-Afters are guaranteed, but she likes to put her characters through hell to get them there. She's evil like that.

www.natasha-knight.com
natasha-knight@outlook.com